Felony Murder Rule

Thonie Hevron

Aakenbaaken & Kent

Felony Murder Rule

ISBN: 9781938436901

Dedication

None of my work would be worth anything

without the loving support of my husband, Danny.

FELONY MURDER RULE: California Penal Code § 189[1] classifies a homicide as first degree murder when it is a murder committed during the commission of one of the following predicate felonies: Robbery

CHAPTER ONE

What the hell was that noise?

Meredith Ryan's eyes shot open, her mind racing at the sound of glass breaking.

That was a window.

And Nick was working, graveyard shift. She and the baby were in the house, alone.

Davy's even breathing whispered over the monitor on the nightstand, verifying he was asleep in his room. Yesterday the ten-month old almost took his first step. There was no way he could've climbed out of the crib and walked into trouble.

Soft moonlight streamed through the window. Meredith sorted through the possibilities. Then, she punched a sequence of buttons on the box beside her nightstand. The gun safe opened with a click. Meredith wrapped her fingers around the grip of a Glock 43 and clicked off the safety. Ready to fire.

Out of habit, she grabbed her duty flashlight, a Streamlight she kept next to the bed. She used it on patrol, but currently it was helpful navigating her unfamiliar house when the baby cried at night. She eased her feet to the hardwood—an old floor, prone to squeaks. As she slipped into a pair of flip flops, the cool Petaluma night air greeted her. Wearing a tank top over an old pair of Nick's boxer shorts, she felt the chill raise goosebumps. Or was it fear?

After six months at their new house, Meredith was still learning the old girl's quirks. As a century-old Cottage-style bungalow, it had plenty. She padded down the hall, trying to minimize the floor's groans.

Meredith paused at Davy's room; gun muzzle up. The door was wide open. She'd closed it at midnight when she checked on him. A breeze slid across her bare skin. Silent as death, she ducked around the door jamb and slipped into a fluid three-point posture. In the moonlight a shadow leaned over the crib. A thin, bony-shouldered male shape.

She aimed. He was too close to the baby. She couldn't pull the trigger.

Her son was below her line of sight; the stranger filled her view. Her adrenaline kicked into high gear. "Police! Stop or I'll shoot!" The warning was automatic. Shoot? No, he was too close to Davy. She couldn't put her child in jeopardy. "Step away! Let me see your hands!"

The figure lurched sideways, arms reaching for the windowsill. He plunged through the screen, ripping it from its frame.

Six feet below, she heard a thump like a sack of sand as he landed on the patio. A sharp breath and a curse, then scraping. From the window she saw the intruder stumble trying to balance against an aluminum trash can. The metal shattered the night as it clattered to the ground.

Lights flicked on in the house next door. A neighbor's window screeched open and a woman's voice demanded, "Who's out there?"

"Tina! It's Mere."

"Meredith! What the hell's going on?"

"Come over here right now. I need you!"

The window slammed shut. In less than a minute, Tina banged on Meredith's front door, wild-eyed in a faded chenille bathrobe.

Meredith pulled Tina inside and pushed her sleepy son into the neighbor's arms. "Stay here with him. Call 911. Someone broke into my house."

"Where are you going?"

"After him."

She peered out the window, down the steps to the yard. With a soft eye, she scanned the property. Through the tattered screen, a shadow skulked from bush to bush in her back yard. Then it reached the gate. Limping.

At the back porch, a 10' X 24' screened-in area—the door hung open, the glass pane shattered. The intruder's point of entry.

Meredith crept around glass shards to the wall, then made her way to the exterior door and scanned the back yard again. Outside, the heavy wooden gate leaned open, no one around. Scented lilacs and mock orange shrubs rustled with the wind, belying the startling intrusion.

At the top of the outside stairs she stopped. The baby would be safe with Tina. Meredith heard her neighbor harsh whisper to the 911 dispatcher. At no protest from Davy, she decided. The last of her doubt evaporated

She ran down the stairs, missing a step and twisting an ankle. No time for the indulgence of pain. She flew along the rough, hundred-year-old concrete path through the yard to the back fence, flung open the gate and took cover behind a metal garbage can. Then she listened, Glock pointed skyward. She heard only what the breeze stirred up; rustling leaves, the crack of a twig. No footfalls, nothing—

Then, across the alley, she heard the scrape of a shoe, the rattle of gravel. A slim-shouldered outline, male, running with a limp through a neighbor's yard behind her house. That was her suspect.

Meredith's house was built on the flats in the historic Northern California town of Petaluma. A block behind her home loomed La Cresta Ridge, a steep hillside forming a natural barrier to Petaluma's dairy pastures. As she watched, the intruder hobbled away out of sight toward La Cresta Ridge.

"Stop! Police!" After a decade as a deputy at the Sonoma County Sheriff's Office, Meredith's warning was second nature. It occurred to her she should've yelled, "Sheriff's Department," but the Ryan home was in the city limits, police jurisdiction.

Stupid thought. She huffed in frustration. Damn, she should've grabbed her cell. Too late. Ankle throbbing, it was all she could do to get back to the house. Furious at losing the intruder, she hobbled into the yard, slamming the gate behind her.

Tina's strident voice called, "Who's out there?"

"It's Meredith. I'm coming in."

CHAPTER TWO

The dashboard clock showed shortly after midnight. Monday nights were often easy—Nick had learned early in his career not to say quiet. He never even tried to fight that superstition. It was as proven as all the crazies coming out for a full moon. Driving a circuitous road back to the station, he combated the human tendency to follow habit—in this case, the same route. It was basic officer safety not to be predictable. Besides, it gave him time to think.

Something on last night's shift bothered him.

As graveyard sergeant, he collected, read and approved patrol deputies' crime reports. While most were cleared, some had to be returned to the deputy for grammar, accuracy, or to make sure all the elements of the pertinent statute were met. Nick Reyes' San Francisco State Bachelor of Arts degree featured an emphasis on English composition. Because he was raised in a Spanish-speaking home, Nick worked hard at being comfortable with college-level English. Now that his career position included approving or denying reports, he found it ironic that some native English-speaking deputies had trouble writing at a sixth-grade level.

Still, he was serious about his responsibilities. Last night, for instance, he had to call in a rookie female deputy over a routine matter. Her report was unclear—the order of events in the timeline was off. The home-invasion robbery statement would be scrutinized by Violent Crimes Investigators. If a suspect was arrested, a Deputy District Attorney would tear the report apart looking for holes before deciding to prosecute. Defense attorneys lived for weak police reports. The details had to be accurate. Nick could not allow his deputies to be inept or careless.

Nick sat at his desk in the patrol sergeant's office, reading his hundredth report of the shift, when rookie deputy Evelina Marquez rapped on the door jamb. He stood up—manners ingrained—and said, "Deputy Marquez—Evelina."

"Sergeant." She flashed a toothy smile and eased her way into the small office. Nick first met Marquez after she'd completed field training, when she was assigned to his graveyard team. Mostly quiet during roll call, she'd never talked to him except in the briefing room. Evelina was attractive, in a dark, brooding way. Nick wished she didn't remind him so much of his ex-wife, Angela.

He waved toward a chair and she sat, back straight and hands clasped demurely in her lap. "I've never been called into your office, Sergeant," Evelina said, her long dark lashes fluttering and a hint of a smile on her lips. "Am I in trouble?" Nick heard the faintest intonation giving away her Spanish heritage: the soft consonants, the animated cadence.

"No," Nick smiled.

Was she flirting? Meredith always told him he was dense about these things.

"A minor problem with this report, easily fixed."

He pulled a piece of paper from the printer behind him and placed it before her. "Here," he pointed at the text. "This has to be cleaned up. The timeline of the crime is off. You can't have this observation mixed up. 'The reporting party sees lights moving around in the house. He confronts the suspect before he calls 911.' It must be clear to a person who's reading it for the first time. Go back and fix it."

Evelina looked at the paper, a flush rising in her cheeks. Any hint of the smile was gone. "But that's what he told me."

"You need to re-interview him to get complete accuracy. This has to be right. If you go to court and a defense attorney sees this gap in the timeline, he'll eat you up on the stand. That's a humiliation you don't need."

"But—"

"It has to be right, Evelina. Contact your victim again and make sure."

"Yes, sir."

He hoped he wasn't too tough on the rookie. She was just starting out. A lot of what he said and did now would remain imprinted throughout her career. He spent the next five minutes explaining why the report had to be done this way. He ended with, "Do you see why the progression of events has to reflect all the elements of the crime?"

Evelina's large eyes met Nick's. No humor there, he thought. Good, she's taking this seriously. She reached for the paper, her hand briefly touching his. She didn't pull away. Nick jerked back, reacting to the touch like it was fire.

Evelina smiled ever-so-slightly as she turned to leave.

Behind her, Lieutenant Rasmussen stood in the doorway, his arms across his chest. He looked in a hurry. Still, he cocked his head as the female deputy turned to leave. His gaze followed the deputy as she left. He was wide-eyed as he stepped inside to the sergeant's desk. When he was sure Evelina was gone, he whistled. "Damn, Reyes. What was that about?"

"I'll be damned if I know." Nick rubbed his eyes. It was almost two AM, time for the brass to call it a day. "Going home?"

"I was, but I just got a call from Petaluma PD. Someone broke into your house."

Nick shot to his feet. "Meredith, the baby—?"

"They're fine. Everyone's in one piece." Rasmussen's hands flew up, attempting to placate. "The PD's asking for you to respond. I'll hold over for you."

Nick was already in motion. "The suspect?"

Rasmussen shrugged, "In the wind, I hear."

Nick realized he was grateful the suspect had gotten away. The intruder hadn't forced Meredith to use lethal means. The guy had no idea how lucky he was. Even though he'd escaped, he'd spared his wife the trauma of shooting him.

His phone vibrated in his vest pocket. Petaluma Police Department.

CHAPTER THREE

The officer from the Petaluma Police was incredibly patient.

"I lost him," Meredith sniffed as she looked away. Anger produced tears, which made her even angrier. Someone had forced his way into her home, was inches from her baby, and she hadn't caught him. The moment she saw the figure in the room, the thought of shooting him had charged into her mind. Even with no shot clear of the baby, she couldn't say why she hadn't fired. She'd wanted him away from Davy.

But now, tears? What the hell? Oh, hormones. Crap.

The woman in blue, Officer Patricia Doran, smiled, her face radiating confidence. "We'll get him." The officer backed up, letting the crime scene tech take a measurement of the room.

The kitchen was large, but the crowd of strangers made it feel like a closet—three PPD patrol officers, a sergeant, two evidence technicians, and a sheriff's deputy.

Where is Nick? Someone said he was on the way from the office in Santa Rosa.

"Glad you're okay, Mrs. Reyes." The sergeant nodded at her. "We'll keep your house on extra patrol, walk the yard off and on for the rest of the night." He turned to make a phone call.

Tina, the frazzled-looking neighbor from next door, came in with Meredith's drowsy baby in her arms. Squinting against the kitchen light, Davy saw his mother, leaned out of Tina's arms and reached for Meredith. "Momma, Momma."

Meredith took her son, feeling whole for the first time in the past hour. She squeezed him and he squeaked, fussing at the pressure. Relaxing her grip, she nuzzled the hair on the back of his neck and savored the smell of his baby sweat. Davy was safe.

Smell?

"Patricia, I remembered something."

Officer Doran turned to Meredith, reaching for her pen.

"The guy smelled like an ashtray." Meredith remembered more. "Not just like he'd been smoking recently; the odor permeated his clothes. I smelled it when he moved."

Voices came from the front of the house. Nick.

Tina secured the knot in her bathrobe. "Nick's here; you're in good hands. I'm going home. Call me if you need anything." She touched Meredith's shoulder. "Are you going in to work tomorrow? Will you need me to watch him?" Tina had been a godsend, assuming childcare duties for her son when Meredith returned to work four months ago.

Meredith forced a smile for this neighbor and friend. "No, but thanks." While grateful for the speedy help, Meredith struggled to be polite when her insides were screaming with outrage. How could this happen? Who did this?

"You okay? Davy?" Nick came through the door looking like he'd aged ten years since she'd last seen him.

Meredith stood with the baby in her arms, unable to speak. When Nick hugged them, she felt overwhelming relief. Needing the comfort of his embrace, she rested in his arms until Davy fussed. The police officers gave them a few minutes, tactfully busying themselves with one of the evidence techs.

Even after all this time, when Meredith saw her husband in uniform it felt like he filled the entire room. She must not have been the only one to feel this way; everyone in the room focused on Nick. Tall for a Latin, over six feet, he'd always been active, including gym time. She secretly thought it sexy the way his uniform strained across his biceps.

After introductions, Officer Doran briefed Nick. "Your wife awakened to the sound of breaking glass. She checked the house with her Glock, there," Doran nodded to the kitchen table where the handgun sat, magazine out, slide open. "She surprised a male standing over the baby's crib and cautioned him. He bailed out through the screened, open window. She chased him, twisted her ankle, and followed him through the back yard to the alley. She lost him behind a neighbor's house. We're checking back yards now."

"What kind of evidence are you finding?" It was early yet in the investigation. There would be more info compiled and collected tomorrow. As a previous Violent Crimes Investigations detective, Nick wanted to know everything PPD had.

"Entry through the back porch door—he broke the glass, reached in and opened the door from inside. No footprints around the perimeter of the house, so it's unlikely that he scouted the area before he broke in. But we'll come back tomorrow to be sure."

Nick nodded. "We have automatic irrigation, so it'll be wet out there." He glanced at his watch. "Sprinklers are set for six AM."

A sigh escaped Doran's lips. "I'll come back to check before they go on." She'd be knee-deep in reports by six. Meredith was impressed. Taking time out for this follow-up was a sign of Doran's dedication—and the seriousness of an intruder in a law officers' home.

"How does it look for finding any usable prints?" Meredith rocked Davy on her shoulder, thankful he was falling asleep.

Doran nodded to the evidence tech, giving her the okay to report.

"We got a few," the tech said. From across the room, the gangly young woman held up the tape she'd just pulled. "If he's in the system, we should get a name. He wasn't all that careful about leaving his signature behind."

CHAPTER FOUR

The officers left, one by one. On her way out, Officer Doran leaned toward Nick, her voice low. "We'll be driving by your house more often for the next few days—just in case."

He nodded. A nice thought, but pointless. He'd be sitting right here with his Glock—waiting. At least, figuratively. It wasn't in his nature to let others do for his family, and he wasn't going to wait for PPD.

When Meredith, Nick and Davy were finally alone, Nick stood at the doorway watching them. Meredith was as beautiful as the day he'd first seen her. Fresh from the academy, she'd been assigned to him as a trainee in the Field Training Program. She was just twenty-two, a tall, athletic graduate of San Francisco State. Nick thought she would really be someone special, a natural leader—first in her academy class in academics, third in physicals. Yet her brown eyes hinted at sadness. It had taken many shifts and long graveyard conversations for him to get a glimpse into her past—the bonding of two people who have been tested and know they have each other's back. They'd become fast friends, to the dismay of their spouses: his jealous wife forced Nick to limit his friendship with Meredith. Eight long years passed, filled with death, divorce and loss, before they were both free to love each other.

And now, she and Davy had been at risk, mere hours ago. An early morning breeze drifted through the broken glass, giving him goosebumps.

As Meredith sat at the kitchen table holding Davy, Nick's mind searched for answers. Who was this intruder? Why was he in that room? No burglar would look for valuables in a nursery. Was he interested in Davy? Why? What the hell were they going to do?

Meredith must feel the same anguish. Except for one thing: Nick had already lost a child. Nine years ago, SIDs took his baby daughter, Mia. Afterward, he'd been unsuccessful consoling Angela, his first wife. The baby's passing had broken their hearts, fractured their marriage and sent Angela off on a wild tangent that led to divorce. In the end, he'd lost a child and a wife.

He wouldn't let that happen again.

As he looked across the kitchen, the sight of Meredith holding Davy grabbed and held a place deep inside him. When she looked up, Meredith's eyes were pools of torment. The two people he loved the most in the world had been in jeopardy. Soon, tears trailed down Meredith's face. Her sense of security had been pulled out from under her. As had his.

He touched her shoulder. Davy woke, his dark brown eyes clouded with sleep, and reached for his daddy. Meredith rose and gently handed him over.

Nick moved Davy's arms and legs around to avoid the sharp edges of his badge and name plate. His son had been poked before when he'd hugged the child while in uniform. Davy was a tough little guy, though. It would take more than a poke to make him cry. On the other hand, Mia, Nick's daughter, had been all softness. Even now, it broke his heart remembering the gentle tones of her cries.

Nick looked into Meredith's red, swollen eyes. He'd promised himself not to let his job come between them—ever.

"This might be some jackass we've put in jail." Nick enunciated each word, careful about his word choice. He didn't want to alarm Meredith any further. "The department will help with extra patrol—"

"Who the hell would do this?" Her fingers wiped away the tears. "Was it some random burglar? Maybe he didn't know we're cops. But, why did he stop and look at Davy in his crib?"

A dozen scenarios ran through Nick's mind, none of them good. He didn't believe in coincidence. "Why was he in the baby's room? I mean, it's obvious it's a nursery. There was no reason for him to be there unless he was going to take—" His throat went dry. He had trouble getting the words out. He asked, "Do you have any open cases?"

Meredith's eyes widened. He saw indignation in her posture. "No way. I would've told you about a potential threat." Her current assignment was as a detective in the Violent Crimes Investigation Unit—VCI unit—at the Sonoma County Sheriff's Office. Her astonishment turned to anger. "I wouldn't leave an open case with work undone," she snapped. "And I sure as hell would tell you of any threats to us or our family."

"I'm sorry. I know how that sounded." This was dangerous ground they'd covered before, in another life. They'd grown to respect each other while he was her field training officer. After completing training, having differing assignments, they hadn't worked on patrol together very much. Then two years ago, when she'd been promoted to VCI, he'd been her trainer again. While he could critique her work, he'd learned not to question her decisions or put her on the defensive.

With Davy contented in the crook of an arm, Nick reached out to Meredith. She sank into his chest, next to their child. He whispered into her hair, "We'll figure this out together. You and me, like always."

Her reply was muffled, but the message was clear. She got it.

His body shook, a delayed reaction. Shock, maybe. He shifted, hiding it from her.

Meredith reached up. Her fingers caressed the back of his neck, her other arm clasping Davy. Looking at him, she said, "Together."

He should've known.

Now the hard part. "I want you and Davy to go to Cav's until this is settled."

"You've got to be kidding."

Nick touched her forearm. "Listen—"

She pulled away, angry. "Nothing you can say will make me leave. And Davy's staying with me. With us." She leaned on the counter and looked out the kitchen window—

searching the dark for something to focus on. They couldn't stop being cops. The intruder had been there, just hours ago. "This is not working it through together."

From behind, Nick slipped an arm around her. "Mere." She couldn't help herself. Even angry, the touch of her husband softened her. "I need to know you and the baby are safe. Cav's ranch is the best place that can happen."

Standing behind her, Nick kissed Meredith's hair. The night breeze brought a chill. "Cav says Filomena can't wait to get her hands on Davy."

Meredith sighed. "You've already talked to him?"

Nick nodded. "The timing's right. You'll be off work."

Earlier, she and Nick had put in for three vacation days—upcoming Tuesday through Friday—intending to help Cav around his ranch in the remote Sonoma County hills. It was hard, physical work, but therapeutic—Nick helping the rancher repair fences and re-shingle the barn, while Meredith and Jake moved the sheep and cattle to the summer pasture. All their work was tempered with swims in Cav's pool and evening walks down the country road. The ranch was a prescription for sanity.

Their friend Raymond Cavanaugh had proven his mettle months ago. He'd saved both their skins and helped them stop a domestic terror attack. Since then, he'd stayed close to Nick and Meredith—and Davy.

Cavanaugh had recently shown that same heart with his family, too. Six months back, the man's seventeen-year-old grandson, Jake, had asked if they had a place on the ranch for his buddy, Salvador's mother, Filomena.

It turned out the kid had a great idea. Cavanaugh's housekeeping skills had slipped since Jake came to live with him last year—their meals consisted of dry cereal and frozen dinners—and Cav realized the Cavanaugh men needed help cooking and keeping house and, since they lived so far from town, whoever they hired needed to live on the ranch. Last March, Cav offered Filomena a place to live and a part-time job as the ranch's housekeeper and cook. She'd accepted the offer with enthusiasm.

Meredith's resolve crumbled. Her first responsibility was to protect her son. "What are you going to do?"

Nick stiffened. He dreaded telling her his next news. "I already arranged it with Ferrua." Ferrua was Meredith's boss, and she wouldn't take kindly to anyone going behind her back. Especially since she'd only returned to work a few months ago at the end of her maternity leave. Even her remorse over leaving her son couldn't counteract the guilt over leaving the rest of the unit short-handed.

"I'll be working with Petaluma PD, helping with follow-up and available for questions."

She spun to face him. "Did you get a name to go with those prints?"

"Not yet." But something should come soon.

"Any ideas who it was?"

Nick shook his head, his brows drawn in frustration.

Meredith pulled at a button on his uniform shirt, mulling over his demand. She sighed. "Davy and I are already packed for a few days. We'll just go up there sooner." She looked up. "Cav's okay with this?"

He nodded. "He's ready for you both."

Again, going behind her back. She waffled, but she couldn't argue with the logic of getting Davy out of the line of fire. And there would be trouble. Trouble, not if, but when the intruder was found. Anyone who tried to harm their son—

Well, God help them.

CHAPTER FIVE

Meredith recalled her first meeting with Filomena last March, a few months ago. Cav told them that he had hired the woman as a cook and housekeeper. She would stay in the guest room until the bunk house was ready.

On the back porch that winter afternoon, just days after she arrived, Meredith and Filomena sipped coffee while Cav handed Nick a Pacifico. The sunlight dappled the yard through the oak trees as the four looked across to a small, neglected bunk house. Filomena's aging blue Saturn was parked in front.

"Gonna clean up the place. Make it livable for a lady." Cav looked at the structure.

"Need some help?" Nick was handy with a hammer.

Cav squinted, his lips curling into a smile. "I thought you'd never ask."

"Of course." Nick tipped the beer bottle to his friend. "Jake's gone this week, right?"

Cav shook his head. "No, next week. He and his dad are going to UC Berkeley first, checking out the Ag Operations School. Then on to UC Davis. I'm betting on Davis."

"He's certainly straightened out. Didn't seem that long ago you were worried about him going to jail."

"Yeah." Cav nodded. "He figured out what he wanted to do, and we mapped out a plan to make it happen. He's got a 4.3 GPA at the junior college. He'll go on to get his Bachelors in Ag Operations, then come home and run this place."

"Looks like you'll be able to retire someday."

Cav sighed softly as he scanned his property, "Don't think I'll ever leave this place, though."

Nick drank from his beer. "Let's get started on that clean-up. I just happen to have the next three days off."

Cav nodded toward the structure. "I want to change out the commode, put in a sink and mirror. Probably put up insulation and drywall. It gets plenty cold during the winter…"

Cav's voice faded as they walked to the bunk house.

Meredith pulled her coat around her neck and smiled at the petite Hispanic woman next to her. "Let's go inside. It's getting cold." March in the hills of Sonoma County could be chilly. Meredith noted the old Pepsi logo on the thermometer next to the door into the house. The temperature had only risen to 50 degrees that afternoon. She shivered as the door slammed behind her.

"Do you mind if I make a fresh pot of coffee? I could stand a spoon in this stuff." Meredith grinned.

"Have a seat." Filomena's warm smile filled the room as she took over the coffee-making duties. "You already have your hands full."

Meredith sank into a kitchen chair, Davy spilling out of her arms. Suddenly free, the boy flopped onto his bottom. With a squeal, he grabbed the table leg and pulled himself up. "He's almost walking." She wasn't sure she was ready for a toddler. It was easier when he was less mobile. "You have other children besides Salvador?"

"Yes," Filomena answered, loading the basket and filter with two generous scoops of ground coffee. She lit the burner under the pot. Fanning the match out, she leaned against the counter and waited for the water to boil. "I have five other boys. Salvador is the youngest. The older three are in Mexico. They have good jobs and are starting their own families."

"Salvador and Felix are in college here in the US." The teapot whistled and Filomena poured the boiling water over the coffee grounds.

After a short steep, Filomena's pot of coffee smelled heavenly.

"This job will help to pay for my sons still in school." She poured two mugs full and sat opposite Meredith. "This is much like my home in Tomátlan, Mexico. I was a schoolteacher when my husband decided the boys needed the opportunities the US could provide." She flashed a rueful smile. Meredith wondered what kind of drama surrounded such a decision. "He's gone now."

"I'm so sorry." Meredith knew what the loss of a husband felt like.

Filomena drew back suddenly, her palms up in denial. "Oh no. You misunderstand. He's not dead, he's gone—with another woman."

Meredith's face flushed. Filomena noticed and waved her discomfort aside. "It's okay." She waved a hand again as if to wipe away all the bad times. "The boys and I are better now." She leaned forward, a hand on Meredith's knee. "Besides, I love it here. Mr. Raymond is wonderful. He lets me stay in the guest bedroom until the little house is ready."

"Don't you miss teaching? And your family in Mexico?"

Her dark hair framed a plain but guileless face. Her smile was a little sad. "Yes, but I can see them every year or so. With these wages I can save up the airfare." She looked down at Davy chattering away to his stuffed elephant, Fresno. "I love children, especially the little ones." Her smile radiated contentment. "I have the best of everything right here."

Meredith was pleased. This seemed to be working out for both Cav and Filomena. "And Jake?"

Filomena tilted her head. Meredith could see something wasn't right. She was glad the woman was honest. "It will take more time for Jake to get used to me. I have to learn what's okay and what isn't—like putting on his *abuela's* apron."

"You'll learn the rules fast enough," Meredith said, knowing it had been Jake's idea to help his friend's mother. Meredith guessed Jake hadn't expected her to make herself so at home.

"Mr. Raymond said to give him time."

That sounded like Cav—adopting a 'wait and see' attitude in the hopes the two would find a balance. The less interference, the better.

The Cavanaugh Ranch was not only a sanctuary for the

Reyes and Cavanaugh families, but for Filomena, too.

CHAPTER SIX

A pair of mosquito hawks bounced against the porch light at the Cavanaugh Ranch as Meredith pressed the doorbell. Cav answered the door in his jeans and T-shirt, his curly gray locks hanging to his forehead until he ran a hand through them. He squinted at Meredith as he flung open the screen door. "Come in, come in." She pictured him glancing around the yard as she entered his home.

In the living room a bathrobe-clad Filomena chewed a nail. As Meredith walked in, Filomena extended her arms to take the sleeping baby. "I got the crib made up in your bedroom." She led, holding Davy, Meredith followed, as Cav shouldered her backpack and the baby's duffel. The baby began to fuss just as Filomena put him in his bed. As quietly as possible, Cav and Filomena left the room.

Meredith dropped their bags on the bed. She leaned over her son, tucking in the blanket, whispering words she could only hope would soothe him back to sleep.

Five minutes later, she faced Cav and the housekeeper. Cav's grandson, Jake had roused, sharing the same tousled locks on their foreheads, only the teen's hair was red. So was his temper. "What the hell's going on? It's three in the morning? I have to get up in—"

He was shushed soundly. Meredith heard intense whispers as she went into the room. Her voice low, she answered him. "I'm afraid it's our fault, Jake."

The teen looked at her in surprise.

"We had an incident at our house that made it smarter for us not to be there." She was exhausted, tired from the experience and the adrenaline spike. The long, boring drive up here in the dark did nothing to energize her.

"What the—" Jake began again, his sleepy eyes looking confused.

"Someone broke into our house. I found him standing over Davy's crib."

"Damn."

She shrugged, knowing she'd have to explain it all over again. She looked at Cav sitting in his recliner, waiting patiently. Filomena glided in, handing Meredith a coffee mug. "It's herbal tea. It will help you to relax."

"Thanks." She took a sip, then another as the three waited for her to tell the story.

After it was told, the lines on Cav's face seemed deeper. He chewed his lower lip then said, "Stay here as long as you need. You and the boys are always welcome."

Jake shook his head in disbelief and whistled. "That guy's got balls—or no brains."

Cav frowned, nodding toward Meredith. "She'll figure out which."

CHAPTER SEVEN

The next morning—a mere three hours later, Meredith sat in the rocking chair, too keyed up to sleep. She looked out the bedroom window, watching old Rocket and Denver, the ranch horses, graze on the late spring oat grass.

She loved it up here. It was the picture of tranquility on the Cavanaugh Ranch. "You will ride horses," she whispered in Davy's ear. Drowsy and warm, the baby settled on Meredith's shoulder. She listened to her sleeping child's breathing as she rocked in the chair. He was perfect.

When awake, her son's large dark eyes and curly brown hair riveted her attention. Now ten months, little David—named after her murdered brother—had been a surprise. When she'd told him she was pregnant, Nick insisted they marry right away. A willing minister among the county law enforcement chaplaincy performed the ceremony; Nick had tried his parish priest, but the Catholic Church still viewed him as married to Angela. So, Nick and Meredith were married in a civil service at Raymond Cavanaugh's home. Davy's arrival a few months later solidified their union and changed both their lives for the better.

Meredith touched the dark curls, amazed at the intensity of her emotions as she gazed at his angelic face. Surely every mother in the history of the world felt this when looking at her baby. But Meredith hadn't been prepared for the ferocious protectiveness, the absolute devotion to this product of her love for Nick. This little creature had stood their lives on end—in a good, no, great way.

Meredith had never known such a pull on her heart. Carrying Nick's baby—their child—made every day a new adventure. It hadn't taken long to adjust to the idea of being a mother, something she'd never thought would happen. After a few months of morning sickness, her pregnancy had been easy.

In her early days at the Sheriff's Office she remembered

college friends displaying pictures of their kids. The friends had all graduated, married and sprouted kids about the same time—so many baby showers. Secretly, Meredith vowed never to be that woman. She had a career to build. Yet, after her son's birth, she understood the need to share your wondrous production with the world.

Having Davy changed her perspective and her heart. She was no longer the center of her universe. Every move she made was with his welfare in mind. She loved being a mother, and protecting her child was paramount to that role.

Trust wasn't something that any cop comes to easily. Meredith had her share of life's betrayals. The exceptions were her friend Christy, Nick and Raymond Cavanaugh. They'd all been loyal to a fault. Nick had asked her to trust him and Cav. She could do that—but Filomena? She'd had a good feeling about her and wanted to believe the woman was trustworthy. In the end, Meredith gave in. Cav would be there. She felt the baby would be safe.

CHAPTER EIGHT

Meredith closed the door of Cavanaugh's guest bedroom. Filomena had been in her 'little house' for two months now. In the kitchen, Cav had a cup of steaming hot coffee ready for Meredith at the table.

"Davy's down for his nap, even though he slept on the drive here."

"He's tired. Got woke up in the middle of the night." The old man's voice rumbled like tires over gravel.

She nodded. The back door shut behind Jake as the teen rushed off to after-lunch chores. "You're not going with Jake?"

"Nah." The rancher's thin-lipped smile crinkled up to his eyes. "I'm enjoying a cup of coffee with my friend."

Meredith grinned. "Fine with me." This reedy old man had saved her life—and Nick's—several times. He was something, all right. "Thanks for letting us stay."

"Ah," he waved her gratitude aside. "So, what's going on?" He took another sip.

She drew a deep breath and recounted the story. Nick had given up the basics over the phone, but now Cav wanted specifics.

When she finished, his jaw set like granite. "No idea who the intruder was?"

Meredith shook her head. She should've passed up the coffee—the caffeine was messing with her anxiety level. "Not a clue."

"Any chance he was just some burglar?"

"There's no way to answer that without talking to him." She frowned, wishing she knew more. "Nick's at the house now." After a glance at the kitchen clock, she said, "He was going to catch a nap, see if Petaluma PD got a hit on the prints, then come up here."

They sat in companionable silence. Her family was safe

here, two hours from home under Cav's watchful eye.

The Cavanaugh Ranch had become Meredith and Nick's personal oasis in a crazy world. Set in sheep and cattle country in the Sonoma hills, the ranch sat above the tourist route of vineyards and wine tasting rooms. The remote location was peaceful, quiet: The 1,000-foot elevation also kept the property above the fog and traffic. Vast meadows, rocky outcroppings and verdant groves of conifers and mixed oak cloaked the oat-grass slopes. The hour's drive to Geyserville, the nearest town, promised solitude.

The very air she breathed calmed Meredith. Three days off work in these golden hills usually renewed her and Nick for the grind they endured with the Sonoma County Sheriff's Office.

The Reyes had grown to love the property as much as they loved its patriarch. They savored a rare and secure friendship that started two years earlier. At the last homicide case Nick and Meredith worked together, Cav reported finding a body high in the hills above Lake Sonoma. The investigation led to the discovery of a secretive, radical militia group planning a dangerous assault on the local water supply. Cavanaugh had been sealed into an uneasy alliance with the detectives by a landslide and communications breakdown. After setting out with plenty of suspicion, the three had fused into a force to be reckoned with. They'd arrived at trust with bullets zinging around them; Cav was a tough old dog who didn't run from a fight. He'd risked his own skin to save Nick and Meredith's lives.

After the terrorist incident, Raymond Cavanaugh returned to the home he'd built four decades ago with the help of his now deceased wife, Shirley. It was on this ranch they'd raised and nurtured a family, a boy and girl. Both were grown, had their own families and had settled two counties away. That is, except for grandson, Jake, Raymond's son's boy, who lived on the ranch. He'd gotten into a little trouble in his last year of high school. It had been rough on everyone, and Jake's desperate father had called upon his own dad for help. Raymond's wife, Shirley, had passed away two months before, but Raymond knew what she would've done. So, he took Jake in. The boy would finish high school in Geyserville. Jake, the only family member interested in living on the ranch, had an eye to running it when Raymond retired, so it was a win-win for everyone. Jake straightened out and currently attended the junior college in Santa Rosa.

At the Cavanaugh Ranch, Meredith and Cav sometimes took the horses for trail rides while Nick worked on the barn, spent time with Davy, or swam with Jake in the pool. This all happened under Filomena's devoted care.

Raymond Cavanaugh built the home in the eighties, with help from his volunteer fire fighter friends. The kitchen, updated two years before Shirley's death, wasn't Architectural Digest material but was efficient and stylishly functional. Meredith loved this room. She pictured Shirley Cavanaugh preparing meals for her family, back in the day. She wished she'd known the woman.

Filomena bustled into the kitchen; a basket of laundry propped on one hip. She was small and delicate, yet sturdy. One would never guess she'd given birth to six kids. "You need something?"

Cav grunted a "No," while Meredith smiled at the woman. Cav had struck gold by bringing Filomena here. She'd made the place a home again. Still, Meredith had noted a bit of Jake's teenage resistance to Filomena. The woman worked to earn his respect, letting little slights go without comment.

Even with her hands full, Filomena kept a close eye on Davy during visits. While Meredith was off helping with chores, the housekeeper babysat.

When the door to the back porch slammed as Filomena left, Cav picked up where they'd been. "What are you going to do if you get an ID from the fingerprints?"

"Depends." She ran through the possibilities: Follow-up themselves, leave it to Petaluma PD, or report it to her boss, Lieutenant Ferrua. "If we don't get a match, we reach a dead end. We do nothing."

His lips curled into a grin. "I've never known you to 'do nothing'."

"I can't say what kind of follow-up Petaluma PD will do." She sighed. "I doubt my boss will get our agency involved." She traced a finger around the lip of her coffee cup. She smiled as a thought struck her. "You're right. I'm not good at waiting around."

Cav lifted his coffee cup and took a sip, then plopped the cup down, his eyes sharp. "Tell me, what do you want? I mean, in life—besides finding out who broke into your house."

Surprised, she thought a moment. "You mean, like goals or—?"

His craggy face opened to a smile as he waited.

"Once, I wanted to be the best patrol deputy I could be. Promote to sergeant or lieutenant," She shrugged. "Now, with Davy, all that seems superficial. I want to be a good wife and mother. I want our child to grow up healthy and safe." She shrugged at the ordinariness of it. So what? She couldn't dismiss it because it didn't fit into her former upwardly mobile trajectory. After she lost her first husband, Richard, the impetus for self-promotion floundered. Troubled by the loss and the events surrounding it, she'd been in flux for over a year. Then, when Nick asked her to marry him, and with Davy on the way, everything changed. She was content in a way the job could never satisfy.

"I'll be happy if nobody shoots at me anymore." To be a wife and mother, to keep my family safe. That was what she wanted, to her core.

"Man, you would've loved Shirley." Cavanaugh's voice was deeper than usual; it was clear her words had touched him.

Meredith's fingers covered his fist. Work-hardened, bruised and scraped, the old man's hand clasped hers with astonishing tenderness. She hadn't realized, until this moment, how Cav's presence made her a better person. He asked questions where answers mattered and made her think hard.

"She would've wanted you to be safe here." His voice was raspy. "You and your family are welcome as long as you need to be here."

CHAPTER NINE

Davy awoke, fussing and calling for her from the back of the house. Meredith rose from the table as Cav muttered something about helping Jake with the fencing. In the bedroom, she picked up her son and settled into a worn rocking chair. The wooden arms betrayed battle scars from Shirley's efforts to calm her babies. A midmorning breeze fanned the sheer drapes and cooled the sun-drenched bedroom. Meredith sighed with the rocking motion, feeling the weight of her precious son. She loved this chair.

With Davy on her chest, arms across him, she rocked until they both nodded off.

Her damned phone shattered the quiet. Wishing she'd left it in the car, she looked at the screen. It could be Nick.

The number was an old Santa Rosa prefix, a land line.

She answered, "Ryan."

"Uh, Ms. Ryan? This is Emily from the Haven Convalescent Hospital in Santa Rosa."

Meredith's mind clouded. "Okay?" At first, this made no sense at all. Then, Meredith understood. The Haven was where her father lived. At least he did nine months ago when she signed the conservatorship papers.

"It's about your father, Terence Ryan." The woman cleared her throat—likely a fruitless effort to ease her own tension. "He's passed, ma'am."

Meredith didn't trust her own voice. "Hmm?" No matter how many times you gave this news, it wasn't easy. She'd given her share of death notifications—knocking on a stranger's door, looking at their shocked faces as you tell them someone they love is dead. Getting the call was even worse.

Emily rushed on as if the faster she delivered the news, the sooner she could get beyond this phone call. "He passed away this morning. I'm sorry for your loss."

"Yes, thanks." She imagined all the platitudes: No more

suffering. Easy when you're dead. No, Terence Ryan suffered every day of his life—and made everyone around him feel the pain, too. "What happened? His heart?"

"Dr. Francis, our staff physician, attended to him so he's the one you need to ask. But yes, I believe it was related to his cardiac history."

"What do I need to do now?"

"We call a mortuary. His Advance Directive says Adobe Knolls. Is this still your preference?"

"Yes," she mumbled. She remembered getting his will together months ago, bringing it to him, watching him scratch his signature on the dotted line. Of course, he'd told her what he wanted the will to say. And she'd followed his wishes. There was no one to contest his last testament, no real property to speak of. The job of executor wouldn't be a huge drain on her. In the interest of doing it by the book, she'd run the will by an attorney who'd agreed to handle the income taxes and any other issues that came up.

As if she abhorred a silence, Emily said, "If you want to see him, you'll have to talk to Adobe Knolls."

Meredith hadn't seen her father since the day she signed his estate papers. He made it clear that he didn't want her around, in spite of his reluctant trust in her—he'd named her executor of his will. Still, his last words were, "Don't let the door hit you in the ass—"

"No, I'm up in Geyserville now. Just call the Adobe Knolls. I'll contact them in the morning."

"Ms. Ryan," the woman began in an officious tone. "Do you have any wishes about his personal effects? We can hold them for safekeeping for a little while, but—"

Biting off her frustration, Meredith said with a finality that permitted no further comment, "I'll stop by today."

A minute later, she ended the call and studied the funeral home information she'd scratched on a scrap of paper.

Terence Ryan was dead. Terrible Terence, beater of wives, batterer of sons, a man who never met a holiday or school event he couldn't ruin with his drunken abusive behavior. Dead. Terrible Terence.

Meredith smirked at the irony of that nickname. She'd been ten years old hiding with her brother, David, in the lawnmower shed behind their row house in the Sunset District of San Francisco, Eleventh and Judah. They'd hid out the sanctuary of the shed. Terrible Terence—she'd uttered it from the depths of her fear of him. As they sat, they began to giggle from the anxiety that Terrible Terence had infused in their lives. He beat their mother on a regular basis and slapped and punched David. For some reason, her father hadn't raised a hand to her.

The memories pitched her back to full consciousness. Terrible Terence was dead.

CHAPTER TEN

Meredith slipped her backpack and the baby's duffle to the kitchen tile. Davy held her other hand, unsteady on his toddler legs. Filomena buzzed from the refrigerator to the sink, then to the counter with lunch preparations. Sandwich makings, soup bubbling in a pot, homemade cole slaw, and store-bought oatmeal cookies covered the counter for a buffet-style meal. She looked up from stirring the pot on the stove and noticed the luggage. "You're all packed up. Are you leaving?" Her dark Latin eyes squinted their dismay at Meredith. "But you just got here!"

Meredith flashed a rueful smile. "I know."

"But I haven't had any time with my little man." Filomena dropped the spoon and bustled across the room to put a dainty hand on Davy's back. Dropping Meredith's grip, he reached for Filomena, snuggling into her welcoming bosom. "Meena, Meena, Meena."

Meredith smiled, pleased with how well her son had taken to Filomena. The woman was so good with children. Salvador, Jake's best buddy, was the youngest of her grown family. The two boys had graduated from high school last year. Salvador earned a soccer scholarship to University of California, Riverside, and would be staying down south during the summer to work.

"You miss your children, don't you?" Meredith knew the truth of it. She had trouble leaving Davy behind when she went to work.

Filomena nodded with sadness. "They are all grown. Two in college and three married, one working."

"They're all doing well?"

"Yes, praise God." Pride glinted in Filomena's eyes. "I thank Him every day for Mister Raymond's job offer. Now I don't have to pay rent, and I send money to Salvador and my other son in college. I can save for a trip to Mexico, too. I hope to get my US credentials. Then, I can substitute teach in the Geyserville Elementary School."

Meredith said, "It was a great idea for both of you." Cav had come to rely on Filomena. As independent as he believed himself, Cav needed a firm female hand to manage the house. So did Jake, although the boy spent more time at Santa Rosa Junior College than he did on the ranch. Jake had followed through with his promise to get an education.

"But I miss babies. No grandchildren yet." She nuzzled Davy's neck and made him giggle. "I don't even mind changing diapers."

From the back porch came the high-pitch squeal of a faucet and water splashing into a concrete deep sink. Cav and Jake were washing up.

Filomena's head snapped toward the noise, then back again. Her gaze was intent on Meredith. "How long will you be gone? I can watch him if Mister Raymond says it's okay."

"Says what's okay?" Cav grumbled as he and Jake walked through the back door.

"Mister Raymond, it's okay with you for me to watch little Davy, isn't it?"

"Thanks, but no, Filomena." Meredith spoke before Cav could answer. "I've already talked to his daycare lady." Suddenly, she couldn't send her son away—even to Cav's. Then to her friend, "It's my father. He's died." She surprised herself by how easily she spoke the words.

"Sorry to hear that." Cav frowned. He didn't often let his face express emotion. But now he was open and unguarded, a rare thing she felt honored to see. He stood, hat in hand, murmuring his regret.

"He wasn't well." She'd told him that much before.

Cav's head dipped. "You'll have business to attend to. Want lunch before you go? It's a long drive home." He nodded to Jake, who seemed to understand their unspoken language.

Jake moved around and took Davy from Filomena's embrace, plopping the child in a highchair. After dropping a handful of Cheerios on the tray, he pulled up a chair in front of the baby, handed him a peeled banana and sat clowning as

Davy ate and giggled. Meredith was always surprised at the delight with which both Jake and Raymond held Davy.

Filomena got back to work; bustling between the refrigerator, sink and kitchen counter to load food on the table.

Meredith glanced at the kitchen clock over the sink, 12:30. "Thanks, but I'm not hungry."

"Death is never easy." Cav pursed his lips like he wanted to say something else. After a pause he added, "No matter how you felt about him."

"I guess." She gathered her scattered thoughts and leaned toward him. "I don't know what I feel. I mean, he was awful to us. He beat my mother black and blue anytime she crossed him. He'd whip my brother for no reason." She met his gaze. "He shattered any trace of self-respect my mother had. And my brother was—" Her gaze shifted away, uncomfortable with Cav's riveted attention. "My brother, David, had a huge heart, but ended up without a responsible bone in his body. I think he was afraid of becoming like my father—cruel and hateful."

"But your father didn't harm you?" A tiny squint. "Thank God for small mercies, eh?"

"I don't know." She shook her head. "I never knew what made him so angry."

"And now you might never find out."

She studied her hands. "I know. And it's confusing. His career in SFPD was a dream job. His wife and family loved him. Or wanted to, at least. He threw it all away." Meredith wondered what she was supposed to feel. She thought how screwed up her head must be, to deny the grief this moment deserved.

Cav's face sagged. "I don't have answers for you."

Meredith's thoughts turned from her father to Raymond Cavanaugh. In the months since Cav had come into her life, he'd become the anchor she'd been missing. He was a good friend—the best, after Nick. Sensible and stable, he was someone she could rely on. He had in so many ways, become the father she'd always wanted. Meredith reached out and covered his hand with hers. She knew he felt the same way toward her.

As silent as his grandfather, Jake stood looking over Filomena's shoulder at the soup. When she put the pot on the table, he slipped into his chair and lifted a ladleful. Filomena smacked his hand. "Wait for your *abuelo*," she scolded.

Then, to Meredith, "Are you sure you don't want to leave Davy here? You'll have your hands full with arrangements." Cav's gaze fell to his housekeeper.

From across the room, Jake smirked. "It'll get Filomena out of my hair for a few days."

"I can't." Meredith shook her head. "I need to have him close. My neighbor, Tina's going to watch him."

Filomena cleaned up scattered Cheerios, mopped Davy's mouth and brought him over to Meredith. He settled into her lap and began to nod off.

"I hate to wake him, but it's time to go."

CHAPTER ELEVEN

Meredith slipped behind the wheel of her well-worn Subaru, her feelings a mix of relief and sadness. In the car seat behind her Davy fought against sleep, his head bobbing. She took a deep breath, glad for the travel time to sort things out.

Tina, Meredith and Nick's neighbor and day care provider, had said she'd be happy to take Davy as Meredith wrapped up her father's affairs. While Meredith wanted her son close by, she didn't want to drag him to county offices, care homes and mortuaries. Having him with Tina would allow her more mobility, too.

Halfway down the hill to Highway 101, Davy was sound asleep. Meredith pulled over to the road's shoulder and dialed Nick.

"What's going on?" he answered. Nick almost always knew when she was in turmoil. Even over the distance, by phone, he knew.

"My father died this morning. I've got to go down to Santa Rosa and make arrangements. First to the Haven Care Home to pick up his things." She rushed through the last sentence.

"Damn," Nick breathed. "I'm sorry, babe."

"It wasn't unexpected—"

"I know, but that doesn't take away any of the pain," Nick said.

Pain? She wasn't sure how she felt. She'd had an hour to let it sink in, but she still felt—numb? She guessed this was the mind's way of coping so the grieving person could get through the final arrangements.

"Look," Nick was already planning. "I'm pulling into our driveway. Give me a few minutes and I'll meet you at the Haven Care home—the same one, right? I'll call the office and cancel the range this afternoon." To spend a few days at the ranch, they'd rearranged their schedules, excepting his department-required qualification shoot. This was Nick's last graveyard before his short three-day vacation. Now, canceling the shoot, he'd have to make it up another time.

"I have Davy with me. I know we wanted him out of harm's way," she paused. "but I need him close by whenever possible."

"Well, this puts a whole new spin on the situation."

She was grateful he didn't raise an objection. He sounded tired. Meredith gave him a brief run-down of the call from the Haven.

Nick was silent on the other end. Was he looking for a way out? No, not Nick. She worried about her father's impact on their lives, even now. It was unavoidable for Meredith, but Nick—he was patient, but she knew he hated what Terence had done to her and their family.

"But you don't have to come with me." She chewed her lip. "It's not like I'm mourning or anything. We expected this, and now it's here. You'd rather go to the range, anyway." A smile broke through the feeling of a leaden weight—guilt, was it? She would rather go to the range.

"No. I'm going with you." His voice was granite. He'd decided.

Damn, but Nick Reyes could be stubborn. In this case, she was relieved to have him. "I'll keep Davy with us. Tina's not available today." She sighed. "I'm on my way to The Haven now. I want to get this over."

Nick's voice softened. "You're okay?"

"Yeah. I'm fine. This stuff just sucks the energy out of me."

"I know."

"But I am okay. I'll meet you there." She disconnected.

Was she okay? She didn't feel anything. Shock? No, she didn't think so. Anger? No, obligation, more likely. She didn't care—couldn't care—about her father.

Oh yeah? What about the time he took her to work with him? The spring of 1992. At the San Francisco Police Stables, he'd introduced her to his partners, Jerry and Fred,

time at work. This wasn't work, it was heaven!

He'd taught her how to ride properly, at first using mature horses headed for retirement. The Ryan Family couldn't afford a horse, so she did chores around the neighborhood, saving enough to rent horses at the civilian Golden Gate Park Stables a mere thirty feet from the SFPD Stables. Meredith spent as much time as she could at both places, for the horses and to escape the increasing quarreling between her parents.

When she was twelve, trail riding around Golden Gate Park grew boring. She took up the challenge of English jumping lessons and learned how to groom for shows. Some horse owners even paid her for the work and, putting the wages to work for her, she enrolled in every stable-sponsored show she could qualify for. She often took home ribbons in Equitation and Jumping classes.

Sometimes she'd look up and see her father in the crowd. He didn't always attend, and never stayed; she figured he was on a work break. But when he was in the stands it meant everything to her desire for a normal family life.

At the same time, his behavior to Meredith's mother and brother was anything but normal, so her feelings about him were all mixed up. She loved him—he was her father and he'd passed on a love of horses. But she hated him for how he'd mistreated David and Mom.

In the summer of 2000, when she was fourteen, her father left the family. The riding halted right after.

Her mother sank into a depression: Nora Ryan barely made it through the night janitorial job which paid the rent. Meredith's younger brother, David, had no sense of responsibility, and Terence gave Nora little of what he earned, so it fell to Meredith to help with the family's finances. Washing dishes at a neighborhood Italian café put food on the table.

Meredith occasionally managed an hour's ride at the stables, even participating in one show—her last—between classes at San Francisco State U. in the summer of 2003. She thought she caught a glimpse of her father at that event, but by the time she turned to look, he was gone.

That was her father—elusive and absent. He never laid a hand on her and kept her at a distance. In her father's spectrum of emotions, this benign neglect was about as positive as he got. She'd felt guilty about that; couldn't figure out why. She wondered if she'd have felt more like family if he had beat her.

Now he was gone for good, and her tears were in lockdown.

CHAPTER TWELVE

"We all loved him." The sentiment was shallow, the speaker's eyes tracking to Nick, who stood behind Meredith.

The woman behind the desk at the Haven Convalescent Home was in her late fifties. Her outfit couldn't belt in decades of bad food choices. A hot pink blouse stretched across her full bosom and shiny slacks pulled taut around her midriff and butt. An overstuffed disco bunny.

The receptionist's smile didn't reach her eyes. In fact, her air was that of a person who has manufactured a brand of synthetic sympathy. She pushed her glasses up the bridge of her nose as she looked at Meredith, tipping her head in a cloying gesture. "He was so nice."

Meredith decided the woman was too old to lie outright like that. Then, wondering if she had the wrong patient, Meredith asked, "We're talking about Terence Ryan, right?"

"Yes. Third door on the right, 3A."

Suddenly tired of the woman's fiction, Meredith was ready to dismiss her and The Haven. "Can you get me his belongings?"

"Oh yes." The receptionist looked behind them to an empty hallway. "If you'll wait a few moments, please. We have them secured in the Administrator's Office. The door is closed now."

"We'll wait," Nick spoke up from around Davy's curls. The child was asleep on his shoulder.

"Mr. Ryan didn't have many visitors."

If the woman was trying to make conversation, she was doing a poor job. Meredith didn't feel guilty in the least. "No doubt."

"We don't keep track of visitors so much anymore, but there was one lady who came sometimes. The last time I saw her, she used a walker. I just assumed she—"

They heard a door open in the administration hallway, and the receptionist stopped talking and rose. As she waddled down the hall, Meredith realized how depressing the place was. At least it smelled of disinfectant instead of urine, as had several other facilities they'd visited. The staff had seemed attentive when Meredith and Christy had first scouted this place for Terence. Now, the same people seemed nosy and officious.

Meredith glanced sideways. Her father's room was right there, third door on the left. She saw the shadow of movement in the room. Curious, she walked toward it, Nick following.

The sun shone through the window at an attendant's back, creating the silhouette. A dark-skinned man in his forties wiped what looked like food off the wall. His muscular arms swung an industrial-sized sponge in broad strokes. Juice spattered behind the bed confirmed that Meredith's father hadn't been a model patient. Something bad had happened here.

Meredith caught the attendant's eye. "This is—was—my father's room. What happened?"

The man shrugged. "Sometimes the patients get excited." A slight accent gave away the man's Hispanic heritage.

"It looks like there was a fight," Meredith commented, eyeing the food mess and bed clothes on the floor.

He nodded.

"What? What happened?"

"The man got mad and then they were fighting."

"A fight or an argument? With who?" That sounded more like Terence Ryan. Still, it was doubtful her father was up to it physically. "The receptionist said everyone loved him."

The attendant frowned, a parent telling his child the disagreeable facts of life. "She always says that." He shrugged again. "It's what you people want to hear."

Meredith let go of any hope that Terence Ryan had redeemed himself before he died. Even ill, her father was a prick who went down fighting. "What about the other guy?"

"He was okay." The attendant looked away. "He left.

I've never seen him before." The man resumed cleaning her father's dinner from the wall, muttering. "They figured out how deal with 3A."

Hmm, her father's room and bed assignment. She had to know. "What do you mean?"

Looking sorrowful, his head moved from side to side. "Medicine and hobbles."

"Hobbles?" She flashed on her father training a young horse: hobbles—stout leather straps shaped like a figure-8 to prevent the animal from moving around. It wasn't inhumane if it was done properly. Uncontrollable prisoners were sometimes hobbled for transport. Again, done correctly, it wasn't inhumane.

"Restraints." Nick startled her from behind. She turned to looked into his eyes. Did he feel the same dismay? His stone face gave nothing away. She had the lead on this.

Shock? Embarrassment? Shame that her father had been so difficult? Anger at the staff that had to restrain him physically?

Nick looked like he was waiting for her reaction first. "Mere?"

She sighed. Terence Ryan, even dead, made life difficult for those around him. But it didn't matter anymore. It was over.

Suddenly she wanted out of his room, now almost sanitized for another unfortunate senior. She wanted out of The Haven—this place that was anything but a haven for her. She needed to get away from the memory of Terrible Terence.

Meredith bolted, making for the entrance. She burst through the automatic doors, taking a huge gulp of fresh air. She trotted across the parking lot, trying not to sprint, and stopped at their truck. She bent over the hood. The sun-warmed metal felt good against her skin, doing battle with sudden goosebumps.

"Mere, take a deep breath." Nick stood beside her, balancing Davy's wobbly head.

She inhaled again. The smell of road dust from the

truck's hood brought her back to reality. "Damn. I don't know what happened." She shook her head, amazed at her own reaction. "I had to get out of there."

Nick put a hand on her shoulder. "Understandable." He handed Davy to Meredith. "You wait here. I'll go back in and get your father's things."

In minutes, Nick was back with a battered maroon briefcase. He tossed it in the Subaru's back seat—far enough away from a certain toddler's reach. "Let's drop your car at the house. We'll take the truck to the funeral home."

CHAPTER THIRTEEN

She settled on embarrassed.

Over a year of therapy sessions had taught her to sort and label her feelings. As a cop, this helped her and the therapist, Dr. Kathie Servente. Identifying what bothered her enabled Meredith to put those things on a shelf with a new label, "Something to work on." Being raised by a taciturn cop and a hysterical Irishwoman had taught her to bury feelings. Being a deputy with Sonoma County Sheriff's Office reinforced this natural reluctance to show emotions. Then, in 2013, it all boiled over after she'd shot a man. She was ordered to seek professional help. She had grown anxious of the job's potential for killing, afraid she'd be forced to do it again.

Then, less than a year later, she killed another man with her bare hands—strangled him. The brutality of it still shocked her. Knowing she had no choice didn't silence her inner critic. The man was trying to kill her. She'd learned some hard realities the past few years. No matter how much you give the job—and life—more could always be extracted.

Her father's brutal estrangement was one of the worst lessons—one that was winding to a close. She hoped. Just when Meredith thought she could be left in peace to savor the wonderful change in her relationship with Nick, marriage and a baby, Terrible Terence surfaced to grab center stage again. In some ways, she felt sorry that Davy would never have grandparents to spoil him. But then again, Terence wasn't one of that kind.

She sucked in a determined lungful of air. Well, she'd get through this. Then it would be done—forever. At least Davy would never witness his grandfather's rage. She was free to explain Terrible Terence when Davy asked—sometime in the future. She suspected he would be in school before he learned about the role of grandparents. Nick's father had died years ago, and his mother passed away just and glowed with pride as he showed her how to groom horses. Terence even put her in the saddle.

She couldn't have been more than six, but she still remembered how her heart thumped the first time her fingers touched a horse's soft nose. With her father's rough hand guiding, she reached up to the reddish-brown behemoth called Patrick. Scared, yet fascinated, she let her father push her trembling fingers closer to the animal.

Patrick, Terence's quarter horse/thoroughbred cross, dipped his head obligingly. He was just as curious as Meredith. Huge gentle eyes blinked as he sighed into her hand. His warm breath energized her. Contact! His nose felt like her mother's velvet Christmas dress, but wrinkled.

"He likes you," her father smiled. "But then," he continued, his smile hardening, giving her a look saying she wasn't anything special. "He likes everybody." A small corner of her mind curled up with hurt, but she made herself shrug off his slight. Even at that early age she was used to his disapproval.

"I like him." With that, she was hooked. Patrick's musky smell, his gentle nudge as he looked for a carrot, his immense kindness—all of it captured her heart. She'd ridden him that day, squished between her father and the saddle horn. At the walk Patrick paced rhythmically, jerking Meredith's head against her father's chest with each step.

"Tighten up your belly muscles, Mere." Then, "Look between his ears at where you're going." Then, "Press your legs into his sides to make him go."

Already tall for her age, her six-year old legs had little effect on the horse's motion. Then Terence guided them into the lope, an easy, rocking motion where her father moved with the horse like a dancer. At first Meredith jammed up against the black saddle horn, but she soon found a comfortable position and let the motion do the work. Her pulse pounded in her ears at Patrick's magnificent tempo as he carried them around the ring.

Thus began a life-long passion briefly shared between father and daughter. This was why her dad spent so much after Davy was born.

Nick snaked an arm around her waist, and she sagged into him. They stood like that for a few minutes, until Meredith collected herself. "You're right. Let's go." She would've loved the luxury of someone else taking over, but this was her mess. She was the only one who could untangle the chaos her father had left behind. Now, she wished she'd thought to ask the janitor to describe the man who fought with her father. She wondered if she knew him. Then dismissed the thought.

She had work to do. Serious, get-this-over-as-soon-as-you-can work.

Nick glanced at his wristwatch. "Do we have time to stop at Christy's? I think you should tell her about your father face to face. What do you think about taking her out to lunch? She loves hamburgers and there's…"

"Love the idea, Nick." Meredith smiled, delighted at the growing affection between her husband and her best friend. "Let's let her pick the restaurant."

They strapped the baby in, and Nick got behind the wheel. When he turned on the engine, the radio blared a vintage Marty Robbins song. Meredith reached over and turned it down.

"Hey," Nick began.

"You're the only Mexican I know who listens to old Country and Western music." Meredith stifled a smile, glad she was driving home in her Subaru.

"This takes me back. My Dad used to listen to it. It's how he learned English."

Meredith smiled at her husband's fond memory. A small part of her wished she had something like it from her father.

It wasn't long before they had dropped Meredith's Subaru in their driveway and were on their way to the mortuary.

The morning fog had burned off, and the City of Petaluma basked in late spring warmth. Predicted to top out at a comfy 80 degrees, the town was alive with the business of maintaining its image. A quaint suburb at the northernmost end of the San Francisco metropolitan area, Petaluma was bisected by Highway 101. The east half of the mostly residential city sprawled over yesterday's dairy cattle pastures. The old part of town sat to the west, where Queen-Anne-style turrets towered over Craftsman's bungalows that sidled up to mid-century moderns. The area west of the highway included the Victorian era downtown. The Masonic Building at Western Avenue and Petaluma Boulevard South with its ornate 135-year-old clock tower stood as the unofficial center of town. The downtown buildings were the real deal—the devastating 1906 earthquake completely missed downtown Petaluma. From San Francisco, the San Andreas Fault line zigged out to Tomales Bay and zagged inland to Fort Ross, where it shook the alluvial plain on which Santa Rosa sat twenty miles east. Santa Rosa suffered devastating damage, while Petaluma went unscathed. Thus, the historic iron fronts stood proudly, their legacy secured by the efforts of history-minded citizens. population comprised pioneering Italian and Portuguese dairy families and millennials who'd grown up in the area, gone to college and returned. Both factions found the town comfortable to raise their own families. The gentle balancing act between the demographics made Petaluma a tolerant, welcoming place to live.

Meredith had fallen in love with the town on her first exploration. When her home sold in Forestville three years before, she chose Petaluma as the place to start her new life. And now the city was the new Reyes-Ryan home. Meredith's best friend Christy was another reason to move to this town.

Adobe Knolls Funeral Home was a half-mile away from the Reyes home, while Christy lived two miles north at the city limits. Adobe Knolls was a seventies-vintage mortuary in the dark-wood-and-Mansard roof style, well established and maintained. The business's welcoming façade belied the fact that it held dead people. If you were alive, you were grieving.

Once again, Meredith acknowledged she was not

mourning. She was grateful for the lack of emotion so she could conduct the business of burying her father without the interference of messy feelings.

As she opened the door, a chime echoed from the back of the building. In the foyer, sedate paneling lined walls decorated with pastel oil landscapes. Here and there, small end tables held vases of silk flowers, the kind that would never die. Strategically placed bowls of potpourri masked the musty smell. With couches and chairs arranged in three distinct conversation areas, you'd be quite comfortable—if you didn't know where you were.

Meredith noticed the doorways to the dark rooms adjoining the foyer. She'd been to enough autopsies to be familiar with what they were doing to her father's body. A tiny shiver shot down her spine.

She stole a glance at Nick and Davy—her anchors in a tumultuous storm.

Soon, a plus-sized woman in a black-and-white sweater-skirt set met them. Her shiny auburn hair bounced as she walked, a candidate for a shampoo commercial. "Ms. Ryan?"

Meredith nodded. She'd never changed her name to Reyes. When they'd talked about it, Nick shrugged. "You're not my possession. I mean, you're still Meredith Ryan to me. It's your choice." She'd thought it odd that he'd been upset when his first wife, Angela dropped his surname. He didn't feel that way with her. It pleased her that he was satisfied with her decision. She'd kept Ryan, but not over any loyalty to the family name. More, it was who she was. It didn't have anything to do with a man.

"I'm Phyllis. I'm so sorry for your loss." Sincerity pooled in the woman's brown eyes. She was well-practiced in the decorum of mourning.

"Thanks." Meredith turned. "This is Nick Reyes, my husband."

A polite handshake followed, then Phyllis' attention swept back to Meredith. "If you'll come this way, we have some paperwork to finish up." They followed her down a dark corridor to a small, orderly office and a desk with two chairs on one side and one behind it for Phyllis. A lone file folder sat dead center on the desk's shiny surface. Phyliss ushered them to the chairs.

"I notice that you've already made arrangements." She waited for Meredith's assent. "To make sure nothing has changed: You still want cremation?"

Oh God, yes, Meredith thought. A precursor of things to come for Terrible Terence: She flashed on her mother's desperate shouts as her husband walked out the door many years ago, "You'll roast in hell for this." She saw him surrounded by fire, suffering unimaginable pain for his sins.

"Yes." Her voice sounded strong. "Nothing's changed."

"I see you've decided against a funeral service."

"Right." What if I gave a funeral and no one came? "There isn't any family left, and his friends are all gone." Except for Uncle Desmond. Crap. He probably needed to know. She'd do anything to avoid talking to him. She wondered if Desmond's phone number was in her father's belongings. She hadn't spoken to her honorary uncle in years. He'd been Terence Ryan's partner, thereby awarded to her father in the divorce. "Maybe we'll think about a memorial at a later time."

"Fine," Phyllis said, with what Meredith thought was disapproval. The woman opened the folder and pushed a paper across the desk. "You'll see here that the arrangements have been paid for in advance." She used a pen to point. "If you'll sign here, please." The woman glanced over at Nick who stood, holding Davy's hands as the child wobbled in his effort to stand. "Will ten certificates of death be enough?"

Irritation spiked in Meredith. Phyllis should focus on her, not Nick. He wasn't the boss. He knew the plans, of course. Meredith had filled him in on the details as they'd driven over. She'd been grateful for his ear; she'd wanted to do the right thing for her father. Nick was a good sounding board.

Meredith answered. "Yes, that will be fine."

Handing Phyllis the pen, Meredith realized she was being hypersensitive. "Thank you for all you've done.

You've made this easier than I thought it could be."

Phyllis' smile was genuine. "It's my job, Ms. Ryan. We try to facilitate the easiest transition possible for those left behind." She stood. As Meredith rose, Phyllis asked, "Would you like to see him?"

"No." The word erupted from her chest before she could stop it. Davy looked up at the force of her answer. She'd almost shouted.

Meredith's voice softened. "No. I'd prefer to remember him as he was." A simple banality would suffice. Phyllis didn't need to know why Meredith chose not to see her father's body.

She shivered. Her mother used to say it happened when someone walked over your grave. Superstition. She felt like a veil dropped over her heart.

In her mind, she finally said the words: her father was a criminal—he'd battered his wife and son. It didn't matter that he never saw the backside of a jail door. That didn't change what the man did. He was dead now, but Meredith couldn't shake the premonition of Terence-generated troubles to come.

Nick grabbed her hand and gripped their son as they left the office.

CHAPTER FOURTEEN

In the truck on the way to Christy's, Meredith found her father's address book/calendar in the briefcase's outside pocket. She leafed through it. "I don't see Desmond's phone number anywhere. Maybe he had it in his phone." She tossed the calendar back in the pocket and picked up a flip phone. She'd left the service on so he could make or receive phone calls if he wanted. Month after month, the statement showed nothing but base charges. She almost felt sorry for him.

Lying in that nursing home bed, in a disinfected room with several other men, the faces changed often as patients healed and went home or died.

But Terence was difficult to get along with. She suspected many roommates simply requested another room. She'd pieced enough information together to determine even while he acted comatose, he'd sit up with a start, yelling at a roommate to turn down the TV or an attendant to remove the stinking food tray. The doctor had told Meredith that his heart was weak—aortic stenosis meant his heart wasn't getting enough blood flow. She knew that. But medically, Terence had chosen not to pursue treatment. He was firm in his decision to lay there and die. He'd even sent Hospice away. He had done it his way to the end.

No, she couldn't make the leap to pity. He'd done all this himself.

Meredith scrolled through the phone's contact list. "Desmond. Here it is."

"You going to call now?" Nick asked.

Meredith looked around. Another mile or two before they got to Christy's. "Yeah. It won't take long."

She selected the number, then pressed the call button.

"My man." Desmond Rollins' deep baritone answered. "What the hell's going on?" He greeted his old friend with familiarity, but his words suggested it had been a long time since they'd talked.

Meredith cleared her throat. "Uncle Desmond? It's Meredith. I have some bad news." She hated calling him "uncle."

She told him, giving him details as he asked but deliberately keeping distance between them. Yes, it was his heart. She felt no obligation to tell him that it had been especially taxed after he'd jumped out of bed and attacked a visitor. No, no funeral. Besides you, there isn't anyone who would attend. Yes, cremation. That should make her mother happy.

"Meredith, m' darlin'," Desmond said in the faint brogue she remembered him using when he wanted to charm. "You should come see me." The idea was absurd. Why would she want to see her father's old partner? He'd shown his loyalty lay with Terence. He'd made no attempt to keep in contact with her or her brother.

Yet, when her mother died, Desmond was there at her funeral. A small wedge of gratitude angled its way into Meredith's heart. While she had paid for the services, Desmond had opened his bar for a fitting wake—and picked up the tab. Plenty of friends showed to give Nora Ryan a proper send off. "Yes, I'll do that next time I'm in the City."

"No, really, Mere darlin'." His voice took on a practiced earnestness. His use of the contraction of her first name irritated her. Only Nick used that—now that her father was gone. "I have a box of your father's things here. I been keeping them for him." Why would she want any of Terence's stuff?

"Just toss it." Her voice was sharper than she'd meant to be.

"Meredith, these are your father's worldly possessions." His charming tone was wearing thin. "You should take them yourself. If you want them dumped, then you do it."

"I'll call you." After a vague promise to stay in touch, Meredith ended the call.

Nick flashed a wry smile as he pulled into Christy's driveway. "You didn't tell him about your new family." Was Nick upset?

She grimaced. "I debated, it but I didn't want to spend that much time with him."

He shrugged. "I guess I don't blame you."

CHAPTER FIFTEEN

"You should do something." Christy folded a stained dish towel. "I mean, he was your father." The three sat at Christy's tiny kitchen table, Nick holding the baby. Lunch in a restaurant had been a great idea but less than practical with a squirmy ten-month-old. In the end, they stayed at Christy's for sandwiches.

Nick watched his wife—the warring factions battling it out on her face. With a grimace, she presented an argument. "He wasn't a very good one. One day when David was eleven, he'd told Dad he'd written a song about him, that he was going to play it in the talent show at the school assembly the next week. David had left notes all over the house to remind Dad, but in the end, David played to the school. His father's guest of honor chair sat empty. David was crushed."

"Yeah, yeah," Christy waved the incident away. "But he was your father. It counts for something. You need to close this chapter of your life. You need to do it for yourself." Nick thought Meredith had already settled it years ago, but it looked like Terrible Terence was the gift that kept on giving. Annoyed that she was avoiding something so important, he put Davy on his knee. Leaning back in the chair, he waited for her response while the baby was busy spreading cracker crumbs all over daddy's pants.

Meredith spread a hand over her eyes, a sign she used when thinking. Nick waited, more patient now because he had Davy in his lap. He never tired of holding his son. This person, this being, was here because of his love for Meredith. What a treasure they'd created! Their son was an easy baby, slept through the night almost right away and cried little. Nick felt full of love for the four people in the room. He believed he'd always loved Meredith, long before he admitted it. And he loved Davy the moment they'd created him—well, the moment he'd known they'd created him.

His feelings for Christy had taken longer. She was a pale

twin to Meredith, as blond and short as Meredith was tall and auburn-haired. They'd been friends before Christy had married Mere's brother, David, their son's namesake. Christy was always there for his wife, especially during the darkest period of her life when she'd lost her first husband, Richard. Both Richard and David had been killed by Meredith's stalker four years ago. Richard was killed to eliminate competition. Shortly afterward, David had been mistaken for a new suitor and killed by the same man.

The two women's shared grief strengthened their friendship.

Meredith dropped her hand and sat up straight. "I don't believe in 'closure.' My father will influence me for the rest of my life, whether I like it or not." She looked across the table at her friend. "But his time of haunting me is over. That I can memorialize. You're right. I should do something."

Nick sighed with admiration. Meredith could admit she was wrong and not assume the requisite Irish-Catholic guilt. She didn't take time for that. His girl was always in motion, either physically or emotionally. But pragmatic as always, she added, "But no funeral. He was adamant about not having one." A sardonic smile swept across her face. "I think he figured no one but Desmond would come."

The sun coming through the kitchen window gleamed on Christy's blond hair as she nodded. "At his burial, then?"

"He's being cremated."

"Okay," Christy was a terrier unable to let go of a bone. "When you get his ashes, we'll scatter them, bury them or whatever—"

"He wanted to be interred next to my mother." Meredith shook her head with the absurdity. "Desmond bought a niche for them both when mom died."

Christy's brows drew together. "Funny, huh? I mean, wanting to spend eternity with the woman you beat and abandoned. What d'you suppose—penance?"

"Who knows?" Meredith's eyes settled on Davy. He had changed everything, even her long-held animosity toward her father. Nick had seen forgiveness take hold and was pleased she was moving in this direction. Still, she hadn't seen her father in months. He guessed it was out of respect for his last comment to her, "Don't let the door hit you in the ass on the way out."

"When you put his ashes in the niche, then." Christy's eyes drilled Meredith. "And his time at SFPD? Wouldn't they want to know? I mean, doesn't he get a flag or something for his twenty-six years of service?"

Meredith sat up straighter. "I hadn't thought of that." He loved that Christy challenged his wife. What a good friend she was.

Then, Nick considered all the paperwork needed to bury a person. Social Security Administration had to know, SFPD's pension plan and health insurer, county recorder for the death certificate, his bank, and more. He was happy Tina would watch Davy tomorrow while he and Meredith sorted through the details.

The baby sighed as if the weight of the world was on his shoulders. His son would never hold a burden like Terence, Nick would see to it.

CHAPTER SIXTEEN

At home in their Petaluma kitchen, Nick brought in Terence Ryan's briefcase and set it on the buffet. He crossed his arms, savoring the quiet moments before the incoming storm—hurricane Terence. His wife sat at the dinner table cajoling their son into eating vegetables. Squashed peas, nobody's idea of good food. "You get him to eat that and I'm asking for a paternity test. No way he's my kid."

Meredith frowned, dropping the spoon. "I wouldn't eat it either."

Nick peeled a banana. "Try this."

A minute later, Davy giggled as he shoved mashed fruit into his mouth with both hands.

"Hon, you want tamales for dinner? There're some in the freezer." Nick had assumed cooking duties when they got married which helped keep Meredith away from the kitchen. He said it was for the sake of their survival.

"Yeah, just one, thanks." She stood and stretched. "While you get that ready, I'll look at my dad's stuff."

"You got that list of things you have to do? The Will and all?"

"It's in the office. I should keep all this together, though. Can you manage Davy and cook at the same time?"

Nick rolled his eyes. Of course.

"I'll be right back."

A certain amount of clutter came with the baby, but Meredith worked hard to keep their little bungalow in order. The briefcase looked out of place in the kitchen. Nick watched Meredith walk away, noticing how she didn't see the toy truck Davy had left on the floor. She almost tripped but veered around it at the last second. Normally she'd pick it up—his wife was a terrible cook but a very tidy housekeeper. He knew her mind was far away.

After putting the toy in a toy box, Nick put a pot of water on the stove. He dropped the tamales in the steamer basket and opened a can of chili.

Meredith walked back into the kitchen studying a yellow lined legal-sized paper, a manila folder clutched to her chest. "I've got most of this stuff under control. There's a copy of his Will in this file. The cremation and niche are paid for. I'll have to update the list of creditors, the nursing home, but I don't think there's anyone else. I had his checkbook. He had no real property or cars." After ticking the items off her list, she looked up at Nick. "I don't remember any jewelry. Maybe there's something inside."

Meredith picked up the battered leather case, placing it on the kitchen table. Weird that it held the material possessions of a man's entire life. Nick wondered where the important things went. On top? Was there anything significant? Her father didn't have much.

Nick shuddered, knowing how quickly one's life could be yanked away. Not much to show for Terence's—no loving wife, adoring children, warm home. He had none of the blessings Nick counted as his own now. Showing a distinct lack of faith, Terence had specified that there was to be no priest or Funeral Mass. He'd died alone, a sick, bitter man.

Meredith must have been thinking the same. "Not much of a legacy, is it?"

Nick sighed, not wanting to gang up on a dead guy. "He gave you life. For that, I'll be eternally grateful."

She smiled, the sentiment resonating with her own thoughts "Where do I fit in? I mean, I'm not like my mother. She fell to pieces if someone looked cross-eyed at her. Dad was demanding, hard, and unforgiving."

"His traits aren't inherently bad. It depends how far you carry them. You demand a lot of yourself—and others, too. You're not hard, but I'd say you're incredibly strong." He turned to the stove. "As for unforgiving—he should've been the one seeking clemency, not demanding it."

"I guess I can learn from him, how not to be." She looked at the damaged briefcase. "I want to check it out, but I'm nervous."

"There shouldn't be any surprises. You already looked in his address book." Nick shrugged, glancing on the slim volume. "Maybe he won the Powerball or invested in Google."

She gave a crooked smile at the improbabilities. "I feel like I'm gonna get my hand slapped any minute."

Nick bent to wipe Davy's hands as the boy shouted, "Dada, dada, dada." The baby's dark curls shook with delight at his father's attention. For the first time, Nick pitied Terence Ryan. Meredith's father would have missed all this. He would have been at work, or too drunk to see his children. He never bonded with his son, and barely with his daughter. At least he'd made enough time to pass on his love of horses. Still, Nick was sure even this passion had been more about Terence than his daughter.

Nick loved that Meredith had something of her own besides the family and career—her love of horses. It gave him a warm feeling that their friend, Cavanaugh, had welcomed them to his ranch for visits. Cav had made it sound like he needed Meredith to help round up strays at the end of the season. Nick saw how much help she'd been last summer, when Cav's grandson, Jake had been away visiting his father.

As Davy snuggled into Nick's broad chest, Meredith opened the briefcase. Nick watched her face harden.

"What's this?" She pushed aside the address book and picked up a bulky envelope. "He had a life insurance policy. What the hell?" Flipping open the pages, she read out loud. "April 1st, 2018, beneficiary is Brenda Houston. Twenty thousand dollars." Meredith's eyes closed for a moment; her lips pressed together. Then, "Who the hell is Brenda Houston?"

Nick kept quiet.

"This was just last week. Who's this woman he's giving money to? And why?" She slammed the papers to the table. "I can't believe he had a secret insurance policy."

The noise startled her dozing son. He fussed awake. She stomped around the kitchen table and took Davy from Nick.

Caressing the baby's forehead, she said, "I'm sorry, little man. Let's have a nice bath, then you can go to bed."

"Maybe there was a good reason—"

"Don't even try defending him, Nick." Her ring tone chimed from a back room. She was gone before he could finish.

Nick stood, his arms empty and his mind in a whirl. Damn that stupid, senseless man for hurting Meredith—even from the grave.

Nick pulled down the briefcase and leafed through bank statements before he even thought about it. The checking account balance was minimal but more than he'd expected—$3000.00. Statements going back four years—before Terence fell ill. Several thousand dollars from the San Francisco Employees Retirement System directly deposited the first day of every month. His electronic funds transfer to The Haven ate up most of the pension deposit when it was paid on the third of the month. A stack of statements from a modest deferred compensation account was rubber-banded together. He opened the top statement—the most recent. The pay-out of three thousand dollars quarterly to Brenda Houston. It showed a declining balance allowing for two more payments. Who was this woman? No wonder Terence didn't have anything else. He couldn't have afforded it while paying Houston and the care home.

Nick scanned the statements but found nothing that would tell him why Meredith's father would give most of his income to this woman. In his main account, the one with Meredith as a co-signer, the progression of Terence's illness was recorded in his increasingly scratchy handwriting. Nick bundled the bank records together with a rubber band and set them aside. He sat down, looking at the remaining papers. A few letters addressed to Terence, in a woman's cursive handwriting, care of Desmond Rollins, the Crazy Eights Bar, Ninth Avenue and Irving, San Francisco. The return address was Brenda Houston in Rohnert Park, California.

Nick picked up a letter and sat back in the chair. He should wait for Meredith. He wanted to read the letters. If there was anything hurtful, he could tear them up. Save his wife some pain.

No. He couldn't do that. Nick had learned how harmful it was to take power away from Meredith. She didn't need him to censor her father's letters. She understood Terence was a jerk. He'd proven it time and again. Besides, he trusted her to manage this new wrinkle. He fingered the envelopes. She'd handled much worse.

"Couldn't wait for me, huh?" Meredith came into the kitchen.

She still amazed him. He'd seen this woman dressed up and dressed down, beaten up, crying and tired. With resolute courage, she'd fought through battles most people never could imagine. But the way he thought she was the most beautiful was at this minute: her face flushed from bathing Davy, shirt sleeves rolled up, her long chestnut hair down with wisps in her eyes.

Nick smiled with the irony. "I had some strange idea I should protect you from your father."

Meredith stopped; eyes wide.

"But then I remembered who you are." He tossed the letters back in the briefcase. "I'll wait for you to read them."

She smiled back. "I've got to get Fresno out of the dryer." Referring to Davy's stuffed toy, an elephant, she nodded toward the utility room off the kitchen. "I'll be back when I finish reading him a story and put him to bed."

"Dinner will be ready in twenty minutes."

She crossed the room, leaned over Nick and kissed his forehead. She nudged his ear, whispering, "I love you." Then from the utility room, she pulled the stuffed toy from the dryer and was gone.

Twenty-five minutes later, Meredith slumped into a dinner table chair. Her hair hung loose, small tendrils curling around her forehead. "God, I'm tired."

Nick slid a plate of food in front of her. "This emotional stuff drains a person, doesn't it?"

"You mean, on top of raising a baby?" The shadows on her face cleared to a soft smile. She picked up a glass of

Coppola Winery Merlot. "This is nice, Nick." Her deep brown eyes caught his. She tipped her glass in a toast as he hoisted a clear bottle of Pacifico beer.

CHAPTER SEVENTEEN

Dinner and dishes were done before Meredith reached for the packet of letters on the sideboard. Gripping the stem of her empty glass, she sat at the kitchen table, staring at the packet.

Nick worried at her stress level. Most importantly, Davy was asleep. He'd checked while Meredith dried the dishes. Nick knew if Davy was awake, the baby would be her priority. Nick was deeply gratified that Meredith put their son before the hubris of her dead father. He couldn't help but compare his first wife, Angela, with Meredith. He still wasn't sure what Angela wanted out of life, but she'd made it clear it wasn't him. What had been heartbreak at the time, he now saw as a blessing. In Meredith's life, Davy was the most important person and Nick knew he was a close second. As it was supposed to be.

Meredith had her work face on—an expression that said her armor was in place and nothing could hurt her. Nick felt a vague sadness that she needed to brace herself to find out her father's secrets. Nick's own father died soon after he'd been hired by the Sheriff's Office. They'd enjoyed a mutual respect. While he wouldn't call his father a "friend," they were able to talk with few barriers.

Meredith flipped open the briefcase and pushed the papers aside. "I'll sort through the bank statements later."

She picked up the letter on top. Squinting at the mailing address, she said, "Dad must've used Desmond's address for mail. Weird, right?"

"You mean like, where was he living?"

"Yeah." She untucked the flap and pulled out a sheet of binder paper. "It's dated November 21st, 2008—ten years ago." She scanned to the bottom of the page. "It's signed, by Brenda." She read to herself for a few moments then said, "Listen to this. This woman was crazy pissed-off. She wrote, 'Terence, when you left last night, I felt awful. You hurt me.

I won't deny it. But no way did I deserve what you dished out. Therefore, there will never be more to our relationship—even with what we have together. I won't ever be able to believe you again. Honesty is a real problem for you, isn't it? You say you're being honest, but your honesty only hurts me. It's like you don't believe that I could care deeply for you. You shut me out. Your only friends are Desmond and the Crazy Eights. I won't share you with them. I can't. I want the money. Otherwise, leave me alone. Brenda'."

"At least your father was consistent. He hurt everyone."

Meredith reached for another letter. She read, then dropped it like it scalded her fingers. "Yuck, it's a love letter from this woman, dated the year before."

Nick glanced at the letter and found an interesting phrase. "I wonder what she meant by 'what we have together'?" A secret? A kid? A safe deposit box?

Meredith shrugged as she scanned the remaining half dozen letters. "These are all the same. In some she says she loves him and in some she hates him. And she still wants money."

At the bottom of the case, Meredith found a handful of yellowed newspaper clippings. Most had photos of Officer Terence Ryan and his mount, Casey, on the job, chasing down a purse-snatcher; a picture of Terence and Casey searching the polo fields in Golden Gate Park for a rape suspect; a profile story about Ryan's daily activity on mounted patrol; and more. Two articles were about an armed robbery at Harrison and Sixteenth Street, the Potrero neighborhood. The incident was newsworthy because a truck driver was shot during the crime. The second article followed up with the death of the driver—the armed robber was now a murderer two days after the original robbery.

She opened an envelope labeled 'employment' stuffed with papers. Something to shine a light on Terence's career? A copy of her father's SFPD separation papers dated August 1, 2001. Nothing new here.

Wedged in the corner was a plastic-capped, silver-colored key hung on a gold 18-inch linked chain—very masculine. A common Master Lock brand key.

"I wonder what this opens?" Nick picked it up. Nothing engraved, stamped or otherwise identifiable, other than the brand. "No way to tell."

She turned. "And why would he save letters from this woman?" Her face flushed. "I'm going to find out about Brenda. Why he was paying her after wounding her so deeply." She dropped the papers, her brow furrowed. "Tomorrow. The next four days are available for bereavement leave if I need it."

He'd expected that. Her natural curiosity was ramping up with every bit of Terence's history. It was odd, though, how her father, who cared for so few people in his life, must have loved this mystery woman. Of course, Meredith would have to find out about her.

"I have to go in tonight for a couple of hours to clear my desk. But I'm off for the next three days. I'll take the rest of the week off if you want. This qualifies as bereavement." He'd taken days off to work on the barn up at Cavanaugh's ranch and catch up on some chores and a little relaxation. Being physical had always been a stress-reliever, whether it was sports or construction. "Tina will take Davy. I told her we'd drop him off early."

"Thanks for arranging that. But there's no need to take time off. I'm fine." Meredith waved away his offer. Her face flushed as she reconsidered. "Okay, maybe take off the rest of the week."

Nick was pleased she wanted him with her. Her normal response to anything to do with her father was to withdraw. While their relationship had been refined by the fire of doubt and ordeals, Nick suspected that on this subject there was a lot he'd never know.

Should he push her? He watched her pull Terence's address book from the briefcase pocket, toss it inside and snap the case shut. No, he'd wait. He had a deadline for a few personnel evaluations that couldn't wait until he returned next week. There was a schedule to inspect. His patrol lieutenant was notorious for screw-ups with staffing levels. "Okay. I'll go in tonight and get this done as soon as I can, then be home for the week."

CHAPTER EIGHTEEN

That night, another patrol briefing over, Nick packed up his briefcase and headed to the patrol car lot. Graveyard shift ran from 9 P.M. to 7 A.M. Tonight, he'd marked a year as a graveyard patrol sergeant with no fanfare. His wife didn't make cupcakes for the team—his deputies were lucky to escape Meredith's culinary exploits. But Nick was content as he settled in for what his life would be—at least, for the next few years. He loved the work.

Nick shut the trunk of his marked unit and slipped behind the wheel. He'd already done the equipment check, the siren, PA system, and MDT—mobile data terminal—his technological lifeline to dispatch and the other deputies. His posse box—containing report forms, criminal codes cheat sheets and other resources—sat in the passenger seat. He tugged at his vest, stiff and uncomfortable under the seatbelt. Earlier, when he'd come into his office, the patrol lieutenant pressed him to fill in for a sergeant's sick call.

While this was not unusual, it was inconvenient. Nick had made some quick phone calls and arranged to have the day shift sergeant relieve him at 4 A.M. An hour, maybe two, in the office during shift would be ample to complete the paperwork. Then he could head home for a few hours' sleep.

"Sam 12 respond to 418 Dawson Street, Santa Rosa. On scene unit, Frank 19 is requesting a supervisor." Inside the normally even tone of the seasoned dispatcher, Maria, Nick heard an urgency. He tapped a command on his MDT. The Dawson Street call popped up as his assignment—an attempted suicide.

Dang, he hated these calls. According to the detail notes, the ambulance and fire company were still on scene. Their short time on the premises could mean anything. They might be stabilizing the victim for transport. Or, if the patient suffered catastrophically fatal injuries, there'd be no use trying to revive him. He glanced at the address again, feeling it tug at his memory. No, it couldn't be.

In the reporting party's information, only the first name was recorded: Donna. The dispatcher commented that the caller was hysterical. The victim was in the back yard. Gunshot was the method. Not many survive gunshot wounds when they're intent on killing themselves. The word gruesome didn't do enough to convey the horror of seeing someone you loved ending up like that.

Asking for a supervisor meant the victim likely didn't survive. The sergeant's approval was needed to call out VCI. Suicides were treated as a crime scene until the coroner made the determination on the cause of death. But the worst part about suicides was the people left in the wake of such despair.

418 Dawson Street, Santa Rosa. No. Please God. Don't let it be him.

CHAPTER NINETEEN

Meredith threw the sheet off and lay in bed, bathed in her own sweat. Petaluma lay northeast of the top end of San Francisco Bay. Nighttime fog in the summertime was typical. But this was early spring, and the evening failed to cool as was normal. She got up, went to turn on the floor fan but decided against it. The white noise might cover the sounds of another break-in.

She pushed aside the anxiety of a repeat incident. Chances were, the intruder was more spooked than she'd been. Rationally, she doubted he'd return. He'd know they were on alert for trouble.

Opening the bedroom sash window, she let anger guide her—she wouldn't live locked up in her house and be uncomfortable, by God. She opened the kitchen, dining room and living room windows, but left Davy's closed. A light breeze wafted through the house. That was better.

She lay down, resigned to elusive sleep. From the baby monitor beside her, she heard Davy's even breathing. What impact would her inquiries have on her son? What if Terence had done something bad? Why couldn't she just leave things alone?

She couldn't. It was part of who she was—she had to know. Was there something in her heredity that leaned toward the shadowy side of the law? If so, she could fight it if equipped with the knowledge. Couldn't she?

Ridiculous, right? She'd never felt the inclination to take something that wasn't hers. What had her father done? Had he been on the take?

A childhood memory popped up—Terence dragging her brother David back to the corner market to pay for a pack of bubble gum he'd shoplifted. She thought back, searching her memory for a clue of dishonesty. There was certainly no extra money in the household. The Ryans struggled to pay the rent, even with Nora's job. No, he wasn't crooked.

What was he involved in? She had to know, for Davy's sake and her own. What kind of man had her father been?

CHAPTER TWENTY

The neighborhood was in northeastern Santa Rosa, on the border of the burned and randomly spared homes of the October 2017 wildfires. In an inferno that rolled out of the hills into Santa Rosa, 5,643 structures were destroyed, including more than 2,800 homes. The area was scarred by the devastation of lost family members, lost homes and lost dreams. Twenty-two people died in Sonoma County. The sheriff's office employees suffered disproportionate losses in Larkfield and Coffee Park developments: 30 active duty and retired deputies, and corrections officers lost homes. A total of 166 Sonoma County employees were counted as fire victims. In addition, the homes of eight Santa Rosa police officers and one civilian technician, along with 16 retired employees' homes burned, many while rescuing and evacuating others.

The air was thicker here, weighted with emotion and loss. He remembered that night as a blur. Every time he drove this area, he marveled at the ferocity of nature and the resiliency of Sonomans.

Nick traveled the familiar roads with an increasing dread. An eerie silence had descended on the region seven months ago. In each lot, solitary chimneys, charred tree skeletons, and sometimes a toppled building frame testified to the incredible heat. Some clean-up and demolition had begun, but seared, caved-in homes and cars burned to cinders still populated these residential blocks. No one lived there now, except on the peripheral streets where a few houses had miraculously escaped the conflagration.

He pulled up, neighbors stood in their yards, hunched against the evening chill a. When he saw the home, Nick fought the urge to bolt. It was no surprise there were several patrol cars parked outside.

A fire truck's engine rumbled across the street, and an ambulance was still double-parked in front. The medics were apparently still with the victim. Nick had expected two Sheriff's units; there were five, now six counting his, bearing witness to the gravity of this call. One of their own was down.

The house was modest, not much in the way of improvements during its' thirty years of its existence, but it was tidy and comfortable. Now, it was aglow with interior lights. The porch fixture shone, as well. A knot of uniforms clustered in the living room—large, intrusive men.

Through the front window Nick caught the eye of Deputy Manolo "Mano" Paniagua. The man stepped away from conversation with a fire fighter and strode toward his sergeant. Nick waited on the porch. He wanted to know what he was getting into before facing the family inside.

"Sarge." Manolo's terse greeting confirmed this was going to be bad. The deputy struggled to meet Nick's gaze. "It's Eddie, Sarge. Eddie Moran. He did himself in the back yard. Shotgun to the mouth."

"Fuck." Nick's worst fear had come true. The victim was his friend, Eddie Moran, a Sheriff's Office senior patrol deputy.

A few years ago, Ed and his wife, Donna, had taken Nick under their wing, helping him through the insanity of Angela's departure. After, he and Ed stayed close at work but hadn't socialized much—the Reyes' lives had changed drastically with Davy's arrival.

Assigned to Nick's shift as a field training officer, Moran's last trainee was Evelina Marquez. Moran had gone out on a knee injury and, after three surgeries, faced disability retirement. Though he hadn't talked to him, Eddie wouldn't have been happy about that. Nick mentally kicked himself for not staying in touch.

His shudder passed, and Nick knew what had to be done. "Where's Donna?"

"In there, with a neighbor." Manolo nodded toward the dining room table, his eyes glistening in the artificial light. "She found him. He left a note on the front door. Typical Eddie."

Mano handed the evidence bag over. Nick read Eddie's terse message, carelessly scrawled. "Don't go inside. Call 911 for a coroner."

Nick groaned, pulling out his phone. "I'm going to get some outside help. Give me a minute." Nick didn't need to explain himself. He was the acting Watch Commander; Mano would follow his orders.

Nick punched the number for Gil Ferrua, the Lieutenant in Violent Crimes Investigation. Ferrua needed to be briefed. When the lieutenant answered, Nick spoke in clipped tones. "Gil, I'm at the scene of a suicide in Larkfield. It's our jurisdiction but the victim is Eddie Moran."

The sooner he got relief for his team, the better. Nick barely gave Ferrua time to express his dismay. "Since this's so close to home, I'm invoking the county-wide shooting protocol." He didn't need to ask permission—it was Nick's decision to make. The protocol would relieve the deputies of the onerous task of investigating the death of one of their own, as well as providing an impartial report of the incident. "Will you notify the sheriff and outside agencies? Use my cell for whatever questions the responding agency may have." They were all too emotionally connected to investigate this death. Eddie Moran and his family deserved an investigation driven by clear-headed thinking, not emotion.

Nick pictured Ferrua in his shorts, sitting on the edge of his bed, frantically scribbling information that came at him too fast. Nick didn't care. He had to get back to his people—and Donna.

"Mano, can we route everyone through the side yard? I mean, is it accessible? I'd like to minimize Donna's trauma."

"Yes, sir. The fire captain already made his crew use it, so the lights are on."

"Okay, Mano. We're handing this over to another agency—Santa Rosa PD, probably. Ferg was primary on this. Has he made assignments?"

"Uh, no sir."

"I'll go talk to him in a minute. You got a list of

everyone here, including the fire guys? Good. When the allied agency gets here, give them all your info."

"Okay." Manolo reached into his breast pocket to pull out a small notebook and pen.

"I've got to make another call." Nick turned away. Nick pushed the key for Dispatch and made his call-out request for a police chaplain. Then, he dialed the patrol captain. As acting watch commander, Captain Gerry Greene was next up the chain of command. The captain and Eddie had gone to the academy together. Ferrua had already notified him. He was on his way.

One more call to make. Hunched over the phone, Nick remembered bass fishing on Clear Lake near Bayliss Point, sitting in Eddie's old twenty-footer, just the two of them. It'd been so peaceful, their lines in the water before dawn, the sky pink along the water's edge. Suddenly, Eddie told him the story of his father's last words in the nursing home. The old man, dying of emphysema, grabbing Eddie's shirt, whispering between breaths. He told how years before, in his thirties, he killed a prostitute. He'd buried her body in a bean field outside Ukiah and was never caught.

Eddie's face was dark in the pre-dawn shadows. "I thought I came from the right side, Nick. What am I doing in this job? Can you tell me?"

CHAPTER TWENTY-ONE

"Hey, babe. Sorry to wake you." Nick's voice was raspy.

Meredith felt it before the words formed in her head. Something was up. "I wasn't asleep."

"It's eleven thirty. You should be."

"Well then, thanks for waking me up." She smiled into the phone. Then, the import of his call sunk in. Not good. "What's going on?"

"Eddie Moran is dead. Suicide."

"Jesus." Meredith knew Eddie and his wife, Donna, but they were more Nick's friends. Eddie had been Nick's training officer out of the academy and was on Nick's patrol team. Jesus. "I'm so sorry, Nick. I know you were close." She wished there were words to take away his pain. "This must be a shock."

"Yeah." She pictured her husband holding the phone with one hand, running a hand over his face with the other. "No one saw this coming."

"And Donna?"

"She's here. She found him." Nick blew out a breath, clearly troubled. "I'm going over to her now. I'll talk to you later." He hung up abruptly.

The weight of Nick's duty settled on Meredith. Sharing in the anguish that he felt was something she'd done since they were first partners. Nick would support Donna, reassure her that she wasn't to blame, tell her that Eddie suffered from an incurable depression—anything to lessen Donna's grief. When all that failed, he'd sit with her, holding her hand in silence while she cried.

And later, when he handed Donna over to her family, Nick would manage the paperwork, stowing his own grief until he could make the time.

As if he didn't have enough on his plate.

CHAPTER TWENTY-TWO

The deputy sniffed over his notebook. "Mano, you okay?"

Manolo took a millisecond to search his sergeant's face. "I guess," he answered. Then, he shrugged. "I don't get it. He didn't seem the type—" Mano's sentence dropped off. There was no type. "I'll deal with it."

"You know if you need anything, come to me. I can help; the department also has resources. The Employee Assistance Plan offers counseling."

Manolo's smile emanated gratitude. Nick would check with the rest of the deputies when he could, making sure not to be obvious. No one wanted a fuss to be made over them, particularly around Donna.

The department debriefing would follow in a few days. Ed was the third law enforcement officer in the county lost to suicide in the past five years. Debriefings were good starts, but more was needed. No one talked about the toll the job takes on first responders like deputies, fire fighters, dispatchers, and corrections officers. The damage was cumulative. The pain of a devastating call could be swept away by a night of binge drinking, but corrosive debris accumulates in the corners. The pile grows, slowly and unnoticeably, until one day, it becomes a mountain that cannot be ignored. He'd seen Meredith wrestle with this and was quick to apply the lessons she'd learned—and shared with him—to his team.

When official notifications were done, Nick turned his attention to the interior of the house. "Call-outs are being done," he told Mano.

Inside, the deputies were quiet. Nick took a deep breath. Some were in silent shock, some whispering, some helping the fire fighters collect their gear. Mano had spread the word—no more work here. Photos, note-taking, and measurements would be done when the other agency's crime scene techs arrived. This was no longer the Sheriff's crime scene. But Nick's people needed to feel useful, even in a situation where no one could really help. He sent the four deputies from the yard to help with traffic around the emergency vehicles.

The feeling of helplessness had been the same when he'd lost Mia, five years before. Nick had tried CPR on his daughter's blue, lifeless body. When the medics arrived, they'd whisked her to the hospital, his then-wife Angela alongside the baby. Nick followed in his truck. He didn't know how they'd been notified, but soon the Sheriff's tan and olive-green uniforms filled the ER waiting room. Their presence was meant to soften his pain and show support. He'd met each one with a grim acknowledgement of the tragedy.

After Mia was pronounced dead, Nick found a sliver of purpose when Angela's hysteria set in. Finally, there was something he could do. It gave him momentum to move on, instead of wallowing in his own grief. He needed to take care of Angela. But with his co-workers, as now, no one knew what to say. Words couldn't assuage the torment that threatened to swallow him whole. He was sure Donna felt the same.

Two women sat at the dining table. A skinny blond looking at the best part of her fifties, Donna Moran sat pale-faced. She made like she was listening to the bathrobe-clad woman sitting across from her.

Nick remembered Donna Moran organizing shift parties every year. She threw herself into providing food, drink and planned fun pranks to pull on everyone. He saw her laughing nearly to tears when she herself got punked. Now all that energy was gone.

As he approached, Nick listened to the other woman. Hearing shallow platitudes and few words of comfort, he didn't feel bad for interrupting. "Donna?"

Donna Moran half-turned, her eyes swelling with tears as she recognized Nick.

"Nick." She stood and reached for him. "I was hoping

you'd come," she said with her face buried in his chest. She sobbed, unable to restrain her emotion.

He embraced her, whispering, "I know, I know." He let her cry, knowing this was all he could offer for now. Her cries were the only sound in the house. He stood there, bearing the weight of Donna's pain, pushing his own aside. His sergeant's mind catalogued what should be done for the real victim in this tragedy. He caught movement in the backyard, paramedics moving through their duties.

When Donna's sobs slowed, Nick turned away, asking Mano, "Has family been contacted?"

He nodded. "The chaplain just got here," the deputy answered. "And, I got hold of the daughter. She's on her way from Sonoma; should be here in twenty minutes."

Pulling from Nick, Donna slowed to sniffles. "Amber is on her way?"

"Yes, ma'am." Mano's voice was soft. "The chaplain just arrived." Mano turned to a tall, thin man with a shock of gray hair on his forehead. "Doctor Billings, this is Mrs. Moran."

Nick watched Donna welcome the newcomer. She had the same well-mannered quality as Nick's mother had. But he'd liked her for more than that. Donna was smart, clever and quick to catch on. Even in grief, she was a woman with a caring heart. She led the chaplain to the living room sofa, where a deputy was quick to hand them bottled waters. Doing something, no matter how menial, was better than nothing.

Nick always thought Donna was the perfect wife for Eddie Moran. She'd understood the toll the job took on her husband. She always put him first. Nick wondered why Eddie hadn't leaned on her in his desperation.

Why do this? His first thought was Eddie's impending retirement. While retirement is normally a good thing, to a cop it represents a separation from the brotherhood. Not to have a say in his own future removed the control most cops need in their lives. Now, his identity would be yanked out from under him, leaving him in a vacuum. He wasn't a civilian. but he wasn't a cop anymore, either. Then, Nick wondered about his relationship with Donna. Though outwardly solid, Nick suspected Eddie had begun to drink more than usual. He was close enough to Donna to know that she couldn't tolerate a drunk.

Maybe all the above: the complete and irrevocable loss of his job and identity, drinking to numb the pain and the subsequent alienation of his wife. Eddie would've felt boxed in.

Donna listened intently to the chaplain, freeing Nick for a moment. Time to do another thing he hated.

He had to see the body.

Cutting through the room, Nick let himself through the glass slider. Deputy Martin "Ferg" Ferguson, a tall, wiry redhead, stood beyond the body near the back fence. The fire captain paused for a word with Ferg as paramedics and firefighters made their exit. The crew exited at the side yard. Nick was grateful for their thoughtfulness.

Ferg resumed studying the scene. Knowing the process, Nick waited at the back slider and did his own review. Beyond the fence, illuminated by the Moran home lights, he saw a neighbor's undamaged roof. To the east, burned trees spiked skyward into the bleak night. Closer in, the Moran backyard was a patch of lawn anchored by a wooden deck. Mature trees dotted the perimeter, with scrawny shrubs at their base. Staked in the bushes were three life-sized pink flamingoes. In the middle of the yard, a stamped concrete circle held the fire pit and several chairs—and the body of Eddie Moran.

A pair of Santa Rosa uniformed officers arrived to relieve Mano and Ferg of their grisly duty.

VCI detectives Jerald Mossi and Eric Lanza had walked through the Moran's front door. In the living room, Mossi's big Italian frame dwarfed Donna with a hug. The chaplain moved aside, searching out Mano. After a minute, Mossi introduced his gangly partner, Lanza. Donna's face puffed up with tears as she sank back into the couch, Mossi holding her hand. She dabbed at her eyes with a tissue and nodded to the detective as he spoke to her.

Nick got the SRPD officers' names, left Ferg to brief them and went inside.

"What the hell," is all Mossi could choke out. His eyes avoided Nick's as their hands clasped in a tight handshake. When Mossi's gaze came to him, Nick pulled the detective into an embrace, giving Mossi a moment to collect himself. They were family who had lost a brother. Mossi, Nick and Eddie Moran had been on the same graveyard team several years ago for four rotations. They'd functioned as separate arms of one body, each thinking the same thing at the same time. Going call to call to call together, hooking and booking. Rescuing citizens during fires and floods, directing traffic around car wrecks, picking up the pieces after domestics, rapes, and other trauma caused by their fellow man. They'd been work partners and much more, bonded by the terrible things nobody wants to hear about and cemented by the suppression of their own emotions. Only they understood.

"This is just fucked," the detective whispered as he pulled away from Nick's hug. "Why couldn't he call either of us?" Why?

As one, the two men turned toward the backyard and their friend's body. Now, they would never know.

CHAPTER TWENTY-THREE

Ed had polished off two bottles of Budweiser before he'd gathered the nerve to end his life. The empties lay on the concrete. His body slumped in a lawn chair before an unlit fire ring, the Mossberg shotgun on the ground beside him. The gas created by the explosion of the powder in the shotgun shell blew everything to pieces from his neck up. He sat away from the house, so when Donna came out the back slider, she didn't see the damage the shell had done. Until she realized he had no head.

Nick couldn't imagine the rage or desperation that drove Eddie to do this. Donna must've been horrified when she found him. No way she could've anticipated this. How could anyone expect it?

Nick ached for Donna, having to live with what she would eventually consider her own failure to help her husband. Two weeks from today Donna would have to go back to her bank job, dragging this burden behind her. There was no way to escape from the pain of a shattered life. What was left was the wondering: what could she have done? How could she cope with this loss? What was her part in it? Would her life ever be normal again?

He couldn't imagine the pain Eddie must have endured if he thought this was his only option. What had gone wrong in his life? Had he wanted to punish or hurt Donna? Maybe they'd had an argument. He'd always felt Eddie and Donna were close, that they talked to each other. One time at dinner, watching them, he remembered wishing he and Angela had that kind of relationship.

Ferg came inside, greeting each detective with a solemn handshake as Nick stood behind them. "Oh, sorry, Nick. I didn't see you there," Ferg said.

"You were doing your job."

Ferg looked at his boots. "Pretty shitty job, today."

Nick gave a curt nod. "You okay?"

"Yeah," Ferg sighed. "I guess."

Nick let the implications of this answer settle. "I'm here for you, dude, if you need anything."

"I'll be okay." The deputy sucked in a breath. "What about you? Weren't you friends?"

Nick nodded. He pictured the last few times he'd seen Eddie. Were there hints that he hadn't seen? He wasn't aware of any trouble Eddie might have gotten into. He hadn't heard any rumors. No, Eddie hadn't given away anything. "No one ever understands this." He cocked his chin at his friend's corpse. "But I do know this happens more and more. We're not the good guys anymore. Sometimes it's hard to live with what we do every day." Nick resisted the inclination to over-talk this situation. The increase of law enforcement suicides wouldn't be resolved in a suburban tract home in Northern California tonight. His father had taught him that sometimes silence was the only suitable reply. Still, Nick's own guilt pushed him to construct a mental checklist of Eddie's motives.

Ferg nodded.

Nick collected himself. "If you need anything, call me. We can find help, if you need it." Nick almost said that word—feelings. It wasn't a word many cops acknowledged, much less admitted to. "You can't ever un-see this, but you can learn from it."

Ferg looked away. "What a fuckin' lesson."

Nick made a mental note to check in with Ferg that afternoon. Nobody on graveyard would sleep much today. Maybe an unofficial debrief after clearing the scene would be in order.

On his way inside, a woman's voice punctuated the hush. "Donna, oh, I'm so sorry." Evelina Marquez.

Nick sensed the change in the room even before he got inside. All eyes were on Deputy Marquez, hugging the widow. Marquez had been assigned to South Beat today and thus was, with minimum traffic, thirty minutes north from her assigned area. Even with this tragedy, the job had priority. She shouldn't be here.

Searching the room over Donna's shoulder, Evelina found Nick. Her eyes changed shape, but he couldn't read what it meant. Hm, she must know she's in trouble, he thought. As he walked toward her, he considered the words he'd use to get her out of here and back to the South County-Petaluma area. He wouldn't dress her down in front of her peers, but he'd make it clear—

Then, she broke away from the widow and darted across the room to him. With surprising force, she slammed into him, almost bouncing off his chest. Shocked, he took a step back. She followed, tears rimming her eyes, a fierce gasp, and jumped toward him, their vests resisting the closeness. She was small enough to his six feet three height that her badge caught on his portable radio case. "What has he done? Oh, Nick."

With the eyes of everyone in the room on them, Nick extracted himself from the embrace and pushed her away. "Deputy." The words he'd prepared failed him, so he relied on instinct. "Marquez, who's watching your beat?"

Marquez was silent, tears streaming.

Ah damn it, tears. Nevertheless, he had a shift to run. "Go on back," he nodded. "We'll talk later."

Damn, he thought, as Marquez turned away, sullen. Why did he feel such a strong reaction? Did she have a thing for Eddie? No, him?

At any rate, Nick hadn't handled that well.

CHAPTER TWENTY-FOUR

Normally Evelina Marquez loved being the center of attention. But tonight, her cheeks felt like they'd been scorched by flames. After her sergeant's abrupt order, she hurried from the house into her patrol SUV. She took the 101 southbound on-ramp and reached for her phone. "Siri, call Felicia."

Felicia answered after two rings. "Hey, sista. Whassup?"

Evelina cussed at the car in front, driving below the speed limit. She hated it when drivers freaked out at cop cars. "Felicia. I gotta talk. You got a minute?"

Evelina was pleased when she heard Felicia's attention sharpen. "Of course."

"My FTO—the guy who was my patrol trainer after I got out of the academy—shot himself tonight." Evelina paused, waiting for Felicia's reaction.

"Oh my god, honey, I'm so sorry. What happened?"

Evelina blew out an exasperated breath. "I don't know. He was looking at a disability retirement. Maybe the injury just got to him. Maybe he got hooked on painkillers, maybe—"

"It's always so sad when someone commits suicide. It seems a lot harder to take when it's someone who's a cop or something."

This insight surprised Evelina. Felicia wasn't usually so deep. But she understood this and how it affected Evelina. "Cops have a hard time asking for help. In fact, most don't."

She changed lanes, hitting the accelerator in the number-one lane. Driving southbound toward her beat, she recalled how strong Nick sounded when he kicked her out. She was in the wrong and she knew it, but still couldn't pass up the chance to see him, even if it meant exploiting a terrible situation.

"You never have trouble asking for help, sista. Especially when you been a naughty girl." Felicia's throaty laugh gave away her recent cannabis intake. "Did you see your man?"

Evelina thought before she answered. "Nick? Yeah, and he was all like a boss and everything. Not happy to see me."

"How come?"

"I'm not s'posed to leave my beat unless it's an emergency. I'm south county—Petaluma, Penngrove, Cotati. That's a long way from Larkfield. If a hot call came in for Petaluma and I was up in Santa Rosa, I'd get days on the beach."

"Jeez, that's a little harsh, isn't it?"

"Not if you want a deputy at your crime scene in a hurry." Maybe she didn't get it. Really, Felicia was trying to make Evelina feel better about getting in trouble. She was probably the wrong person to unload on. But if not her, then who?

She didn't like most of the other deputies. They were all business with no time for her. Nick was married with a kid. Evelina knew the deputies she worked with were all fiercely loyal to Nick and his wife, detective Meredith Ryan.

Evelina knew Meredith. They'd been to a few training sessions together. Women in predominantly men's professions seek each other out—mostly for the companionship that only they can understand.

But Meredith hadn't warmed to Evelina. She didn't know why, but Meredith Ryan kept her distance. She was never rude but refused invitations to go have a drink together or meet for coffee. Evelina had grown to believe Meredith Ryan was a stuck-up bitch, even if her man was a fine piece of cheeseburger.

CHAPTER TWENTY-FIVE

Meredith inhaled deeply—a diver going into the depths—standing outside the Crazy Eights at Ninth and Irving. The brick warehouse style building from the late 1800's towered two stories above the rest of the block. The ground floor housed three businesses; the upper spaces rented out as residences. The Crazy Eights Bar on the corner featured black subway tile lining the bottom three feet of the outside wall. Interior shutters were topped with curtains blocking any view inside of what promised to be a seedy dive. She pushed the grimy door open.

Desmond Rollins' smile was professional, the expression of a career barman with plenty of experience in the pretense of welcome before a customer paid for his drinks. The Crazy Eights Bar was dim and musty and smaller than she remembered. The odor of past miseries and celebrations weighed down the air. Yellowed newspaper clippings and photographs were tacked to mahogany-colored 1970's paneling, news from decades ago. Much of it was of SFPD officers in uniform. Two sweat-shirt clad men nursed beers on the far end while Desmond mopped the bar with a towel.

He greeted Meredith smartly. "G'day, miss."

"Hello, Uncle Desmond," Meredith said.

Desmond worked nineteen years as a San Francisco cop; long enough to know how to hide his surprise. He squinted at her. She knew he was at a disadvantage—she stood in the doorway with the glow of the morning fog behind her. She stepped into the gloom of the bar, taking in the surroundings, wondering where he'd been two nights ago. No, he couldn't move as fast at the intruder. That guy was younger.

"Meredith, m'dear. Why didn't you call?" He cocked his head while chiding her. "I've an appointment in a few minutes."

Meredith slung a hip onto a worn Naugahyde bar stool.

"No worries, Uncle Desmond. I won't take up much of your time." It wasn't like she'd come to drink with him. "I came for my father's things."

He stood in the front of the hallway to the back room. From behind him, a bleached blond woman in the toughest part of her forties brushed past. "I'm here, Des."

"Thanks, Ramona. I won't be long." Desmond tugged off his apron and wadded it up. He tipped his gray head toward the stocky blonde who looked like she could wrestle any man to the mat. "She's holdin' down the fort while I'm gone."

When Meredith didn't say anything, his hand waved her toward the interior hallway.

Steeling herself, she ducked under the bar gate to follow Desmond. Reluctantly. In her childhood, he'd led her places she never wanted to see again.

Like, the first time he took her father away. Her parents had an argument, then a punch, and a split lip. Neighborhood doors opened and sleepy eyes watched. One of them called the cops and well, SFPD couldn't very well arrest one of their own, could they? The cop called Terence's buddy Desmond, who turned up within minutes. There, in uniform, two patrolmen carried her staggering father to Des' car. While the uniforms waited, keeping an eye on Terence, Desmond returned to the family apartment. He pushed open the door, knocking Nora to the floor. Holding back an outraged Meredith with one hand, he spit on Nora. "You stupid cow. He could get fired for this. Don't ever call the cops again. You call me."

The slamming front door obliterated her mother's sobs. Meredith's eyes stung with humiliation for her mother. But she'd learned; they both had. It came to be a routine. Instead of the neighbor calling, her mother telephoned her husband's best friend when her husband got physical. Meredith's relief at the halting of hostilities was tempered by the feeling of brokenness. As violent as Terence was, she'd never seen hate and disgust like that on Desmond's face on that first night. Her family was divided by "Uncle" Desmond. No one did anything to repair it.

The bar was dark, but the storage area was even darker. Pausing to let her eyes adjust, Meredith found herself in a storeroom with shelves packed to the ceiling. Bottles of alcohol lined three walls; cases of mixers, glassware, napkins and snacks were on the fourth.

"Step into my office." Desmond smiled at his own silly cliché. Beyond the liquor storage area, she came to another small room. A cot with a threadbare blanket and stained pillow faced opposite a solid, decades-old desk piled with newspapers, ledger books, and invoices. In the corner sat a beat-up aluminum locker with no lock.

Desmond stood three inches over Meredith, looking distinguished with his wavy iron-gray hair and square jaw set for a fight. He wore what he'd always worn behind the bar: a white button-down oxford shirt and dark slacks. At almost six feet, Meredith was tall enough now to drop all pretense of being subordinate. When she was a kid, though, this man had always acted like the wise old uncle. Even before her father left, though, she'd seen the real Desmond—shifty-eyed and sneaky, telling lies and constructing stories to get his way. After he lost his job as a policeman, Des had bought the Crazy Eights. Meredith remembered her mother yelling at Des, saying he'd taken Terence away from the family as much as the job had.

"Your father slept on that cot most of the fifteen years after the divorce."

"He didn't get an apartment?" This was a surprise. She always assumed Terence had found a place to live—not flop in some dark storeroom. Where did Brenda Houston fit in? Was she the woman Terence left her mother for?

"No, he had a lady-friend up north he visited from time to time. He kept telling me he'd find another place, but he never did." Desmond shrugged, then reached into the locker and pulled out a large shoe box. "He even rented a storage unit up in Sonoma County. Then, he got sick."

"But—"

"Here're his things. There isn't much, but my man

always traveled light." Desmond seemed proud his friend had nothing; that he'd lived his life on a rung of the ladder somewhere below seedy bartender. "I took the liberty of donating his clothes when he got sick."

Nice. What a jerk.

Meredith took the box. It was light, dimensions 12" by 18" by 12," printed on the side. It had been sealed and re-sealed with packing tape. Distrust fired in her brain. "Did you open this?"

"My God, no." Desmond reared back like she'd accused him of treason. He looked harder at the box. "Likely, he put something inside then needed it again." He frowned. "No, young lady, not me."

Her mother's voice echoed in Meredith's head, telling Desmond's story—how Terence and he had met in the academy and been fast friends since. They'd continued their association after Desmond was assigned to the Tenderloin. "Your father never told me the specifics, but he mentioned that Des had gotten into more than his share of trouble." Her mother had shaken her head at the waste of it all. "In the end, even his nineteen years seniority didn't save him. He beat a junkie at a fleabag hotel. This was nothing new for Desmond—you know how brutal he could be." Her mother's chin stuck out with vindication as she finished the story. "Except he got caught. It turned out the junkie was the grandson of a local congressman. Desmond got fired for the beating and lying about it." She ended her story with the moral. "Just because they're police doesn't mean they're honest. So be warned. "

Meredith was sure Desmond had opened the box. Dismissing his protests, she tucked it under her arm. She wondered if she could wait until she got to her Subaru to open it. But she still had questions for Desmond. He glanced at his watch, to her irritation.

"Okay, Desmond. I give. When can you spare the time to tell me about him?"

Desmond turned, grabbing a worn leather jacket and slipped it on. "Ah lass, I thought you'd never ask." He looked down at her and in the dim light, she made out an artificial smile. Good God. "Your father was a troubled man, but he had a good heart."

Right. She had never met anyone who said her father had a good heart—no one who knew him, anyway. Not even her mother. The Irish had a name for his character—Blackguard. Scoundrel. Only worse. "This afternoon?"

"No, I won't be available."

"How about tomorrow?" She felt her face warming. He'd won control of the conversation by making her return. He was a sly bastard. She cleared her throat. "Before you open?"

"Sure, darlin'. I open at nine AM."

He opened the back door and waited while she walked out. A blast of cool air blew inside as a muni streetcar rattled by. Suddenly remembering outside—the neighborhood—behind the bar startled Meredith. She had forgotten what it looked like, smelled and sounded like. It was a familiar thoroughfare—one she and her brother, David, had taken a thousand times on their way to school. Seeing it now brought an instant memory, too, of David tugging a ball cap over a bruise on his forehead. Other than the hat, he had made no attempt to hide his injury. The teachers never asked. In their defense, David was a quiet boy who spent most of his spare time in a dark corner learning chords on a school-supplied guitar. He was unremarkable and flew beneath their radar. Meredith clearly remembered her fury at seeing a fresh bruise.

She'd known memories would be jogged loose when she came back to the old neighborhood. Still, she struggled to reconcile it with the reality of today. Her teeth clenched. "See you at eight."

CHAPTER TWENTY-SIX

"You don't have to come tomorrow." Meredith picked at the sealed lid of her father's shoe box. She'd made it all the way home without opening it. Now, seeing Nick feeding Davy, going through the box dropped on her list of priorities. The baby was in his highchair, singing and bouncing to an unidentifiable tune. She wanted to hold her baby and kiss her husband. She wanted to thank God for the life he'd given her. Sure, she'd done the heavy lifting, but marrying Nick and having Davy were miracles she never felt worthy of. And her career. Even though she'd gotten her Bachelors in Phys Ed with the intention to teach, she'd applied at Sonoma County Sheriff's Office instead. Now, she thought she'd always be a cop.

All of this, in spite of her father. Funny that, in the end, she chose the same career.

"No, Mere. I want to come with you." Nick mopped greenish dribble from his son's chin. "I know how draining this is." He straightened and met her gaze. "My mom and I got along great. But after she died, handling everything was still exhausting." He stirred the zucchini and aimed the spoon at Davy's mouth, airplane style. "It must be tougher for you, carrying around all the crap Terence dished out. Tough, considering the old dog never changed."

"But there's more to it than just grief." Meredith sighed. "He wrote gave her money and made her beneficiary of an insurance policy. He had a relationship with Brenda. Who the hell is this woman?"

"Maybe she had something on him—"

"A guy like my dad doesn't get blackmailed."

Nick dabbed green slime from his son's chin. "You hungry?"

"Nah," she said, shrugging out of her jacket. She'd lost her appetite on the drive home. Pouring a glass of Merlot, she looked at her father's box. It was as if his self-centeredness had slopped onto her.

Nick. He'd made dinner. She rested her hands on his shoulders. "Jeez, I'm so sorry." A pot on the stove, avocado and tomatoes gone from the fruit bowl. Eventually the aroma of barbequed beef awakened her senses. "Nick, you made dinner." She ran her fingers through his dark bristly hair. "What did I ever do to deserve you?"

He stood, reaching his hand to her cheek. "I don't know. Maybe if you do it again, I'll remember." His arms enveloped her.

Meredith smiled, for the moment happy in his embrace. "Count on it."

Davy sang out, pounding an empty spoon on his table. "Mama, mama."

Wiping food off her son's face, Meredith pulled him from the highchair. She nuzzled his neck, tickling him with kisses. He laughed a baby laugh that came from his toes, then squirmed toward his father. "Dada, dada, dada."

"You stay with your mother while I get our dinner on the table," Nick spoke softly to their son. Meredith didn't think she'd ever seen her husband so content. Keeping Davy occupied, she stole glimpses of Nick expertly serving up a beef tri-tip, roasted red potatoes and an enticing green salad.

With Davy on her knee, Meredith ate. "This is great." With what seemed so little effort, Nick made food taste so good.

"I called Tina," Nick said, filling a water glass. "She'll take Davy tomorrow at 6:30 A.M."

Feeling the mix of emotions that she was sure every mother felt, she concluded it would be better if the baby wasn't around. The meeting on the following morning would dredge up memories—her parents arguing, cops arriving, and calling Desmond to take her father away for the night. She could shelter her son from that turmoil. "That should work fine. We need to leave here about 6:30 to allow for traffic and be in the City at eight."

Nick nodded, jaw set. He wasn't looking forward to this, either.

After dinner, Meredith did the dishes. When Nick held up a freshly bathed little boy for inspection, the child showered his mother with nighty-night kisses and hugs. Ten minutes later, with the baby in bed, Meredith sat at the dining table staring at the container her father had left behind. It was a large shoe box, the kind that held hiking boots. A white logo swirled on the cover, Nike lettering marched across each side and packing tape sealed the ends together.

"You gonna open it?" Nick sat beside her.

"Yeah." I'm ready. She cut the tape and pulled off the lid. On top lay an envelope addressed in her father's hand—to her. Meredith placed it squarely before her on the table. So, he'd thought about her going through his things. There was no wrestling over opening the letter first. It was meant to be read after his death, so her reaction couldn't touch him. His sheer selfishness quashed her curiosity. It would wait.

The box's contents were the leftovers of a life—a life in which she had rarely been invited to participate. The box held prescription sunglasses, a worn bundle of family documents, and a receipt from the property division of the SFPD for a service revolver. Tucked behind the receipt, a photo of a teenage boy standing under a tree in what appeared to be a suburban neighborhood. Scribbled in pencil on the back was, 'Jamie 1994'. Flipping the photo over, Meredith reluctantly decided the boy had Terence's short turned-up nose. Who is this kid? Why is he so important that her father kept only this photo in his box? Why no pictures of David or her? Had Terence fathered another child?

Each item brought more questions than answers, but what really tugged at her detective's brain—why was her father's service weapon in police department evidence? The date was July 9, 2001. The year her father left the family.

She smoothed the wrinkled corners of the receipt. "I don't get it, Nick. What's with his gun? The date is just before he retired. What the hell happened?"

"You're off for the next week." He cocked his head, thinking. "Treat this like a case. Investigate. Talk to people in your father's life. Maybe you can get an insight."

She felt herself distancing tangled feelings for her father. There was danger ahead unless she numbed herself to his bombshells. Yes, Nick was right—as usual. Treat this like a case. After seeing the evidence receipt and photo, she decided to read the letter. The other documents could wait.

Her fingers trembled—just a little—when she slipped a dinner knife under the envelope flap. A lined, legal-sized paper was inside, folded in thirds. She opened the page.

There was no sentimental apology for past sins, no remorse for the pain he'd caused. As she read the words, she wrestled between anger and curiosity that he didn't address the turmoil he'd spread among his family.

"I did it because I had to, not that you'd understand. Leave it alone or you're another girl cop with her head blown off. No snitches on this side of the fence. No reason to think you're smart enough to catch a dead man. I got nothing to apologize for."

Nick stood behind her. "What the hell does that mean?"

She looked at him, wondering the same.

CHAPTER TWENTY-SEVEN

Meredith dropped the letter back and closed the box. She shoved it on top of the battered black briefcase she'd stored on top of the hutch. Leave what alone? Is this a warning? What's he afraid of me finding? He didn't know me if he thinks I'd be scared off by some nameless peril. He should know I won't back off.

She knew exactly what to do, although Nick would have some ideas, too.

She expected him to bring it up at the dinner table, but he was silent. Nick would wait until she asked for his input. He was respectful of their relationship, which included the job. He'd let her think it out, as he had when she was in patrol field training nine years ago.

"I've been thinking." She took a deep breath. "First, I'm going to see what caused my father to get so excited that he had a heart attack."

Nick's eyebrows drew together. "What difference does it make?"

Despite his skepticism, she wanted to know what agitated Terence to the point of a heart attack. The Haven administration hadn't told her of anything other than a natural death. As he'd been seen by a doctor within the past day, his death was not deemed suspicious. It was probably a non-starter, but she had to know. And who was his visitor?

"Then, I'm going to call Deb at Rohnert Park PD. She works detectives. If there's something to know about Brenda Houston, she'll know."

Meredith glanced at the time on her phone. "I'll have to wait until tomorrow to visit the Haven. But, it's not too late to call Deb."

Her friend picked up right away. Ten years ago they'd gone through the academy together. The sweat, terror, and fear during their cop schooling created a bond that transcended normal friendships. They'd seen each other in tough moments and held each other up through doubt and anxiety. Trust, Meredith thought. A friendship forged that could weather months of no contact and shine forth as soon the phone rang.

After asking about Davy, Deb vented about her divorce for a few minutes. "But you didn't call at this time of night to hear about my misery." Deb's voice took on a curious tone. "What's up?"

When Meredith told her of her father's death, Deb said, "Oh yeah. I saw the name on the coroner's report this morning. I wondered if he was related. I'm so sorry for the loss of your father. It's so difficult to lose family."

"We're related only by blood." Meredith remained focused as she told Deb about the situation.

Deb read the tone and offered an idea. "I'm at the office in front of my computer. You want me to check this woman's history? I can contact her if you want."

"No, thanks. I'll handle that. I'm not sure what I want to ask her yet. It needs to be face-to-face." She took a breath. "What I need from you is info. Are you familiar with her? She lives at 1807 Arbor. Does that address ring any bells?" Cops knew troublesome addresses in their jurisdictions as a matter of self-preservation. While all officer safety tactics are based on situational awareness, knowing a particular address is where a criminal element resides is intel providing another layer of safety.

"For starters, that's the low-life section of a trailer park—Evergreen Estates. We get lots of criminal activity there. Anyone who lives on Arbor should be approached with caution."

"Really?" Meredith found it hard to believe the suburban city had any such neighborhoods. She'd never spent much time in Rohnert Park, but knew it was a planned city dating back to the 1960's. It had grown into a bedroom community to San Francisco and Marin. The town had always seemed pretty quiet to her.

Deb tapped on the computer keyboard. "What's her full name?"

"Houston. Brenda."

Deb tapped some more. And suddenly, Meredith realized her friend could get in trouble for checking on someone without a legitimate reason. If there wasn't a good one—such as an open, active criminal case—you weren't entitled to the information. The California Department of Justice enforced a myriad of restrictions about accessing data—even cops were forbidden from using these programs for personal use. Every department in the state participated in annual information audits to ensure agency compliance. The laws were put in place to prevent law enforcement personnel from selling or giving away privileged information. "Hey, close out that inquiry. I don't want you to get in crap over my problems."

Deb breathed into the phone. "Here it is, an Agency Assist call-SFPD. I don't see the name, but an address search shows a guy named James AKA Jamie Houston was paroled to that address last week. In historical data, there was a guy arrested for armed robbery out of there—May 20, 2001. Maybe the same guy."

"Damn it, Deb."

"Oh, don't worry so much." Deb's smile radiated over the phone. "This is another Agency Assist, right? I mean, I'm helping the Sheriff's Office VCI. It's historical, before computers, so just the barest info is here." Houston—same last name.

"Stop." Meredith had confirmed what she needed. The computer search could get them both in trouble. But now the onus was on Meredith should this inquiry come to light in a records audit. Crap. Deb had offered up too much help. "Let's get together for lunch next week."

"Hey, before you go," her friend paused. "I don't think this should wait until we're face to face. There's something I've got to tell you." Deb's voice was serious.

"What?"

"My sister—you met Felicia—well, her BFF's a sheriff's deputy, Evelina Marquez. And, Evelina's been talking about this guy from work named Nick. She's got a thing for him and it sounds like she's been hot after him."

"Deb, what're you saying?" Meredith almost couldn't hear Deb over the pounding heartbeat in her ears.

"I'm warning you, Mere." Deb let out an impatient breath. "Evelina is relentless when she wants something. If she's after Nick, you better sharpen your claws."

Crap. Crap. Crap. We don't need this.

"Thanks for the heads up, Deb. I—we—appreciate it." Then, after setting a date to meet in the next week, Meredith disconnected. Eyes fixed on the phone but her mind a million miles away, Meredith wondered if she could assume Nick didn't know about Evelina's intrigues. Almost six years ago her husband Richard was murdered on the way to his girlfriend's home—revealing a six-month long affair. Meredith hadn't a clue about the relationship until she'd been notified of his death. She must be the most naïve cop on the planet. She had trouble with jealousy. Wasn't that one of her mother's issues? Turned out her mother was probably right about Terence.

Was Nick cheating on her? No, it wasn't in his nature. Should she say something to him? No, he'd think she was listening to gossip. Still, she'd better wise up. Here's where relationships were weird: this should be something to discuss right away, but who does that?

Nick was still at the kitchen table. She looked over at him and said, "In 2001, a young male was arrested for armed robbery by SFPD at that address. Same guy, Jamie Houston, was paroled to there last week."

He frowned. "This is no coincidence. Maybe I'm reaching for straws but maybe he could answer some of our questions."

"It's 'Grabbing for straws.'"

He brushed the correction aside. "We go together when you talk to this woman."

She smiled, her heart warming. "Of course."

CHAPTER TWENTY-EIGHT

The pounding in Desmond Rollins' head made him lean into the door frame after locking the door to his studio apartment. The heavy fog dampened everything, deadening sound. He sighed with the effort it took to move, but the chill had begun to work its way into his 67-year-old bones. He walked downstairs, craving the hair of the dog—just a tad.

But no, he wouldn't give in to the weakness. He would never admit he was hung-over; he considered himself a non-drinker. Still, his tongue had a cottony texture that a cup of coffee did nothing to disperse. Last night before closing, he'd savored four glasses of Kilbeggan Irish Whisky as a kind of celebration. There'd be no fine Irish send-off for the son-of-a-bitch. After seventeen years, his old partner, Terence, was gone. Finally.

Things were looking up.

When he reached the bar's exterior door, the padlock dangled—the shank cut, and the hinge drooped from two loose screws. Desmond's headache quickly fled as adrenaline shot through his system. He reached back to his waistband and pulled out a 2-inch Colt .38 caliber detective special.

The portal was open just by inches. He stood poised for a second, barrel up, listening.

Nothing. He pulled on the door, the hinge squealing in the wet air. Damn, that would announce his presence to a burglar. He dropped any pretense of his former glory days as a cop and shouted, "I've got a gun and I'll shoot your ass if you don't come out." A silly command. I won't shoot your ass if I can't see you. But he kept that to himself.

Silence. He slipped into the bar, through the back room, scanning for the burglar. Flipping on two weak light bulbs dangling from fixtures, he glanced behind shelves that had been loaded with bottles of alcohol and mixers, sodas and restaurant-sized coffee packets—all now broken and scattered on the floor. Passing through to what he considered his office—an alcove containing a government-surplus desk and chair, a dented metal file cabinet and, leaning up against the wall, Terence's folded cot. The cabinet drawers had been jimmied open, papers pulled out, many of them bills stamped in red, "overdue." Boxes from the shelves were cockeyed, some tossed to the floor among scattered cellophaned bags of popcorn and pretzels.

Stumbling through the mess, Desmond's mind flew in one direction. Jamie. What if the kid found something? What if he found out where the storage units were? And the key? He assumed Terence had dumped the money in with the bodies. That friggin' Jamie couldn't remember where the storage place was. He couldn't even remember what town it was in. Nothing had changed since the kid got out—he didn't know where the money was, either. Ramona had followed him, but he hadn't gone any place where the cash could've been hidden. And God knew, he hadn't figured out the silly mystery. Damn Terence's eyes.

It dawned on Desmond that he'd have to do what Terence had directed so many years ago. Give it to Meredith. He'd let her unravel Terence's damn riddle to get to the money—and the truth.

This whole thing was a mess. It was fucked from the minute he'd heard Terence tell Jamie about the new gang in town up to this moment. The robbery was fouled up. Oh, he didn't care that Jamie had been caught or those others had been killed. That's the cost of doing business in the criminal world. No, he'd wanted to get his hands on that cash. He'd known his tenure at San Francisco Police Department was in jeopardy. The brass didn't hide the fact that he was persona non grata. Treated him like shit, they did. No, he pressured Jamie into pulling the robbery because that was a sizeable enough wad of cash to start over with. But the kid and his pals messed up the whole deal. Now the money was concealed somewhere by a sanctimonious ex-cop who didn't trust anyone but his daughter.

Desmond picked up a bottle pair of highball glasses and

threw them across the room. Then a barstool followed, splintering among the shattered glasses. "Fuck, fuck, fuck."

It took him ten minutes to finish his search of the bar. Des noted a pair of Jameson's whiskey bottles missing from their perch. They'd been there last night. He recalled debating his choice of the Kilbeggan over Jameson's. Other than the whiskey and the mess, there was nothing taken.

Still behind the bar, he grabbed the Kilbeggan and poured a half-glass. He could bear this loss—a couple of cases of booze. He slumped onto his stool—his lower back had been giving him fits lately—and powered down the whiskey.

Des was sure Meredith Ryan would find the money. He'd see where the daughter would lead and when she found it, he'd decide how best to relieve her of it. While she was a cop, she was a county deputy—not the real thing like he'd been. Even at his age, he was sure he could take her.

Desmond stretched his cramped back, taking in the mess. Terence had been gone, sick, for two years and now he was dead. Time to get rid of the cot.

CHAPTER TWENTY-NINE

It took Desmond five minutes to answer Meredith's knock. At the door, his face registered hard disapproval as he looked Nick over. Then, Des flashed a false smile to Meredith while swinging open the Crazy Eights front door. As they entered, Meredith introduced Nick.

"Ah, needed back-up, did you, to interrogate old Uncle Desmond?"

She bit her tongue at the smart come-back. Des was a cop from the generation who believed women didn't belong in law enforcement. "Nick's my husband." She was instantly pissed at herself for justifying Nick's presence. Des' opinion didn't matter. "And this isn't an interrogation."

While her eyes adjusted to the dark, the familiar sour smell of the bar assaulted her nose. Spilled beer, stale cigarette smoke and unwashed patrons stunk up the place. It was a long narrow room, bar on one side and two pairs of tables and chairs on the other. Near the bar, small boxes of snacks were scattered on the floor. Bottles were knocked over and a chair lay on its side.

Something had happened here. "Have a little donnybrook in here last night, uncle?" She didn't try to keep the snark out of her voice. Her taunt was phrased like she was from the old country—the kind of speech Desmond used to charm people.

"None of your concern, darlin'." His smile was strained.

She shrugged, ignoring the mess. Odd that Des didn't clean up after it. Maybe a burglary? Desmond wouldn't volunteer information. But it wasn't her business, was it?

Tucked in the farthest corner of the room sat a battered parquet dance floor and an aged juke box. Unwelcome, a childhood memory drifted in. She and David sat in the shadowy nook. She remembered struggling to be quiet while her father hunched over the bar, his voice morose like it always was with the drink, while deep in conversation with

Desmond.

But it was difficult to quash a child's enthusiasm for music. Quarters jingled in her pocket. She was in charge of the juke box. Meredith and David listened to the vintage music of Cindi Lauper, Foreigner and Janet Jackson—and kept out of Terence Ryan's way. Meredith often felt her brother's interest in music began out of boredom at that seedy bar in the Sunset. The Ryan kids savored the moments out of their father's line of fire. A thought struck her: Her mother had never been there. Meredith had never speculated about her mother's frequent absences from the Crazy Eights. It was normal for her to be absent. Now she thought about Nora, and how out of place she would've felt. She would never have approved for her wake to be held there.

Desmond waved them to a table near the bar. "Coffee?" He reached for a pair of mugs. In silence, he filled both from an aluminum pot. He shoved the mugs across the table without asking about cream or sugar and, a moment later, slid heavily into a chair facing Meredith. He straightened, like a knight girding himself for battle. As he sipped his coffee, he lifted an eyebrow. "Interrogation or not, you said you had questions."

Meredith reached in a pocket for her phone. Her father's note was folded inside its leather case. She dropped the paper in front of him.

He sniffed, glancing at the letter like it had typhus. He picked it up with two fingers, scanned then dropped it. He shrugged, sagging back into his chair. "Okay. What's this supposed to mean?"

Meredith held her disappointment at a distance, a practice honed into a fine point over the past decade as a deputy.

But this was different—this was her life, not work. Even so, she wasn't willing to give in to emotion yet. Was there an intersection between her career as an investigator and her role as a daughter? At the moment, those lines seemed blurry.

"You tell me." Meredith crossed her arms. "You were

there; you're his best friend. Were."

Terence looked at the letter as if reading it. "'I got nothing to apologize for.'" He blew out a disdainful huff. "This could mean anything."

"Does your answer mean you know but don't want to tell me?" She leaned across the table, disgust making her words terse. "You and your good friend, Terence." She shook her head in controlled frustration. "You both go to the grave with your secrets. The rest of us have to endure not knowing. There are things that need to be put right." Either Des didn't know, or didn't want her to know, her father's secret. She bet on the latter. Meredith had to find out what happened. There were too many strange variables surrounding Terence's demise.

She had no doubt that he died a natural death. Didn't he?

"I have questions, Uncle Desmond." She pushed aside a stab of shame for trying to butter him up with the childhood name. "We'll start with this one: why is there a police department evidence receipt for my father's service weapon?" The newspaper article burned a hole in her pocket. She'd brought it in case Desmond's memory needed refreshing.

Des glanced over his shoulder at the bar. With a small sigh, he answered. "There was some unpleasantness at the end of his career. Nothing was ever proved."

"What kind of 'unpleasantness'?" Unpleasantness? Nothing was ever proved. Did that mean her father did something and the law didn't have evidence enough to prosecute? Or that he didn't do what he was accused of?

She sat up in the chair. "Define 'unpleasantness.'" Meredith's temper had never gotten the better of her. Today, it threatened.

He huffed his reluctance. His face was a mask, his voice strong as a former cop. "One day, your father and me was walking down Turk Street. It was one of those rare Indian summer nights that was warm. No one had air-conditioning in those days and everyone left their windows open. We'd just come from our lunch break and heard a man and woman yelling at each other in an apartment two floors up from the street. We got into the building and up to where the trouble was. We found the apartment, knocked at the door. At first no one answered. We ID'ed ourselves, told them we weren't gonna leave, and the woman finally opened the door. She was a little thing, five foot one if she was an inch." He held up his hand to illustrate. "She was all banged up. Her lip was split, an eye was swelling fast and her clothes were torn. We pushed past her to find the pussy who beat her up, but she jumped on my back, screaming, 'Don't take him away.'"

Desmond took a breath, eyeing Meredith for her reaction. She had her own mask to wear.

"Terence knew I could handle this little gal, so he went inside looking for Mr. Big Man. He caught him with one foot out on the fire escape, ready to bail. Terence wrestled him to the ground and cuffed him. I got the woman under control and brought her into the living room. Terence and I questioned her for a half hour, but she wouldn't budge. She insisted she'd fallen, that he hadn't hit her, and swore she'd never go to court if we arrested him."

Meredith waited.

"So, before we left, Terence gave Mr. Big Man a taste of his own medicine." Desmond's lips spread into an ugly, self-satisfied smile. "Beat the ever-livin' crap out of him, while I held the woman back. That's justice."

Meredith sighed, weighing the chance that a debate would have on her uncle. "That's not justice. That's brutality."

"It was street justice. Something a Mayberry cop like you wouldn't understand."

"I understand it." She thought back on the times she'd curbed her own anger, frustration or disgust with failures of human nature and the system. She hadn't crossed the line, but she'd felt the temptation.

"It doesn't have anything to do with his passing, Meredith." Des straightened in his chair. "There's naught to be gained by digging up old fictions."

"Since when does the SFPD consider confiscating a duty

weapon over a fiction?" Nick's question held an edge, like a sword ready to strike. Meredith was gratified her husband didn't buy this crap, either. The question hung in the air between them.

"You don't understand." Desmond leaned toward Meredith. To him, she was the one person in the room that counted. "In a lot of ways, the PD was old fashioned. The merest hint of an accusation was enough to bench an officer—if you weren't one of the boys." Two fingers hung imaginary quote marks around "boys."

"And my father wasn't one of the boys?"

"He knew how to get what he wanted from them, but no. He wasn't one of them, not by a long stretch." Des slouched into his chair again. "Even though he had the plum assignment in the Mounted Unit, he wasn't one to play their game." Des' gaze drifted to somewhere Meredith couldn't see. "Let me tell you a story; show you how real policemen operated. Your father was told to train the first female patrol officer on night shift back in the 1980's. He figured he'd pick someone who'd get along with everyone, so he selected this gal, Linda something. He put her through the training, not being too tough on her. Then, when she was about to be released to go out on her own, he axed her." Des' laugh was ugly as he savored a belief system that Meredith had battled for the last decade. "He used the catch-all 'doesn't meet expectations for field service.'" He snapped his fingers. "Just like that, he sent her packing." Des clucked. "The idea of a woman in a barney surrounded by street toughs was more than he could handle. He did us a service. He put off getting more split-tails on the job for a few years."

In an instant, Nick shoved the table, pinning it to Desmond's chest. Nick stood, leaning over Des, his hands gripping the table. "My wife is one of those women you're dissing. She's a damn fine cop. You owe her an apology."

Wide-eyed, Des' gaze stayed on Nick, a schoolyard bully keeping an eye on a kid who chose to fight back. Nick was angry, as was Meredith. Nick had endured his own prejudices and understood this kind of discrimination. As brutal as Desmond's words were, she'd heard them all before during her career.

Desmond's slimy reply didn't conceal his contempt. "Meredith, my dear. I never meant to hurt your feelings. I'm sure you're good at your job."

She waved his shallow regrets aside as her impatience seeped out. Des' fake Irish charm was wearing thin. The words of an apology were there, but Meredith didn't feel it. Nick released the table and crossed his arms over his brawny chest. Thinking he might get physical again, she asked, "Why did they take his gun? He must've done something more to—"

Desmond waved the thought away. "He pissed off the wrong people, is all."

He wasn't going to tell her about Terence's gun, so Meredith fired a question in another direction. "Who is Brenda Houston?"

"Who?" He glanced at the bar, buying time to formulate his answer.

Meredith didn't repeat the name. She waited.

"Ah, yes. Brenda." Desmond's eyes widened at the memory. "Brenda filled in for me, some years ago, when I couldn't be here. Like Ramona does."

"Why would my father pay Brenda Houston a significant amount of his pension every month?"

A shallow shrug. "They, ah, they had a thing for a while."

"What kind of thing," Nick snapped. "An affair?"

Desmond's face twisted like he was getting a tooth pulled. "Yes."

Meredith eyed the older man. She didn't want to sound like she was accusing her father of anything—even though she thought it. "Did my father have this affair while still married to my mother?"

"What does it matter?" Desmond waved the question away. "I can't remember what he was doing on what date. This is silliness, young lady. You should be living your life, happy that you—"

"Was there a child?"

Desmond's lips curled.

Meredith snatched up the note. She wasn't going to get what she wanted from him. What the hell was he hiding? "Things happened seventeen years ago that have an impact today. I need to know what my father was up to."

"Well, I'm not one to be talking ill of the dead, so you won't hear it from me."

"You mean Terence, not the woman, right?" Nick tapped an index finger lightly on the table.

"I lost touch with Brenda a long time ago. I was referring to your father." Again, Des ignored Nick's presence but answered the question.

"Was my father forced to retire? Did something happen? I mean, he loved the horse assignment. He would've stayed there until he was too old to sit in the saddle."

"He got transferred from the unit." Meredith strained to hear Des's voice.

She'd always thought Terence had retired from the Mounted Unit. She was confused. Transferred? Why would he do something to endanger his precious horse duty?

"Transferred to where?" Nick asked, while Meredith processed the last bit of news.

Des looked away, then back again. "To a desk job, where the powers could keep an eye on him."

"'Keep an eye on him?'" Meredith repeated indignantly. She stood, steeling herself against Desmond's evasiveness, but too full of energy to stay seated. "What was he accused of?"

Desmond stood, the chair legs skidding across the rough floor. "Nothing you need to worry about, young lady." He shoved the chair under the table.

Nick stepped in front of her. "Desmond, why was the Admin watching him?"

Startled at the physical imposition, Des looked into Nick's eyes. "The gun used in the robbery—it was Terence's service weapon."

"What robbery?" Nick's jaw locked into place, waiting

for an answer.

"The spring of 2001. The Bay City Moving Company courier was held up at gunpoint as he left their office on Harrison at Sixteenth. The job went south. The courier got shot and died. The murder weapon was Terence's." Desmond failed at holding back a thin smile. "The dicks called your father a thief and a murderer."

Meredith fingered the thin newspaper article in her pocket as the shock settled in. She'd suspected the gun had been in evidence for a violent act—but not a robbery, and especially not a homicide. "Why didn't they charge him?"

"The evidence was too circumstantial to prove he fired it. It was his gun, but it was wiped clean, no prints. Terence claimed it was stolen and used before he could report it."

"If SFPD found the gun, did they recover the money?"

"They didn't pursue it too far. It was tainted money, anyway. Bay City Moving Company belonged to some underworld types." Des' eyebrows rose, looking at her with incredulity that she didn't know this already. "Besides, they had a suspect in custody for the robbery, didn't they?"

Meredith thought she knew the answer. "Who was in custody?"

Des' brows drew together. "Young Jamie Houston, wasn't it?"

Finally, a tie to the murder and the Houston kid. Nick asked, "Houston didn't give up the money in exchange for a deal with the DA?"

"There was no dealing. It involved a homicide." Des snapped, like they should've known this. "It was so much gangster money, wasn't it? Who cares if they get their filthy, ill-gotten lucre back? And, the cash was never recovered."

That damn fake Irish. "Gangster money?"

"The moving company was starting up to cover as a money laundering operation. Just getting organized, according to the Gang Unit guys."

"What gang?" Nick pressed him.

Des stared at Nick, a challenge in his shrug. "Some dirty Mexicans or another."

Nick stepped back, ready to take a swing. Meredith anticipated his anger and put a hand on his bicep. Feeling his muscles tense under his shirt, she held her grip. This wouldn't help.

Des seemed to realize he'd pushed too far. With a quick glance at his wristwatch, he said, "Look at that. Time to open." At last, he acknowledged Nick—in a dismissal. "Nicholas, leave the door unlocked when you leave." Desmond turned to loop his arms around Meredith. "Ah, it's good to see you, young lass."

She shrugged out of his embrace and stared at him.

A faint smile curled his lips and he leaned against the bar. From the back room, a door opened and blew shut. Ramona strolled in. "Hey, what happened in here? The back's a mess." She looked around and caught Desmond's eye. She held up a fist full of letters. "I got the mail. On top is something for your buddy, Terence." She slapped them on the bar in front of Desmond and returned to the back room. Bottles rattled as she set to cleaning.

Des' eyes widened as he pushed the letters aside, picking up a legal-sized envelope.

Meredith hurried across the barroom, snatched the envelope from his fingers, and whirled around to leave. He reached for it but too late. Meredith was halfway to the front, the envelope already tucked into her jeans pocket.

"Oh, one more thing," Desmond called after her as Nick pulled open the door.

Meredith scowled at the man who could rile her up as fast as her father.

"Even if you do bring up the bad old days, there's good ones you're ignoring, young lady."

CHAPTER THIRTY

The door slammed shut behind the Ryan girl. Desmond picked up a plastic bowl with last night's happy hour snacks—a dozen peanuts—and flung it across the bar. Nuts flew everywhere as the bowl clattered to the floor.

Something important had been in the envelope, he just knew it. Des figured the con home must've had instructions to mail the letter upon his death. He hoped it contained directions to get to the cash. Terence hadn't trusted anybody, but he'd had that letter sent to his daughter at this address. It pissed Des off that he'd use the bar but not send the letter to him. Like he didn't trust him enough.

Why send it to the daughter at the bar? Terence wouldn't know where Meredith lived, would he? The bar was the sole point of reference in the old boy's life. Terence's horses were gone, so the stable was out. No longer a cop, he couldn't use the station address. He hadn't a home of his own since dumping Nora so many years back. Brenda wouldn't have him, nor was she trustworthy. Not enough money in his pitiful pension to afford an apartment of his own; he was left with a cot in the back room of a neighborhood bar.

Now the envelope was out of his hands. He followed his instincts—they'd not failed him yet. Keep an eye on the daughter. He'd figure out a way.

Meredith Ryan had always grated on his nerves, that one. Even as a girl, she'd never had the sense to accept things as they were. Always asking questions, ruffling feathers. She'd be a pain in the ass to her sergeant, for sure. And he would have hated a partner like her, always bucking the way things are meant to be. Even so, she took after Terence, which accounted for their rocky relationship. Her traits were tolerable in a male, but deadly in a female.

And Terence's boy David was like the mother—passive, accepting, and morose. Mother and son had the Irish in their melancholy dispositions. Meredith was like Terence; even sounded like him, although he'd be pissed if you told him so. He would have been pissed. Past tense. The old asshole was finally gone.

Terence's death had put things in motion that had been on hold for a long while. It was time to get conditions rolling to Uncle Desmond's benefit. He didn't believe in letting life dictate your future. Even when the San Francisco Police Officers' Administration and the Union forced him to quit or be fired, he'd taken control. He'd gotten caught lying, by the brass. Lying, for Christ's sake. It wasn't like he was the only one who embellished. Everyone did it. But times were changing. The department had been facing up to past transgressions and was cleaning house. So, he'd cashed out his own nineteen years of contributions to his pension fund and bought the Crazy Eights. The bar wouldn't make him rich, that was for sure. When he opened, it'd been a cop bar and he'd made a fair bit of coin with the old guard. As time passed, he'd become out of style. The new guys never came around. Now, the neighborhood rummies barely kept his rent paid.

Then, in 2001, Terence's troubles reached the boiling point and provided Des with the possibility of a brighter future. Even lying for the old bastard—giving Terence an alibi—hadn't helped Des' former partner. Like him, Terence got railroaded out of the job, except that Terence had reached that magic date—twenty years on the job. 'Retire or get fired,' they'd told Terence. He'd retired. Taken his pension, cashed out his vacation and compensatory time and ended up with a pretty penny. Terence had literally left town. Not like Des, who stayed in the city that he loved, in spite of the department.

Unfortunately, by then Brenda had her hooks sunk deep into Terence—her and her young son, Jamie. Des looked around the bar: bottles knocked over, cupboards open, towels and paper napkins scattered on the floor. And now that fucking Jamie is out of prison, looking for the money. Like he'd keep it here, Des thought with disgust.

He was getting tired of it—the monthly struggle to pay bills, the ostracism from what used to be his family at the PD, waiting for better days, the loss of Terence, Brenda. Yes, and Jamie. His eyes settled on a photograph of a guy he'd worked and partied with before he quit. Rich Peyton and he had gone to the academy at the same time. In the snapshot, smiling under a blonde handlebar mustache, Peyton stood arm around the shoulders of a sweet-faced Mexican girl. Palms swayed on white-sanded beaches, giving way to the aqua waves of the Gulf of Mexico in the background. Peyton had scribbled, "The good life," across the bottom of the picture.

Then, Des had an idea. He'd use all the tools at his disposal. Where had he put Brenda's phone number? She'd know how to get hold of Jamie.

Ramona's sweeping got his attention. Desmond brightened at the good timing. She'd asked for more hours just yesterday. Her fiscal misfortune suited his needs quite well. "You still got that old Corolla?"

After Ramona's quizzical nod, Desmond asked, "Is that gray truck still across the street?"

"Yeah."

"Follow it—on the clock. Call me when they get to their next destination."

Between the two of them, he'd know what Meredith Ryan was up to.

CHAPTER THIRTY-ONE

The black leather jacket did little to keep the cold out of Jamie Houston's bones. He hated coming to the Inner Sunset in San Francisco. It was always cold and foggy when the rest of the state was sunny. He shoved his fists into the pockets, still pissed about the phone call that brought him here.

Pushing open the door of the Crazy Eights Bar, he stepped into what seemed a murky cave. The stink of cigarette smoke and stale beer assailed him as he let his eyes adjust to the dark. Narrow, with a half dozen tables and accompanying chairs, the room was bisected by a curtain draped open to what he assumed was a storeroom. A tall old guy behind the bar studied him as he weaved his way through the tables to the bar.

The old man flipped a dingy towel over his shoulder and leaned against the bar. "You Brenda's boy?"

"Yeah, I'm Jamie." It had been years since he'd seen Desmond. He used to call him 'Uncle Desmond' years ago, but after they moved, his mother had blistered his butt when he did. On the drive to the City, Jamie had counted the years at fourteen since he'd last seen the old man. And the old boy had aged. Desmond's wiry salt and pepper hair had gone almost white. Tall, still over six feet but shoulders rounded and his wrinkled neck slack under an open collared shirt.

The old man broke into a smile that didn't reach his eyes. "Good to see you, my boy." After a brief, damp handshake, he motioned Jamie to a stool at the bar. "What'll you have?"

"Bud draft," he answered, looking around. The wood paneled walls were covered with yellowed snapshots of cops from the 70's, 80's and 90's. Broad mustaches, hair a little too long, and glassy eyes were like a uniform for cops in those days. Many of the photos featured the faded image of a young, athletic-looking Irishman—a younger version of the man who stood before him. For the first time, Jamie saw the man as he had been so many years ago.

Des slid a glass of beer across the bar. "Been a while, eh?"

The old man cocked his head like he expected Jamie to say something witty. Wit had never been Jamie's strength. He was better with his hands. "You wanted to see me?"

Des straightened. "I did." He took the towel and wiped his hands, although Jamie saw they'd been dry. "I'd like to talk over something that happened."

"Shoot." Jamie took a drink, the beer flat and almost tasteless. He braced himself, figuring Des would want something. This couldn't be good. He was on parole, after all.

"You know, of course, that your mother's paramour, Terence Ryan, has passed away."

Paramour? What the hell is that? "I heard." But he hadn't heard. He felt a jolt and suppressed it. Jamie had served time and Terence was never even charged. Filthy cops.

Des leaned in, his voice low—which was a hoot because they were the only two in the place. "Did you ever get a sense of where Terence hid the money?"

Jamie's suspicions were confirmed. What made this asshat think he had any information to share? Like he'd sit on it after serving nearly fourteen years in prison? Besides, Des didn't do him any favors by setting up that job. Got his buddies killed and him locked up.

"Nope." Jamie forced himself to look into the old man's eyes. The answer was easy—and a dead end. "I thought he dumped it in a storage locker—with some other—stuff. But I never could get back into it." He didn't tell Desmond that he'd been so scared that he couldn't remember where the storage building was.

Desmond's eyes sparkled.

Alarm spread though Jamie. The old man's expression was evil, a borderline maniac. He half expected Des to reach under the bar and grab an axe. Jamie backed up on the stool, trying not to be obvious. Shit.

Des said, "What if I had an angle—how to get the key to the locker?"

"Oh yeah? How?" Jamie felt his bullshit-o-meter swing off the chart. Did this guy know where the storage locker was? He'd play along to see.

"You work with me and I'll clue you in." Des winked, like an uncle with a birthday surprise.

"Why do you need me? Why don't you just get the key and check out the locker?"

"Jamie, me boy. I feel like I owe you for encouraging the foolishness that got you into trouble." Desmond straightened; a liar caught but still trying to make Jamie believe. "And, truth be told, I'm not the man I was. I need the young muscle and energy. And I need the money to keep this place going." Desmond waved a hand to include the walls around him.

Jamie wondered what Desmond's real angle was. The bar was a dump even though it'd been Desmond's home for a long time. And Des had sucked him into a shitload of trouble eleven years ago, then hung him and his two buddies out to dry. Then Jamie envisioned the bag of cash. Cash that he'd held in his very own hands—briefly. He needed that money for his mother's cancer treatments in Mexico. He didn't plan to share it. Still, half was better than nothing. "What do you need me to do?"

Desmond smiled again, and Jamie shivered at the sheer wickedness.

CHAPTER THIRTY-TWO

A block from Market Street, Nick found a pocket-sized parking lot off Eighth. His Chevy truck was larger than any of the other vehicles. He knew he'd have trouble parking in the city, but it was either that or drive Mere's Subaru. He'd rather be caught dead. He huffed at giving his truck keys to these guys. After reluctantly handing over the valet key to the attendant, he followed Meredith down Eighth, hustling to keep up with his wife.

He read the set of her shoulders as she leaned into the muni buses' raucous wake. The diesel, street dust, and car exhaust were preparing her for battle. Anyone who crossed her was in for trouble.

She hadn't said much on the way over, likely stewing at her uncle's lack of cooperation. She'd carry this attitude into the San Francisco Employees' Retirement System (SFERS) offices. Heaven help them if there were any glitches.

Nick hoped for no surprises from the SFERS but dealing with a bureaucracy was a wild card. Mere had a copy of her father's benefit designation. The purpose of their visit was to give the staff an original death certificate to close out the account. It was a formality that could've been done through the mail, but Meredith insisted since they were in the City anyway, they may as well get this done. Truthfully, Nick wondered what curveball might be thrown next. Terence Ryan's "estate" hadn't been predictable, no matter how much Meredith thought she'd prepared. There wasn't much in his checkbook.

He caught up with her at Market Street, wind gusts from the bay tempering the bleak summer sunshine that dodged between tall buildings. She shivered, clutching a portfolio to her chest, but he knew it wasn't from the cold.

At 1145 Market Street, they took the elevator to the fifth floor. The building smelled like everything in San Francisco—the step just before mildew. The structure had been here for generations and was close to the Bay. Moisture was a constant companion which seeped into everything, food, textiles, buildings. Nick smelled the mustiness on people when they were close enough. San Francisco might be his wife's childhood home, but he was glad they would return to Petaluma at the end of this day.

At the SFERS front counter, they waited as a trim young woman approached. When her attention wandered somewhere over Nick's shoulder; he pegged her as an experienced government employee. Dyed blond hair pulled into a practiced yet sloppy bun, artfully applied make-up and enormous gold hoop earrings said she was compulsive about her appearance. A name tag, "Amber," sat on the side of gray-sweater.

The woman's attention arrived at Nick. She didn't even try to smile. "Help you?"

Nick pointed to Meredith. She slapped the portfolio on the laminate counter.

He heard the tension in his wife's voice. "I'm here to notify the retirement board of my father's death. Here's his death certificate." She pushed it across the counter.

Mumbling a vague phrase about being sorry for their loss, the woman took the paper to a desk. Tapping on a keyboard, she scrutinized the monitor. Four desks away, a sheet of paper rolled from a printer. Amber retrieved it.

"Here's the account closure confirmation. You'll need to keep a record of this." She slipped the copy between Meredith and Nick. "Anything else?"

Nick said, "Uh," at Amber's back as the woman retreated to her desk. Meredith studied the paper. He waited for her to compare it to her own copy. Nick wasn't sure they were finished.

"Jesus," Meredith whispered. "He changed beneficiaries last month." Meredith's eyes widened in shock. "Everything goes to Brenda Houston." Meredith looked at the confirmation like it was a pile of maggots. "I'm still the executor."

"It's not like there's much money." Nick thought it over.

"And we don't need it."

"That's not the point, Nick." She squared herself in front of him as if he had become the adversary. "He changed his estate, didn't tell me, and knew I'd find out." The hurt leaked from her eyes. She sniffed and turned away. "Just another way to get to me." Then, facing Nick again, she stared into a place that said she wasn't looking at him. "What did I ever do to him?"

What an asshole, Nick thought, as he herded Meredith from the office.

CHAPTER THIRTY-THREE

The drive to Sonoma County was a commuter's dream. With no traffic, Meredith held her exasperation until they passed the last Mill Valley exit. "What is—was—he trying to do?" She was furious now. "What motivates one person to hurt another like this? And not just any person—his own daughter."

Nick had no words.

"It's like he wasn't nasty enough when he was alive, he had to remind me after his death. This must be what he meant in his will by 'any other specific monies.' I thought it was just one last poke at me." What had Terence taught her about being a father? Did she have any of his anger or malice in her genes, or was it all taught? She blurted, "Do you see any of my father's behavior in me? I mean—"

"Whoa, whoa, whoa." Nick's eyes left the road for a moment. "Don't go there." That had been their signal to stop an emotional train wreck. He'd been prepared for a distressed reaction—death of a family member is a vulnerable time. Throw in family politics, and executing an estate is a nightmare in the making, or at least a Meredith melt-down. "Don't go there," was her cue to stop and think.

She blew out the bad air she'd been holding. "All right. All right." Breathing again, she whispered, "It's so easy to get trapped into this filth—whatever it is." She looked at her husband, gratitude for his common sense welling up. "Thanks for that."

"De nada."

"I just," she paused knowing how easily she could fall down that black hole. But she had to ask. "Nick, you didn't answer me. I'm not like my father, am I? I'd do anything not to parent like him."

Nick huffed in frustration. She couldn't tell if it was at her or the obnoxious lane-changing Beemer in front of them.

"You're nothing like him," he said.

"He wasn't always that way. When I was little, he wasn't so mean."

She was grateful that Nick let her talk out her dilemma. "Davy changes everything. I feel like I have to know why Terence was such an ass."

"So, history won't repeat itself?" Nick's mouth twisted. "I can tell you all day long what a great mother you are. But if you have doubts, you need to address them. Get back on track with your investigation."

Meredith digested this, then nodded.

"What's your next step, detective?" It's what he would ask when acting as her sergeant.

"The Haven Convalescent Home, then I need to track down this Brenda woman. Talk to her."

Nick nodded with finality. "Good move."

CHAPTER THIRTY-FOUR

Desmond couldn't help smiling. The fool was eating up his lies. It was hard to believe anyone who'd spent fourteen years in prison would fall for this shit. Especially considering how he'd pushed him into holding up the moving business. Jamie mentioned Terence's comment and Des had jumped at the opportunity to score some cash. He'd told Jamie to drop the money off with him for safekeeping, but the kid panicked after his buddy shot the courier.

Desmond was on patrol that night and was in the area when the call came out. Shots fired is a "y'all come" emergency response. He was one of the first units on scene. When he figured out what happened, he knew he'd be in the shit if he didn't do something—fast.

When Granados, the fledgling gang leader, showed up all righteous about being the victim of a robbery, Des corralled him. On the sly, he told the gangster where he could find the suspects. Even gave him the address where Jamie lived.

He was a little sorry that he hadn't known about the gang association before the robbery. He'd soothed his guilt by telling himself that Terence had told Jamie the day they'd driven by. So, Jamie knew. But greed was an irresistible charmer.

His own greed included.

He looked around, taking in the place that had been his home for the past thirteen years. Dark and tired, it reflected his own life. With nothing to show for himself or his business, he had nothing to lose. He was done. Done with the drudgery of cleaning up vomit after patrons, sweeping peanut shells from the floor, calling irate spouses to arrange rides home. He was done with taking money from one account to pay another, from borrowing from the few friends he had left. He was done pandering to the ABC agents who liked to roust him from time to time.

Mexico? His eyes went to Rich Peyton's photograph on the wall. Maybe. He'd heard Thailand was a cheap place to live, too. He wasn't sure he wanted to live in a different hemisphere. But he wanted out.

Now—how?

He needed the money. Ramona signed on for easy cash. He'd promised her a grand for following the girl. And, enlisting Jamie gave him some muscle. At Des' age, he'd need another pair of hands. Oh, he was still powerful. He lifted weights in his garage four days a week. He was proud that he could still lift 250 pounds at the age of 67. But he still needed another man.

And the plan? So far, he figured he'd give Meredith all the lead she needed to find the money. Ramona would keep an eye on her, then he'd get Jamie to take it away. And, when Jamie was to hand it over to him, well, he'd refine that. But Jamie wasn't walking away with half the cash. Nor was Ramona getting any dough.

Mexico or Thailand?

CHAPTER THIRTY-FIVE

Nick pulled his Chevy truck into one of the narrow parking spaces at the Haven Convalescent Home. Meredith was out the passenger door before the ignition turned off.

He hurried to catch up with her. "Mere, wait."

She pushed through the sliding front doors, heading for the Administration office. He heard her ask for the Administrator.

The antiseptic smell hit Nick like a wall. Who knew what the odor concealed? This was a place where people die. And the odd, closed-in feeling reminded him of being locked in a closet. A wave of revulsion shivered over him.

The Administration office was small. Too small to contain the volume of Meredith's temper. Nick felt sorry for the middle-aged woman sitting behind the cluttered desk.

"Do you have an appointment?" The secretary smiled at Meredith.

"No. I want to see your administrator."

"I'm sorry," the secretary began with an officious shrug. "She's a busy lady. Appointments are suggested to—"

Meredith took a half step back. Nick saw her dial her temper down a notch. "Then tell her I tried to get her permission, but I'm going to question her staff." She turned to leave.

"Wait. Wait, ma'am." The secretary half rose behind the desk. "You can't do that."

"Watch me." Meredith said over her shoulder.

On their way to her father's old room, Nick said, "Don't you want the custodian?"

"Yeah." Meredith wasn't acting officially here, but she wasn't controlling her interactions like she'd been trained. "Jeeze, glad I'm not working at the Haven Convalescent Hospital."

Down the hall, Meredith stopped a young woman in hospital scrubs. Then, armed with directions to the janitor's closet, Meredith doubled back to the other wing. Nick followed, feeling a bit foolish. He was there to keep Meredith on track—and everyone else safe.

Just outside the door marked, "Maintenance," Meredith found a tired Hispanic with beefy shoulders—the man who'd been cleaning the walls of her father's room.

Meredith identified herself as a patient's daughter. "Do you remember Terence Ryan?"

The janitor's face scrunched in thought. "3A? Passed away a couple of days ago?"

"That's my father." Meredith's gaze drilled into the man. He fidgeted under her scrutiny. "Remember me? I was there picking up his things when you had to clean up the mess he made."

He nodded; his lips pinched in a look of dread.

"You said someone was there and had argued with him. Remember?"

He nodded again.

"Do you know what the fight was about?"

"Hm, I think your father said something about never finding something."

"Yeah? What else."

"He told the guy that he wouldn't want to find it. There was too heavy a price tag."

Nick spoke for the first time. "Did you see the guy?"

Again, reluctance surfaced. "Yes, sir. He was a white man." He nodded toward Meredith. "About her height, thin. But had ink." The janitor exposed a bicep, flexing a crown of thorns tattoo. "Here."

"Hair color, clothes description? Anything *distintivo*?"

The janitor began a rapid-fire answer in Spanish until Nick put up his hand. "In English, so my wife can understand."

"He look like he belong in jail. Tattoos on his fingers. Letters, I think." Seeming to seek their approval, he glanced from Nick to Meredith and back again.

Evil, wicked, mean, and nasty. A standard non-gang tattoo that reflected the criminal's nature. Like Jamie. Thin.

The intruder?

"What did the young man say?"

"At first, it sounded like he was asking for a favor. I was across the hall fixing a sink. I didn't listen. People in here, well—families have arguments sometimes. Then, Mr. Ryan must say no, because the man yelled and threw the food tray against the wall."

Nick was embarrassed that he assumed Terence had thrown the food. It was easy to paint the man black but when your own ugly assumptions are proven wrong, it sets you back. What else were we wrong about? He glanced at his wife. Meredith must've had the same opinion judging from the red creeping up her neck.

Eyes downcast, the janitor added, "The younger man said Mr. Ryan would kill his mother."

**

"Yeah, but what does it mean?" Meredith slammed the door of Nick's truck. "Terence wasn't going to get out of bed and kill anyone."

Nick wished he could make Terence and his drama go away. "And who's the mother he's talking about? Brenda? That means the guy who upset your father so much was her son, the parolee, Jamie."

Meredith nodded.

Nick didn't like it when Meredith got quiet like this. He suspected that she'd want to go see Jamie, question him. He did, too, for that matter. But they were walking a fine line here: they weren't cops investigating a crime in their jurisdiction. A parolee is released from prison with a specific set of terms. One standard is, subject to search by law enforcement at any time of the day or night. Some search stipulations relate only to a criminal investigation. The conditions of Jamie's parole didn't apply in this case. Meredith simply wanted to know if Jamie provoked her father into having a heart attack. It was more personal than professional. Jamie was not required to cooperate with them. Would he answer Meredith's questions?

Only one way to find out.

Something similar must've been running through her mind, because she shrugged and said, "I have to notify Brenda of his death, anyway. If Jamie's there, we can ask."

Nick started the truck and nosed it into traffic.

CHAPTER THIRTY-SIX

1807 Arbor was in the most run-down part of a trailer park in Rohnert Park, fifty miles north of San Francisco. With an estimated population of 42,600, suburban Rohnert Park was an affordable bedroom community to San Francisco and Marin commuters. A planned city incorporated in 1962, it boasted 16,500 housing units with a building boom in progress. Often the butt of jokes from snobbier Sonomans, the city had no discernible downtown and lacked the turn-of-the twentieth century charm of Santa Rosa and Petaluma. But people who lived here loved the small town feel and strong sense of community. There were no slums in Rohnert Park, no mansions, and more than a few light industrial areas and strip malls. Hard-working people—fast food workers to realtors—not only co-existed but thrived here. The half dozen mobile home parks housed the elderly and lower-income families.

Just inside the western edge of the city, Evergreen Estates Mobile Home Park bordered dairy grazing lands. Some days an offshore wind brought the pungent, earthy smell of the neighboring dairies.

The trailer park was divided into two sections, family and seniors. Meredith and Nick found 1807, a rusty yellow double-wide in the family section. The home sat three feet from the front curb, featured an add-on, currently empty cement carport showing fresh oil spots. Landscaping consisted of overgrown juniper bushes. Drawn curtains completed the picture of the most uninviting home site on the block.

Nick parked his truck in the guest parking space three doors down.

Exposed wires hung where the doorbell should be, so Meredith knocked on the metal door. Instantly, a yappy dog raised hell inside. Meredith was considering another knock when the door squeaked open to continued barking from the back of the house. A small, wrinkled woman balancing on a walker greeted them. Meredith knew, from the info she had, that Brenda Houston was around 65 years of age, but the woman looked old far beyond her years. Thinning, shoulder-length, dyed blond hair and yesterday's mascara smudged under this woman's eyes revealed something that Meredith didn't care to discover. Clad in a shapeless gray sweatshirt, sweatpants and slippers, this woman hadn't cleaned herself up in quite some time.

Meredith introduced herself. "Brenda Houston?"

At the woman's nod, Meredith said, "I'm Meredith Ryan, Terence Ryan's daughter. This is my husband, Nick. Can we come in and talk to you?"

"Terence's girl, eh?" Brenda squinted at Meredith. After a second, she snapped, "The cop, right? We can talk right here. Whaddya want?"

"Really, we should be someplace where you can sit down." Meredith found courtesy to this woman harder than she'd expected. But there had to be more to her. What could her father have seen in this woman?

Brenda shuffled sideways and the door swung open. Nick guided it, to keep it from hitting him as he walked in behind Meredith.

The house smelled of stale cigarette smoke and dog pee. The smoke was the same odor Meredith had smelled on the man who broke into her home. In the time it took for her eyes to adjust to the dark, she'd guessed the intruder came from here. Tamping her initial fury, she balanced it with the knowledge that this wasn't a new smell. She'd been around enough people who reeked of cigarettes to seek another sign of Brenda's culpability. It certainly wasn't Brenda herself. Her son? She'd take bets on him. She glanced around for trouble. Nothing here beyond junk, boxes, newspapers and more.

Brenda moved slowly into the living room, eventually settling into sagging recliner. Next to the chair, an end table with a lamp sat amid papers and empty coffee mugs. Sitting on the edge of the seat, the woman clicked on the light and waited.

Meredith found a clear spot for her and Nick on a sofa. The dog still yipped behind a closed door and Meredith raised her voice to be heard. "I'm sorry to have to tell you, but my father, Terence Ryan, has passed away."

Meredith almost missed Brenda Houston's face sag. His father's ex had been surprised, that much was for sure. But why? Here she was within three miles of where her father lived for the past eighteen months. Didn't she visit?

Brenda nodded; her face blank. "When?"

"Two days ago." What? no show of grief? "Monday afternoon."

"The cause?" Brenda croaked.

What an odd question. Why wouldn't she assume natural causes? "His heart. He had a severe cardiac condition—aortic stenosis. The people at the Haven Care Home said a woman sometimes came to visit. I presumed it was you. Is that right?"

A nod, but Brenda's attention was somewhere else. The dog had quieted, as if knowing its master had fallen into a pit of grief. Brenda seemed to have shrunk, caving in on herself. It was hard to believe that this woman would take Terence's death so hard, as ill as he'd been. She should've expected it. Maybe she'd cooperate—give Meredith answers to her questions in exchange for information.

Meredith wanted to avoid Brenda's attention from wandering, so she forged ahead. "You met Terence at the Crazy Eights Bar in the city, didn't you?"

The question got through. Brenda shook her head.

"You were a bartender there?"

Brenda's eyes were losing their glaze as she worked at focusing on Meredith. "Yes, a relief bartender."

"You worked for Desmond Rollins?"

Brenda sighed as if digging up this old history pained her. Maybe it did. "We were part-owners. Bought the place in 1980. The ABC would let him hold a liquor license while being a policeman, so the place was in my name."

"That's how you met my father."

"Of course I knew him. They were partners." She pulled a wadded-up tissue from her sleeve and kneaded it. "When Des got canned at the PD, he bought me out. That's how I got this place." A veiny hand motioned to the trailer. "Your father found it."

"After he married Nora?"

Brenda's expression was non-committal. So?

Meredith let silence do the work. People hate silence in conversation, particularly when they feel they have something to justify. Like adultery.

Brenda's voice softened. "As you kids got older, he had a hard time at home. His son was such a disappointment, not being very manly. You were more tomboy than his son, and your father began to resent you both. Then his wife, she'd become either a shrew or a recluse, depending on her mood." The woman's eyes met Meredith's. "He needed comfort. I gave it to him."

She said it so simply that the implications almost fell flat. But Meredith was tenacious when it came to the truth. Giving him comfort meant many things. Angry arguments bubbled around in her mind, but she pushed them aside. This was important—too important to let raw emotions dictate her responses. "Who is Jamie?"

Brenda looked away. Her gaze fell to a of a high school graduation photo on the end table. The hairstyle could've been from Meredith's own senior class. "He's my son." It was a simple answer.

But to Meredith, it opened more questions. "Who's his father?"

Brenda's head twisted like she'd been slapped in a John Wayne movie. Meredith was surprised when the woman met her with an indignant gaze. "You're a nosy parker, aren't you? It's none of your business."

Meredith backed down. She was sure she knew the answer. This could be settled later. "I understand your son is on parole."

Brenda's lower lip set in a stubborn frown. "He's paid his debt. Leave him out of this. He's a good boy."

If Meredith had heard this once, she'd heard it a million times. No one believed their loved ones committed crimes. She never took their character appraisals as fact.

"Brenda. I'm looking for answers about my father." Meredith had thought hard about showing any vulnerability to this woman who broke up her parent's already damaged marriage, who probably gave birth to an illegitimate son, and who'd taken money without shame from a bed-ridden old man. She wanted to know why. What could she offer that would make a man throw his family away? And now, she wondered if Brenda had anything to do with her father's forced retirement.

"I don't have to tell you anything." The lines on the old woman's face tightened in a grimace. "You don't have jurisdiction here, not even a warrant."

Meredith sighed. "We're not here as cops, Brenda. This is personal. My father made me executor of his will. You're not obligated to answer anything under the law. This is outside of the job. I'm on moral ground here."

"You're not on 'moral ground,' young lady. You're here to insult me. Rub your father's death in my face. Like I had no hold on him."

"Oh, but you did, Brenda." There was a perverse pleasure in telling her she was wrong; she was the beneficiary, even though the designation overlooked his own daughter. "Terence made you beneficiary of his retirement pension. There isn't much left but the money will be coming to you." As executor and co-signatory, Meredith was bequeathed the small checking account. She'd have to go to the bank to see who the beneficiary on the surprise checking account was. She'd wait to tell Brenda about that one.

Meredith could've predicted Brenda's next question. "How much?"

"It's not much. The balance was three thousand dollars. And there's a life insurance policy. The benefit is twenty thousand." Meredith tried to smile. She was, after all, giving her some good news. "I'll give you an accounting as soon as the estate is settled."

Brenda's eyes widened. Meredith figured she'd have questions, so she waited.

Nick stood, went to the window facing the street and pulled the corner of a curtain back. Meredith had heard the car arriving, too. Not for the first time today, she was glad Nick was with her.

CHAPTER THIRTY-SEVEN

Nick looked onto the narrow lane that passed for a trailer park street. A tired brown Taurus pulled into the carport at 1807. His cop brain registered: A solo white male driver, in his late twenties, thin and tallish from what he could see, brown shaggy hair, wearing a tan plaid flannel shirt.

Jamie. He looks just like his last mug shot. And could match Meredith's description of the guy who broke into our house. Damn, what now?

Nick watched him get out of the car, wrestle with a plastic grocery bag while absently nudging the door closed. Nick walked across the room to the front door. It swung open and Jamie stepped inside, poised to swing an elbow around to close the door.

"They're cops, Jamie," Brenda croaked.

Jamie flung the bag and car keys at Nick, twisting through the door and was on the run. Jamie wasn't wanted, Nick had no cause to detain him, but damn it—the guy ran.

"Stay here with her," was Meredith's heads-up. Not that she needed one. Nick would chase a runner. It was in his DNA.

Nick shot through the open door, scanning the area. No one visible, but he heard footfalls running toward the west. Following, he shouted, "Jamie, you're not in trouble. We just want to talk." Panting with the effort of shouting while at a full run, he gave it up. He reached back to his belt holster, assuring himself his gun was secure—and was there if he needed it.

Jamie ran through two tiny yards dotted with weathered Dollar Store yard ornaments and silk flowers. He hopped over a wobbly three-foot fence, pulled a 50-gallon garbage can over behind him and made for an open stretch of weedy lawn. Nick followed, dodging the garbage can, closing the distance between them. Ahead, a six-foot chain-link fence separated the trailer park grounds from a dairy pasture.

Nick called it at the big fence. He wasn't about to shred his good khakis going over the fence after someone who wasn't wanted. Nor did he want to muck around in cow shit.

He was still panting and sweaty when he got back to his truck. Meredith stood by in the carport, waiting next to Jamie's dented up Taurus.

She held out a bottled water. "You okay?"

He took it, downing the whole thing.

"She told me to get out." Meredith shrugged.

CHAPTER THIRTY-EIGHT

As his breathing calmed, he said what they both were thinking. "Let's get outta here before someone calls the cops on us." While they weren't doing anything wrong, off-duty cops loathed drawing attention to themselves. It would be embarrassing if they were found acting in a manner that could be construed as unprofessional without cause. They were simply talking to the beneficiary of Meredith's father's will. Having to explain this to an officer from another jurisdiction could harm their standing in the county's law enforcement community. The inference was that something was uncontrollable in the Reyes-Ryan world. And in their culture, it was all about control. Word of this kind of thing gets out, it spreads like wildfire. There was another way to handle this.

Hopping behind the wheel, Nick went over all the elements of this visit: Brenda had let them in on her own accord. They hadn't represented themselves as deputies, in fact, Meredith had made sure she emphasized to Brenda they were acting as private citizens. And chasing Jamie, well, that was more reaction than anything. No crime had been committed by either party.

On the way out the gate, Meredith took a page from Nick's playbook. "What just happened there?"

Nick turned right onto Redwood Drive, making his way south toward Highway 101. He glanced in his rear-view mirror. Still no cop cars responding to Evergreen Estates. He hmphed in satisfaction and thought about Meredith's question.

"First, Brenda's hiding something." Nick glanced between the road before him and his rear-view mirror. "Probably a lot of things. You gotta cut her some slack, though. It's not every day, the daughter of your ex marches through your door to tell you that you're the beneficiary of his pension policy. She was emotional about his death, and finds out about the money."

"Then, her parolee son comes home and foot bails when he finds out we're cops," she added. "I didn't get close enough to tell but I'll bet he stunk like stale cigarettes."

Nick's gut clenched. He was surely the intruder. He pressed the push-to-talk button on his steering wheel. "Call Rohnert Park Police Dispatch."

"Rohnert Park Police and Fire," the female dispatcher answered.

"Hi, I'm Nick Reyes from the Sheriff's Office. Can I speak to your patrol sergeant, please?" An explanation, even after the fact, would make this go away. No crime, not even bad judgement, had been committed. After hearing Nick's narrative—leaving out the suspicion Jamie had broken into the Reyes home—the sergeant told him that yes, a neighbor had called in a disturbance. The sergeant was happy to close out the call with a brief explanation as "unfounded." The neighbor hadn't wanted any follow-up contact with the police. And Nick and Meredith hadn't concealed anything from local authorities. Nothing important, anyway.

That crisis averted, Nick signaled his intention to change lanes, the fast way to home. "So, what's our next move?"

Meredith blew out a breath. "First, I should find an attorney to help with this estate business. It was easy—no probate—when I was the sole beneficiary but now, with Brenda, I need some guidance. As far as notifications, I need to go to the bank tomorrow with Terence's death certificate for the checking account, then the Social Security and Medicare people. I've got to put the creditors notice in the newspaper, start a file to keep all this crap straight."

She stopped and looked at her husband. "I wish I knew someone at SFPD who could give us the story on this robbery Jamie was convicted of."

CHAPTER THIRTY-NINE

It was 3 PM when Nick pulled the truck into their driveway.

Raymond Cavanaugh's oxidized ranch truck sat at the curb in front of their house. On the tow hitch rested a trailer full of lumber. Cav and Davy sat in the front seat, Davy gripping the steering wheel, turning it like he was driving an obstacle course. "I was at Friedman's Hardware getting some lumber; thought I'd stop by to see how you're doing. I haven't had time with the boy here in a few days, so I picked him up from Tina's."

Nick smiled. Raymond didn't carry a cell phone, and often showed up unannounced.

Nick opened the driver's door of Cav's truck. "Come on in. You and the boy look like you need a beer."

"Wait a few years, you two." Meredith grabbed the baby's backpack and led Davy by the hand into the house. His waddling made for slow going.

Cav's lined face broke into a smile. "Don't mind if I do. We can chew over that basement project you're talking about."

The Reyes home was a 1911 bungalow that had survived many remodels. The previous owner had put up drywall on one side of the basement and finished off the concrete floor. The structure had passed the home inspection, but Nick put drywalling the rest of the room on his list of to-do projects. Once finished and cleaned up, the space would double their storage area.

With a Pacifico in his hand, Cav followed Nick around to the back of the house. A foot below the ground level, the basement door was a rusted wrought iron affair that gave him a devil of a time.

Yanking the door open, Nick and Cav both ducked. The floor joists overhead, copper piping and spider webs prevented them from standing to their full height. The midafternoon sun cast vague shadows through the 2' X 2' windows, two on the front and back of the house.

Nick hadn't been down her much. Between Davy and work, he'd had little time for home improvement projects. It became more pressing to move items temporarily from their living space to the basement while painting and such went on. It was a shame to let all this space go to waste when the tiny 1911 closets overflowed. The room was beneath the entire footprint of the house. Three of the walls were bare down to studs, wiring and tar paper.

Cav glanced around. "Been a while since anyone was here."

"The inspector didn't spend much time down here. Everything was straightforward—just enough to pass a home inspection but nothing more." He kicked a bucket that held the solid remnants of mud used to tape drywall. "Right now, I want to clean it up enough to use for storage. Later, who knows? Maybe I'll make a man-cave for me and Davy." Nick smiled.

Cav took a swallow of his beer, stifled a belch and said, "Good luck with that."

"Right. Let's go upstairs."

Twenty minutes later, Nick had updated Cav about the box and Jamie. Cavanaugh's bushy eyebrows drew into a V. "What the hell?"

Meredith's face creased in a wry smile. "Right? Why run?"

"He's done something he hasn't gotten caught for." Nick popped a cap off a Pacifico beer and slid it across the table for Cav. "Like maybe break into our house." They sat at the kitchen table, watching Davy play with blocks on the living room rug.

At Cav's indignant look, Nick added, "It's not enough to prove it was him."

Cav sighed in disgust as Meredith pulled the shoe box from the shelf. She picked out the note. Embarrassment flushed her face as she shoved the note towards Cav.

"What do you make of it?"

After he read it, Cav grimaced over the paper.

Meredith sighed. "I wish I had access to SFPD's records so I could read that robbery report and the witness statements. That's where we'll find some answers." Meredith twirled the deep red merlot in her wine glass as she scowled at Jamie's photo. "I'm sure all this is related somehow."

Nick nodded. "Jamie's conviction, for sure. Maybe it has to do with your dad's service weapon being held in evidence, and his forced retirement."

Cav polished off the beer. "Wonder what the key opens up?"

The silence was telling. They didn't know much, that's for sure. Then, Meredith jumped up. "Damn. I forgot about that letter Dad sent to the bar." She ran down the hall, returned and tore open the envelope.

"It's a receipt." Wide-eyed, she glanced from one man to the other. "It's from Handi-Storage on Rohnert Park Expressway, just outside city limits."

Nick asked, "Anything else?"

"No. Just this receipt, stamped 'Paid in full to August 2020."

"Who sent it?"

"I don't have a clue." Meredith squinted, trying to make sense out of this. "But the unit is rented in my father's name."

Nick studied his phone, then said, "The website says they close at 5:30. It's almost five o'clock now. Not enough time."

Meredith shrugged. "We've waited this long. I guess a few hours more won't hurt anything. Maybe we'll find something important."

"You'll get your answers, if I know you two." Cav stood, turning to leave. "Just keep pluggin' away."

CHAPTER FORTY

It was the first warm evening of the summer. Dinner was finished, the dishes done, and Meredith had just gotten Davy ready for bed.

"Meredith, come out here. Bring Davy, too." Nick stood on the front porch holding a beer. His soft smile surprised her. He was relaxed, enjoying the evening. The sun set behind La Cresta Ridge, turning the eastern hills a deep purple. Streetlights illuminated the valley floor, but the distant hills slowly faded to dark. Nick was good about sharing moments like this.

The kid next door flew down the sidewalk calling after a mid-sized mutt. A minute later, an older couple from up the street waved as they walked by at the Reyes family. Meredith flipped Davy's arm in an awkward baby wave. Tired and edging toward cranky, Davy pulled his arm away, planting his thumb in his mouth.

Meredith sat down beside Nick in a wicker rocker. Davy hung onto Fresno while she tucked her son into her shoulder. She sat back in a gentle rocking motion, savoring the peaceful sounds of the summertime neighborhood. Most residents had windows open, embracing the warmth. She heard a TV game show from the reclusive senior next door; teenaged boys playing hoops across the street, and an occasional parental holler for kids to come in.

Davy's deep breathing told her he'd fallen asleep. She had no intention of getting up. She was relaxed, too, savoring the peaceful place in which they lived.

Nick tipped the beer, emptying it. "I'm going for another beer. You want anything?"

He cocked his head, looking up the street. The light from inside the living room exposed his whitening knuckles clutching the bottle.

"What is it?" Reluctant to stand and awaken Davy, she stayed in her chair.

"There's a Sheriff's unit cruising up the street."

"That's funny. Maybe he's serving civil papers."

Nick nodded absently, keeping an eye on patrol SUV. It slowed as it passed by.

"Shit." Nick glared after the vehicle. "It was Evelina."

What was she doing here? Meredith's gut clenched. It was time to tell him about Deb's warning. "Nick, come sit down. I need to tell you something."

The SUV accelerated toward the T-intersection of Melvin and English Street. Nick's words were clipped. "Tell me standing up." His jaw flexed as the SUV flipped a U-turn at English Street back to Melvin.

"When I talked to Deb the other day, she told me Evelina has a thing for you."

"What kind of thing?" Nick's face scrunched in confusion. "And how would Deb know?" Then, he waved away the idea. "Nah, that's just bullshit."

"No, it's not. Evelina's best friend is Deb's sister. Evelina told the sister that she wants to hook up with you." Meredith sucked in a breath. "Nick, don't yell. You'll wake the baby."

"Yell?" Nick turned to her, smiling. "Why would I yell?"

"You're fricking flattered, aren't you?" Meredith shook her head. "I can't believe you. You never get it when a woman is flirting with you. I have to practically hit you over the head with it—and now you're pleased!" Meredith had less tolerance for stalking than the normal person. Not that Nick was being stalked, by the law's definition. But this behavior had to be nipped in the bud.

"Pleased?" He smiled as his glance trailed off at the SUV. He looked back at Meredith and sat beside her. Dropping the bottle in his lap, he took her hand. "I guess I'm a little flattered. But you're right. I've got to do something. She works for me and I can't let this go any further." He looked into her eyes and she knew to her core that he was being honest.

She looked over his shoulder. "Now's your chance."

CHAPTER FORTY-ONE

Nick trotted to the street and flagged down the SUV. When she pulled to the curb, Evelina glanced up towards Meredith, who was taking the baby inside. Nick knew that Meredith was right about the infatuation. He'd never had to deal with this before but knew it had to be handled sensitively but decisively. Shit, what to say to her?

"Evelina." He flashed what he hoped was a pleasant supervisorial smile and rested his hands of the open driver's window.

"Sergeant. I didn't know you lived in Petaluma."

Evelina smiled, tipping her head sideways, much like his ex-wife used to. The pose toughened his resolve. "Sure you did. What are you doing inside city limits?"

Evelina rolled her eyes. "I got a stack of civil papers left over from dayshift."

"It's 8:30 P.M. We don't serve papers this late."

"Yeah, but there were some special ones—with court dates this week. They—" Her voice trailed off at the improbability of her statement.

He frowned at the lie. "Evelina. I've heard a rumor that you're thinking you and I can have a special relationship." He emphasized the word, special. "That won't ever happen."

"What?" She opened her mouth as if to speak, then closed it. Her jaw shot out in a defensive underbite. "No, sir. I'm sure you're mistaken."

Evelina reacted like this was about their rank and his authority. That was part of it, Nick thought, but the bigger notion was how much he loved his wife. Many times over, he'd entrusted his life to her and she'd never failed him. She was everything to him and especially now with Davy, they both had another chance at happiness together. She was the only woman who could stir him like a high school infatuation.

And she'd kick his ass if he cheated on her. He smiled at

the thought. "Nope, Evelina. Couldn't happen." He remembered the first night he kissed Meredith—on a boat in Mexico. They'd been sneaking back into the country after being escorted out by local *policía*. They were detective partners then, and both struggled to deny their feelings. Then in the Sonoma County hills, they kissed one night in a cave while hiding from domestic terrorists. That had changed their relationship.

"I don't care that you're married, Nick." Again, Evelina tipped her head seductively.

He must stop this now. He straightened, irritated that she didn't get it. "No, Evelina. You and I will never happen."

Her face flushed. She threw the transmission in Drive and sped away.

Nick didn't care if she was hurt, angry or both. He'd had to be clear.

CHAPTER FORTY-TWO

"Just go. Davy and I will be fine here." Cav squinted into the morning sun, turning to escape the glare. "I told Tina I'd take Davy duty today."

Meredith chalked it up to Cav needing to help her search for the truth. Spending time with Davy was a plus. The boy was happy to be in Cav's arms, smiling and waving around his new toy Camaro. Watching him vroom the toy across Cav's shoulders, Meredith thought what a delight Davy was—happy and cooperative, yet inquisitive in ways that hinted at intelligence. He takes after his father. She smiled.

"Who're we meeting, again?" Nick was as perplexed by Cav's surprise appearance as she was.

"My nephew, Gareth Cavanaugh. Tall young guy, SFPD cop. He'll be at Marvin's Café in Novato at nine o'clock. He's got a buddy, an old partner of his who worked robbery a decade ago. He'll be there, too. Might know something about the crime in San Francisco that you've been looking into."

Davy made motor noises with the plastic car as it coursed along Cav's chest.

Putting her trust in Raymond Cavanaugh hadn't come easy for Meredith. But once there, it was a solid, visceral thing. He'd saved her life—and Nick's. She took that very seriously. Once done, the indebtedness worked both ways. Lives became intertwined, affecting each other like she'd never considered. And, Meredith believed it never stopped.

So did Cav, apparently. She thought about the weight of him calling for a favor, knowing how much he asked. Maybe the nephew's old partner could help, maybe not. But she'd be a fool to pass up the chance. This was just what she needed. Meredith heard her mother's caution from years past, Be careful what you wish for. Meredith shuddered.

Some quick calculations—twenty minutes to Novato and back, depending on traffic. A half hour with the nephew.

They'd be home in a little over an hour. "We should be back by ten o'clock. Will that work for you?"

Nick started to say something, but Cav interrupted. "You have to check out the storage unit in Santa Rosa, too."

Crap. She didn't want Davy there. She didn't know what was inside the unit nor did she want to be chasing her son. That much was for sure.

Nick began, "We don't want to tie you up—"

"Don't you worry about that." Cav interrupted again, frowning. "Go talk to Gareth. Get some answers."

CHAPTER FORTY-THREE

Novato was a quaint northernmost Marin County town, a bedroom community to the rest of Marin and San Francisco. On the way, the detectives hashed out what information they needed from Cav's nephew.

Once in town, Meredith navigated to Marvin's, a snug sixties-era strip café, on sycamore-lined Grant Avenue. As a red pick-up pulled away from the curb, Nick slipped in behind to a parking space near the restaurant. This was an older section of Novato, which was considered an all-American downtown. Old Redwood Highway was a block and a half away, and, in days past, the town was a favorite travelers' stop until Cal Trans built a bypass in the 70's. Although the new Highway 101 was over two miles away, the restaurant's trade was almost entirely locals, so its' popularity was not affected. The inside was filled with patrons eating and laughing through the breakfast hour. The parking lot overflowed. Out front, where there were chairs for waiting customers and four umbrella-shaded tables, almost every chair was taken.

Scanning the crowd outside, Meredith found a tall, Cavanaugh look-alike slouched at an umbrellaed table on the restaurant's fringe. This location, near the curb, would ensure their conversation's privacy. She caught the man's eye and nodded. Gareth Cavanaugh, as lanky and imposing as his uncle, stood to greet them.

From beneath a full head of auburn hair with a wave in front, Gareth's face gave away his Cavanaugh heritage: angular lines, a straight nose, piercing gaze and a reserved smile. Gareth stood straight, his shoulders filling out the T-shirt, the jeans loose around the waist. This guy had spent some time in a gym—or maybe working at his uncle's ranch. He took Meredith's extended hand in a vice-like grip. She winced, handing him off to Nick. They sat, Meredith glancing at the fourth menu and vacant chair.

"Len will be here in a little bit. Len Rankin. He's coming in from Nicasio—on a bicycle."

Meredith didn't have time to question him. A man dressed in bright yellow spandex bike-riding togs coasted to a stop in front of their table. He hailed Gareth and set to locking his bike to a nearby tree. The bike rider was an incredibly fit man who moved easily even after the exertion of riding sixteen miles from Nicasio to downtown Novato. Len Rankin's eyes glinted at them when he removed his wrap-around sunglasses. A light sprinkling of gray beard covered unshaven cheeks.

Introductions went around the table, then Len excused himself to the bathroom. Gareth took the opportunity to explain. "I worked robbery detail with Len before he retired in 2008. He stayed long enough to break me in. He'd been in the unit fourteen years when I met him. He's one of those cops who remembers everything."

"I hope he can help." Meredith felt encouraged.

Coffee arrived and an extra glass of water for Len. Gareth had been an astute host. When Len returned to the table, a young dark-haired waitress appeared and stood beside him.

With a confident spark in her eye, she asked, "Your usual?"

He finished off the water. "You're too good to me, Natalie. Yes, please." He'd never even glanced at the menu.

Gareth ordered next, giving Meredith and Nick time to peruse the menu. "A veggie omelet for me, please." Meredith sipped her coffee.

Nick ordered last, "Huevos Rancheros with corn tortillas, please."

Gareth went first. "So, what kind of info are you looking for?"

Meredith took a deep breath, her gaze moving from one man to the other. "First, I have to say thank you to you both for meeting us. I realize what an imposition this is."

While Gareth gave an easy grin, Len spoke, "Oh, no problem. We old retired farts love to re-live our glory days."

His sharp gray eyes appraised her as he shook out his napkin.

"We won't be talking about anyone's glory days, Len." Meredith grimaced. "First, let me say that my father was not a saint. He's the reason we're here."

Len cut across her comment. "None of us is. I'm not in any position to judge."

Meredith considered his words, recalling that SFPD was a boy's club. She asked, "Did you know my father? Terence Ryan was his name."

Len sipped his water, thinking. Meredith wondered if he was searching for a tactful way to say, 'Yeah, and he was an asshole.' But he didn't. "I met him a few times but never worked with him. He had a reputation, though."

That wasn't news. Every cop has a reputation within the ranks. Even if a guy has no personality, drive or intelligence, he has a reputation. "I can imagine," was all Meredith could say.

Sitting up, she cleared her throat to get their attention. "Let me give you the synopsis of what we know, and why you're here." Meredith waited while Natalie expertly shoved plates heaped with breakfast food before them. When the waitress left, Meredith continued. "My father was in the Mounted Unit, Terence Donald Ryan. In June of 2001, he was relieved of duty in the Mounted Unit and put on a desk in an admin office. Then, in July of 2001, his service pistol was taken and logged into evidence. He retired in the summer of 2001. I'm guessing it was a forced retirement. His gun was booked into evidence as part of a robbery/homicide case." She showed him the SFPD evidence receipt. "Here's the case number. His official retirement date was—," she pulled out the SFERS beneficiary copy and glanced at it. "August 30th, 2001." Meredith leaned into Len, who sat to her right. "He was never charged with anything. Can you tell me what he had to do with this case?"

Len glanced at Gareth. "You look up the report?" Gareth would have access to archived records, including a homicide/robbery.

Gareth nodded. "An armed robbery with subsequent

homicide, May 11, 2001. The courier who was held up died of gunshot wounds two days after the incident. Occurred over at Harrison and 16th Street, by the brick moving company—Bay City Moving Company was the name. A money laundering start-up with a quiet card room in the back."

"Ahh, I remember." Len sat back as the wheels in his head churned. "Lemme think a minute."

The table was silent when Natalie returned to top off Len's water glass.

Len turned toward Meredith. "It was your father's gun that was used in the crime—both the robbery and homicide."

Meredith thought she'd braced herself for the worst—but she hadn't. Her gut churned. Somehow hearing it from the case detective made it real. Homicide?

Gareth asked, "Wasn't a kid arrested and convicted for the crime? Jamie Houston?"

Len nodded. "The kid had just turned 18. Kind of felt sorry for him until I got a load of his attitude."

Meredith struggled to stay seated and not run from the sick feeling in her stomach. Nick went on. "How did the kid get hold of Ryan's gun? Did Jamie cop to it?" Relieved when Nick began to ask questions, Meredith felt her face warm.

Len poked a finger at a mushy fruit cup. "No, that's the thing. He didn't. I got the feeling he was covering for someone else, maybe Ryan," Len's head cocked sideways toward Meredith. "No prints were found on the gun. Funny, right? Wouldn't you think the officer's prints would be on his own service weapon? But they weren't. The report never said that your father took part in the incident; Internal Affairs thought he might have planned it but had no proof. That's the main reason your father didn't get charged. Still, his alibi was weak—he said he was at the PD stables, but no one saw him there."

"What reason did Ryan give for his gun being out of his control?"

"Said it must've been stolen. He didn't know how it got into the kid's hands."

Meredith straightened in her chair. This was an important question to her. She had to know what SFPD knew. "How were Terence and the Houston kid associated?"

Len's lips pressed together. "There was a woman—Brenda something, last name Dallas, no, Houston. Bartender at the old cop bar on Irving. Ryan was living with her. She was the kid's mother."

"Living together?" Meredith repeated as her temper flared. Her father lived with this woman? Meredith reached into her pocket, then slapped the photo of Jamie on the table. "Is this the kid?"

Len picked up the picture while pulling out readers from inside his spandex shirt. Turning the photo to the sunlight, he nodded. "Could be him. This isn't what he looked like when I dealt with him but yes, that's him. James Houston."

Nick asked, "Was Ryan represented by counsel when you questioned him?"

"Yeah. That's likely what saved his pension. The DA was pissed off. He thought Ryan had more involvement in the planning of the crime. He went for the jugular, but Ryan's union attorney carved out a compromise that worked for everyone. No one was thrilled with it—your father took an early retirement, but at least he didn't lose his pension. The DA didn't get to prosecute, but it saved face to get another "crooked cop" off the street."

Meredith croaked, "'Crooked cop'?"

Len shrugged. "We never found the money—a hundred and thirty thousand bucks. It's like it never existed. The victim was a courier for a small-time protection gang. Probably laundering their money and a card parlor on the side. We weren't sure, because we hit a brick wall trying to get any information from them. The DA believed Ryan took the money and hid it, but I wasn't so sure." Len swept crumbs off the table with the flat of his hand. "For the record, I never thought he was crooked, Ms. Ryan." Len gave her an embarrassed smile. "The DA never said he was, but the public had been following the story pretty closely. The mayor was screaming for blood, so your dad got thrown under the bus."

She sighed deeply at this news. She had no idea how bad it had gotten. Her mother kept both she and David away from the television most of the time and couldn't afford the Chronicle newspaper. Meredith's exclusive social engagement in those days was at the stables and school. In the school yard, she'd been called names, but had assumed she was harassed for being a cop's kid. She was used to it.

She imagined her father's life, this prideful man's name clouded by suspicion. No one trusting him for back-up; pulled from his beloved horse assignment, shunned. Even a hint of criminal activity was poison to a cop's status. Reputation was everything, particularly to Terence Ryan. If the guy—of either gender— beside you wasn't convinced that you had the *cojones* to shoot to save his skin, trust was absent. Going into a gunfight, bar fight or any fight, if you didn't have confidence in your partner it was worse than being alone. You'd be looking over your shoulder, wondering whether your back was safe instead of addressing the threat in front of you. A compromised cop—one who puts his own or someone else's welfare ahead of his partner's—wasn't worth dog shit. This was the truth. A bad reputation followed a cop forever.

Why did Terence sacrifice his career, the thing he loved more than his wife and kids? He was protecting someone— Jamie? The kid got convicted for armed robbery and, under the felony murder rule, second degree murder of the courier. The prosecutor based his case on Jamie's fingerprint left on the courier's truck tail gate, and that he'd stolen Terence's gun—he admitted that. Even with a murder conviction, the state of California had suspended the death penalty. Jamie would have spent a long time in jail, with or without Terence's sacrifice.

Who was Terence protecting? Still?

CHAPTER FORTY-FOUR

"Of course, my father knew him, though I didn't get any hints that the two were close." Meredith's source was Brenda and she couldn't be trusted. "Jamie was the girlfriend's son. But why bury his career over him?" Meredith asked. "Wouldn't Jamie have an accomplice? Surely, he wouldn't have taken on a truck in the middle of the Mission district during daylight hours alone. How the hell would he even know about the cash being moved?"

"Good questions, detective. That intel is what we tried to find from the beginning. It made no sense for a fresh kid, barely an adult, to take on a job like this without help. Your question—how did he know about the cash?" Len shrugged. "How did he know when and how it was being transported?" Len absently brushed spilled salt off the table. "Houston never answered our questions. He barely cooperated with his public defender."

"What about the courier's homicide?" Nick shifted in his seat. There were more questions than answers. "I didn't see a conviction for homicide or even manslaughter on Houston's rap sheet. Only armed robbery."

Len sighed. "Technically, that crime is still unsolved. He was charged, but the jury felt there was reasonable doubt that he fired the murder weapon—" He looked at Meredith. "Your father's service pistol." Then, his attention back to Nick. "No prints were on the weapon and he didn't have any GSR on his hands or clothing. But," Len added. "We didn't catch up with him for nine days. GSR wouldn't necessarily show up by then."

Testing for GSR or gunshot residue involves identifying the presence of microscopic particles consisting of lead, barium, and antimony. These GSR particles are the residue that is produced from the elements in the primer of a cartridge. When the firearm is discharged, these particles are ejected from the cylinder gaps, ejector ports, and the end of the barrel, resulting in a plume of residue in the air around the gun. This residue can land on nearby surfaces and objects, including the hands of the shooter. While not a determinant of the shooter, its' presence can support an argument either way.

Nick watched Meredith process the information. Her father's pistol was used to kill someone. She squinted, her thumb and index finger squeezing the bridge of her nose. "But how was he involved, other than the use of his gun?"

"On the record, we're not sure. He had limited contact with Jamie; both the kid and the mom said Ryan kept his distance. Ryan's alibi was worthless. So, we couldn't prove he was involved in the robbery."

"Did Ryan have knowledge of the money transport?" Nick tried to fill in the gaps in this story. Trouble was, the more information he had, the more questions arose.

Len threw his hands up. Even after all this time, his face twisted with frustration. "Who knows? He denied it, but the popular theory was a snitch told him about it, then he told Jamie. Either they set it up together or Jamie took the info and ran with it."

"But neither of them would talk." Nick summed up the detectives' dilemma. "You had Jamie Houston, at least, so the DA charged him with robbery and left Terence Ryan out of it. In the meantime, the SFPD admin, who also didn't have enough to fire him, wanted this compromised cop off the rolls. His attorney bargained a forced retirement to placate both parties."

"That's it in a nutshell." Len swirled the cold coffee in his cup.

Meredith sat up. "Terence's alibi—he said he was at the stables during the day, right?" She waited for Len's nod. "But no one could say they saw him. It's a busy place, with cops and horses coming and going."

Meredith struggled to contain her excitement. She had an idea. "Did you check the stables next to the PD's?"

"You mean the civilian stables—Golden Gate Stables?" Len sat up, too, as if he'd had the same thought. "Jeez, I'm not sure. I don't remember."

Meredith looked at Gareth. "Any chance you can check your report and let me know? Can you confirm he worked an overtime patrol swing shift on May 11, so that part of his day is alibied? And I need the exact date and time of the crime." She scribbled her personal cell number on the back of a business card, then slipped it across the table. Nick had his cash on the bill by the time Len picked up the card.

"Thanks for your help, Len." Nick shook hands with both men, and he and Meredith left.

CHAPTER FORTY-FIVE

Meredith couldn't wait to get back to the truck to tell Nick. For the first time since Terence's death, she had a hunch that her father was innocent of complicity in the robbery/homicide suspicions. The depth of her hope shook her. Was it possible he wasn't the malicious man she'd thought?

When the doors shut, Nick didn't start the ignition right away. He sat behind the wheel, silent.

Her husband knew her so well. He'd wound up the interview with the detectives in a hurry—he must've known she had thought of something that deserved his full attention.

"Okay, here's what I'm thinking." She sat sideways on the bench seat, facing him. His expression was all business. No emotion. Listening. "Dad put that letter in the box for a reason, right?" After his nod, she continued. "It was there as a message to me. From the newspaper account, the robbery took place on May 11th. That's the same day I rode in my last horse show." A smug smile spread across her lips. "Ask me how I remember that date. Okay, I'll tell you. It was my fifteenth birthday. Mom had to work and couldn't be there. It made me mad that she couldn't take time off." She sat back, her arms across her chest. "Terence was there, I'm almost sure."

Nick looked away, embarrassed he'd forgotten the date. "How can you be certain?" Meredith had to be able to prove it. Terence's innocence might make a difference in a cold case. The homicide was still open—these cases are never closed without a suspect identified and convicted.

Excitement drained from her face. "My birthday show, the first competition of the season and no one in the family could come. David was babysitting at the neighbors. Mom and Dad were working. I assumed Dad was on patrol, but I was still hurt he couldn't find a few minutes to see me ride. I mean, my stable was right next door to the SFPD stable. I think he was there but didn't tell me." She looked at Nick. "Why wouldn't he let me know he was there? I mean, the show ribbon should be proof."

"How could one ribbon be proof?

"This is kind of embarrassing." She sighed. "They were announcing the winners of the hunter/jumper class and it went to Judy Wise. I came in second. Judy got so excited she had an asthma attack. They had to take her away in an ambulance. Her ribbon fell in the mud and got left behind." Meredith paused. "When I was untacking my horse, I found it tied to my saddle. I should've given it back to her."

"You think your father put it there? That's kind of a stretch, isn't it? What time did the newspaper say the robbery occurred? Does it coincide with the horse show incident? I mean, don't some horse shows go on for hours?" He was silent for a second. "Isn't that too much of a timeline we're talking about here? Hypothetically, couldn't Terence have been at the horse show and been present at the crime within the same hour?"

"The paper said the robbery was in the early afternoon. That's consistent with the showtimes, and yes, they can go on. I might be able to narrow the time frame down by using the ambulance response time."

"You'll need access to records you don't have any authorization for." Nick's head dropped to the head rest. "We'll have to talk to Gareth again. Maybe he can look into it, maybe even re-open the homicide."

"I hate to ask more of him." Meredith sighed, then straightened. "The ribbon had the date on it—May 11, 2001. I remember because it was unusual to do that, and it was my birthday."

"Where is it? You still have it?"

She smiled. "It's packed away in an old tack box—that chest we're using as an end table on the back porch."

His voice held caution. This was all very hypothetical. "You'll need to find his fingerprints on the show ribbon."

She nodded, completing his thought. "His prints would be on the ribbon, from handling it. There'd be horse manure mixed in with the mud, making it unique. So, it could be analyzed. That is not enough to claim a solid alibi, but it creates some credibility about his whereabouts."

Nick shook his head. "I don't know. Even though he was on patrol that day, his normal work hours began and ended with the stables. He could've picked up a discarded ribbon any time."

Meredith set her jaw. "It was tied to my saddle. I found it after they took Judy away in the ambulance. Who else would do that? With my statement, it creates reasonable doubt."

"Is there any other way?" She could almost see the doubt in Nick's head. "I mean, what if you don't find proof to exonerate your father? That's what you're after, right?"

What if he didn't do it? What if he did? How could she live with the knowledge her father was a murderer? How would this affect Davy—and Nick?

Her husband leaned toward her, grasping her hand. "This is looking like a dead end, Mere. You can't look up medical records by patient name because of HIPAA laws, even if you remembered her name. Another thought: did the SFPD Mounted Unit have daily activity logs where Terence would've recorded what he was doing during the day?" His gaze held compassion for her pain at knowing how impossible it was to prove her father innocent of these crimes. "This happened seventeen years ago. The attending medics have probably retired or moved on by now."

"I imagined going to the ambulance barn, trying to pry this info loose. As an outsider, I'd get nothing more than the cold shoulder." She looked at her phone. "You're right. We need Gareth."

CHAPTER FORTY-SIX

"Hell yeah, I'm on board. The chance to get some answers in a cold homicide and prove a PD veteran innocent? You bet. Meet me at Stafford Lake. We can talk it over there."

Meredith had called Gareth right away. She wanted to get hold of him before he got too far from Novato. It turned out the SFPD detective had decided to return to his home in Petaluma the back way, on the winding country road from Novato Boulevard to D Street in Petaluma. About two miles west of Novato and nestled in the verdant dairy pastures of Marin County, Stafford Lake Reservoir and Stafford Park were a small pair of jewels in the Marin Municipal Water District.

The Valley Oaks cast full shadows under a late spring sun. Stafford Lake's picnic area lay at the edge of the quiet, pond-like body of water constructed as an afterthought but nonetheless welcomed by bicyclists and families. A half-dozen redwood tables with strategically placed trash cans made up the small area. Gareth's black Toyota Tundra pick-up tic-tic-ticked as it cooled in a parking space ten feet from the tables.

The midday warmth enveloped them as they got out of Nick's truck. A breeze ruffled oak leaves, releasing the heady scent of naturally decomposing plant materials. Meredith inhaled deeply, savoring a smell she identified with Petaluma. Novato was close enough. This countryside had become an anchor in her life—far from the muni exhaust and swirling tailwinds of San Francisco, this area had become a point of never-changing foundation for her. As had Nick.

This was her life now. But to completely close her childhood chapters, she must get to the truth. She owed it to Davy—and the rest of her family.

**

Gareth sat at a table near the path, scrolling through his

phone while he waited for them. When he rose to greet them, he moved like his uncle, smooth energy coiled under a blue cotton T-shirt.

After quick greetings, Gareth swept a hand to a bench. "Why don't you tell me what you have so far."

Fighting the distrust of being too open, Meredith recounted the story of her fifteenth birthday. At Terence's death things were set in motion—memories she would've let lie forever, investigations unsolved and news she didn't want to hear. There were ugly truths about her life and her father's. Into her already dysfunctional childhood, her father also introduced adultery, crime and betrayal. He'd shouldered an impugned reputation that forced him to give up what he loved more than anything—anything she knew about, anyway.

Pushing the shame aside, she moved the greater need to the forefront—to find out if her father was complicit in a robbery and homicide. She needed to know if deceit saturated his life or—had there been anything good about him? Anything worth passing along to Davy and Nick?

Gareth pinched his lower lip absently as he listened. "I'll look over everything before I officially open the case." His piercing, gray Cavanaugh eyes held Meredith's attention. "Can you get me the ribbon for testing? If we're going to treat it like evidence, it'll need to be bagged."

Meredith nodded, reassured Gareth would honor his word. He knew how crucial evidence-handling was to pursue a conviction. Every detective knew of a slam-dunk case sabotaged by tainted evidence. She didn't want this to be one.

They arranged for Gareth to follow them home and take custody of the ribbon. Meredith would write out a statement attesting to the timing of the muddy show ribbon.

CHAPTER FORTY-SEVEN

"I don't have to tell you how bad the odds are on getting anything useable. "Gareth stood at the kitchen table with Meredith's declaration folded in his hand. The house was quiet with Cav and Davy in the backyard. Meredith packaged the ribbon in a brown paper sack. Plastic could've ruined any prints by encouraging mold. "What's your next move?"

Nick glanced at Mere. "We're going to see what's inside the storage unit—now we know where it is. We have a key. So, let's hope it matches the lock. This key was important."

Gareth took the bag from Meredith and caught Nick's eye. "Any idea what you're going to find?"

Nick shrugged. "Could be anything." A quick look at his wife, then back. "Money? More evidence?"

"Bodies?" Gareth supplied the word Nick had been avoiding. "They'd be pretty rank by now, but Houston's two accomplices are still missing."

"Anything's possible," Nick answered, seeing Meredith suddenly straighten. "We don't know about them. The news reports never mentioned anyone but think about it. How unlikely is it that 20-year-old Jamie Houston orchestrated a hold-up involving $130,000.00 all by himself? Especially if the cash was from some start-up wannabe gang. And there would have been repercussions."

Gareth agreed. "There was a comment in the report saying he appeared to have acted on his own initiative. Hard to believe. And if a gang was the victim, there would've been consequences, for sure."

Nick's mind churned. "We need to get to the storage unit. Then, talk to Brenda Houston again to see if she knew of any potential accomplices." As Meredith handed over the paper bag, Nick added another task. "Gareth, let us know if there is a usable print on the ribbon." He stopped, feeling an embarrassed smile. "Sorry. I can't seem to stop giving orders."

With a dismissive snort, Gareth said, "No worries. We're thinking along the same lines here. I'll look into the report a little deeper. We could be missing something."

Meredith glanced at Nick, then back to the detective. "Meanwhile, we'll go to the storage place in Rohnert Park, see what's inside, and let you know."

"It'll take something big to encourage my lieutenant to re-open this case," Gareth said without enthusiasm.

Meredith spoke up. "Maybe finding $130,000.00 in gang money will do the trick."

"That would do it." He smiled a Cavanaugh smile. "I'll get back to you on the results of the prints."

CHAPTER FORTY-EIGHT

"They're meeting with a tall guy, buff. Looks like a cop," Ramona said into the phone.

Her oxidized gold 2000 Toyota Corolla sat across the street and down two doors from the Reyes-Ryan home. She'd followed them from San Francisco and their meeting with some guy at the Novato restaurant, then to Stafford Lake and finally on to this house in Petaluma.

Ramona called Desmond after the Chevy truck pulled into the Melvin Street driveway of an older home on the west side of town. Melvin was a cul-de-sac tree-lined street with tidy early twentieth century bungalows with a high-crowned roadway. Century old sycamores and elms shaded the cobblestone trimmed curbs. The house was one of many similar that sat at the base of a hill. Their backyard would be narrow at best. In the well-established neighborhood a pair of chatting mothers pushed baby carriages along a sidewalk. Otherwise, the pre-noon street was quiet. "This is like some fake world from a movie with rich, advantaged assholes."

Desmond put Ramona on speaker phone while he dried a glass. Ignoring her observation, he asked, "Can you see the license plate from where you are?"

The vinyl squeaked as Ramona strained to see. "Yeah." She rattled off seven digits. He scratched them down on a bar napkin, figuring he'd call in a favor from his traffic buddy. There were still ways to get info, even if he wasn't one of the fair-haired boys. With the registered owner's name and address, he'd confirm who he was dealing with. He was already 99% sure. It would be nice to get their home address, though. If they weren't registered by the Department of Motor Vehicles as confidential.

"You're doing good, Ramona." Des allowed a rare compliment. "When they leave, follow and let me know where they go."

"Right."

CHAPTER FORTY-NINE

At the Handi-Storage off Rohnert Park Expressway west of Five Creek, Nick and Meredith made their way to the locker number indicated on the receipt. The building had seen better days. Access to the unit's roll-up door was from outside at a driveway. The concrete was crisscrossed with cracks, the walls stained by water leaks and the place smelled moldy. Dread gripped Meredith thinking about what could be inside. Davy was safe with Cav so she and Nick could give this the time it required.

The key slipped into the lock. Nick clicked open the hasp.

They were both too familiar with the smell of decay that greeted them. Her stomach turned as Meredith's worst fears were realized. Bodies. Laying in the middle of the concrete floor were two bodies, wrapped in transparent plastic sheeting and secured with rotting bungee cords. Clothing—dark, over-sized judging by the way it was squeezed against the plastic.

Absent was the odor of rotting flesh and fluid seepage—that would come later at the morgue when the plastic was removed. She wouldn't touch the bodies. Besides releasing an even stronger sweet, nauseating stench, this wasn't her crime scene—especially because her father was involved.

She worked to distance herself from this horror. Terence Ryan had a hand in these men's deaths, no question. Whether he'd killed them outright or cleaned up someone else's crime, he'd gotten too far into this. There was no finding out what happened first, then making excuses for her father.

No matter how many corpses she saw, she never got used to the smell of death. The work that had gone into concealing them made the bodies even more grotesque than her first impression. Two homicides.

She looked around the room beyond the corpses. Empty.

Nothing around the bodies except—

A canvas duffel bag, drawstrings shredded from age, tossed in a corner, looking like a sad afterthought.

Nick bent over the bag to get a better look. A flap had opened revealing a clue to the contents. Beside him, Meredith's breath caught at the sight of the corners of bundled hundred-dollar bills. Contain the evidence of the crime in one place. Smart.

"Jesus," Nick breathed. They both straightened, Nick's attention held on the bodies. She knew what he was doing—focused on the forensics, cataloging what he saw.

Meredith sorted through the ramifications to distract her from her rising anxiety. First, jurisdiction. The storage business was on the border of the city of Rohnert Park—just outside, in the sheriff's jurisdiction. Thank God. At least they didn't have to involve another agency in this disaster. It would stay between San Francisco PD and Sonoma County Sheriff. Simpler and easier to manage and contain information; less chance of this ugly situation going public.

Second, the unit was rented in her father's name. It was looking like he was a murderer, as well as a thief.

All variables aside, it was time to bring in her department. She hated, hated, hated that Terence had put her in this position. Why hadn't he come clean before he died? The system would've adjusted for his illness.

"It's time to get the SO involved." Nick turned away, already scrolling through his phone. "I'll call Ferrua," he said, stepping out to the driveway. He'd relieved her of at least a small measure of embarrassment by volunteering to make the call. There wouldn't be any discussion—they'd stumbled upon two murdered men. It was well beyond the scope of their informal questions about Terence's estate.

This was now a homicide investigation. By her agency or maybe San Francisco PD's. It occurred to her that her role wouldn't be an investigator. She'd be an involved party—not a victim in the legal sense, nor a witness. But her actions had uncovered the bodies of two murdered men. She'd have to step aside—formally, although the thought grated.

This was her life. Damn him. Damn her father for this. It just gets worse and worse.

Her keen thirst for information got the better of her. With Nick still on the phone, she stepped inside, reflexively covering her nose with her hand. The smell was bad, musty but not as bad as some she'd investigated. The plastic had contained much of the decomposition.

Both bodies were mummified, encased in plastic sheeting, resting prone on a much used tarp. Two corpses, possibly males, difficult to guess their races, and from the Adidas tracksuit on one and Air Force One sneakers on the other, she guessed they were young adults. They may have been here since 2001. Visible skin was thin, leather-like and chocolate brown, contracted and stretched over their skeletons. Upper and lower teeth showed prominently, forming a macabre grin. The ME would determine causes of death.

The minimal stain on the concrete around the bodies—fluids would have seeped from channels in the sheeting—told her the initial crime occurred elsewhere. No pooled blood, as there would have been at the scene, except on their clothing. No shell casings or any other evidence that this happened here. They'd been killed somewhere else.

When Nick returned, he touched his phone, putting an unofficial timestamp on their actions. "It's one o'clock now. The beat deputy is on the way to secure the scene."

"Who's responding?" She hoped for a deputy with a bit of discretion. She hated being a reporting party in a homicide investigation—on the outside, she was sure of her role. Now, she was involved in a way she couldn't reconcile.

"Ferrua didn't say. It should be either Duggan or Lamott." Nick's face was open. His eyes darkened with concern as he tried to say something to soothe her. His start, then stop, effort tore at her. She knew his heart was bleeding for her—that he was trying to support her in this Godawful situation.

He nodded toward the outside and they moved away

from the bodies. "It's okay, baby."

Meredith reached for his hand. "It's not okay, Nick. I don't like it, but I can deal with it." Now, she really believed that. Somewhere in her brain, she knew the emotions would catch up with her. But right now, she would manage.

She had a job to do.

CHAPTER FIFTY

Nick's truck was parked three spaces away from the storage unit. He noticed a gold Toyota sedan with a woman in it down the alley but dismissed it to deal with more important things. After Sheriff's Deputy Duggan arrived, the scene had become the circus that always followed the discovery of a body. Duggan had acted respectfully to Meredith while getting background on their role in finding the corpses.

A pair of VCI detectives, full-back sized Jerald Mossi and his terrier sidekick, Eric Lanza arrived within ten minutes. They made the call for the coroner response. Nick groaned when Lieutenant Ferrua showed up. It was entirely proper for him to respond, but he often left more mess than when he arrived—usually at Meredith's expense. His lack of action three years ago had left Meredith fending for herself against a malicious stalker, and he'd blamed her for the disciplinary action that followed.

Elbowing Detective Mossi aside, Ferrua had pressed Meredith as if she was a suspect, pushing her to divulge more, asking questions she'd already answered from Duggan. She'd held her ground, a professional. Even involved in a tough crime, she refused to get emotional before this ass in brass. Nick was proud of her.

Ferrua lost interest in her when she told him about the robbery/homicide in San Francisco. In the next second, he decided the coroner would hand this off to San Francisco Police. Sonoma County Sheriff would stay on scene to secure it until SFPD arrived to take over. Ferrua called off any evidence work or further investigation. They'd offer assistance but didn't think San Francisco PD would need much help.

Nick shook his head at Ferrua's certainty over the location of the crimes. He should have waited for the medical examiner to narrow down the place and means of the deaths.

The lieutenant told them to stay to meet with the SF detectives. Mossi and Lanza waited with them, as did Duggan. Ferrua sat in his car, occupied on his phone.

It's a wonder how callous we become to death—even murder, Meredith thought. With nothing to do but wait, she studied the bodies, etching the images into her mind. She knew this wasn't the end of it for her.

Just as Meredith and Nick finished looking over Mossi's notes to verify their statements, a solid black Crown Victoria drove up the lane and stopped at the crime scene tape. Gareth Cavanaugh unfolded from behind the wheel. Meredith watched his casual glance—very like his uncle's—take in the area as he approached the detective lieutenant. Ferrua extended his hand in obvious relief. Sonoma Sheriff's Office would provide scene security, but San Francisco Police Department was now in charge. At the introductions Gareth nodded to each deputy, not acknowledging any previous acquaintance with Meredith or Nick. He listened attentively while the lieutenant ran down the information he had—most of which the detective already possessed.

Ferrua ended his soliloquy. "With that, I'll leave you to it, Inspector."

Gareth watched the sheriff's plain clothes Impala speed off.

"Thanks for not complicating things," Meredith said. Sometimes, it was better for people like Ferrua to know less than everyone else in the room.

Gareth smiled with a polite nod. "So, you did have bodies in the storage unit after all." He strode across the blacktop to the open unit. "Did you take a look at these guys?"

"Yeah, but we backed off as soon as we saw what we'd gotten into."

Gareth nodded. "I've got our Crime Scene guys coming from the City, and my partner is en route, too. It'll be a while. Why don't you fill me in on what's happened since I saw you," he looked at his watch, "—a couple of hours ago."

"Did you get to work before you got this call?"

"No, my captain knows where I live, so he called me on my way to work. I was southbound 101 at Central San Rafael when he got hold of me. I turned around."

CHAPTER FIFTY-ONE

They would just get in the way now. It was time to leave.

Nick slid behind the wheel and said, "They'll inject glycerin for hydration to the finger pads at autopsy to get fingerprints." She knew this, but he felt he had to say something.

"We're off this case, you know." She looked out the window as the Chevy powered up the onramp to 101, heading back to Petaluma.

Nick was silent. People driving, walking, shopping, living their lives as people do—oblivious of the terror life could dish out. It was a good thing they didn't know what he knew—what every cop who'd worked the streets knew.

"Technically," he hated to remind her, but it needed to be said, "We were never on the case. We just asked questions about items found in your father's possessions."

"I noticed the silence about having met with Gareth. Even him."

Nick could almost hear the gears turning in her head. He took his eyes off the road and looked at her. "You're not going to sit the rest of this case out, are you?"

She stared back at his wide-eyed, earnest expression. He knew her answer. She gave him a half-smile.

"Didn't think so." Turning to face the steering wheel, he checked mirrors, then eased into the fast lane. "But you've got to be careful not to mess with evidence or witnesses."

"What now?"

"I know what I'd do, but this is your deal, Mere." He had an idea or two but wanted her to suggest the next move.

"I'll let Gareth know, but we should beat feet over to Brenda Houston's. I want to keep an eye on Jamie."

Nick sighed. "We should keep our distance, Mere."

Ignoring her husband, she reflected on the mess surrounding her. Armed robbery, homicide—now two bodies. What had her father gotten her into?

**

"I couldn't see what she was doing, but they both went to a storage unit place in Santa Rosa." Ramona shouted into her phone. The afternoon coastal breeze swirled roadside dust two blocks from where Meredith had finally parked.

"Where are you now?" Desmond's mind was clicking off the possibilities.

"Just pulled off Wilfred Avenue exit in Rohnert Park."

"Were there other cops around?"

"Hell yeah." Ramona whistled. "A shit load of 'em. Must've been eight or ten cop cars."

Desmond sighed. Bodies. Must be the bodies they found. What about the money? "Did you see them carry out a bag, box or something that would hold a lot of money?"

"Nothing like that. I stayed until they carried the bodies away and didn't see anything like you described."

"Bodies?"

"They took two away."

He snorted. Then Meredith Ryan's got it. She took the money and called the cops on the dead guys.

She's got the cash. Now, how to get it?

CHAPTER FIFTY-TWO

Taking the northernmost Rohnert Park exit, Nick drove toward Evergreen Estates. The early summer had blossomed into a pleasant 75-degree afternoon.

Meredith said, "We need to ask permission and proceed carefully."

When Nick nodded, Meredith put the phone on speaker. Gareth answered on the second ring. "Cavanaugh."

It was odd to hear a young man answer with that name. She was dealing with a different Cavanaugh than she had in the past year and a half. She'd learned that being a cop didn't guarantee dependability. But she knew Raymond would connect her with a Cavanaugh she could count on. She didn't know Gareth beyond their meeting earlier, but she must have faith in him. "Gareth, it's Meredith. Can you check Jamie's booking sheet for the robbery arrest? I'm looking for anyone listed as 'known associates'?"

Nick pulled the truck up two doors down from the trailer at 1807 Arbor. The sound of Gareth tapping on the keyboard filled the cab. "Ah, here. Adam Mejia and Isaiah Renton." She waited as he scanned the crime report. "Both kids were from his juvenile hall days, according to the report. Says here Rankin was never able to find them to interview. The families filed Missing Persons reports on them. No surprise there. They could be your two corpses."

"They're your two corpses now." Meredith opened an app on Nick's phone to record the info. "Do you have home addresses for them?"

"Mejia's and Renton were the same, 1807 Arbor, Rohnert Park." Gareth was all business. "Same as Houston's. What's that tell you?"

"It tells me we're at the right address," Meredith said. "We're in Rohnert Park now. We'll sit on the house until you get here."

"If you have time, sure. But it'll take me over an hour to

get there and I hate tying you guys up. I'll send someone to relieve you."

Meredith thanked him and disconnected. She fumbled putting Nick's Otter Box encased phone into the dashboard carrier. It clunked to the floor mat. As she picked it up, she glanced sideways. A gunmetal gray 80's vintage Dodge Charger was parked in the street three trailers down, facing them. Nick's fascination with cars had made her notice anything unusual. He was a Chevy snob and never passed up a chance to diss a Mopar product.

"Nick, see that—"

"Got it. One guy behind the wheel—alone."

"Looks like he's watching this place."

"Yeah. He's not from parole. They don't get rides like that."

"Well, let's go find out." Meredith's huffed, irritated that this clown was watching the Houston place. Debt collector? Maybe. Whoever he was, she didn't want him to be a complication.

Damn. Meredith wanted to twist his arm and make him tell her who he was and his business. She was half out of the cab, one foot on the asphalt, when the Dodge thundered awake. She paused at the deep-throated rumble.

Nick was still behind the wheel. The Dodge driver's face was a blur as he jammed the accelerator and burned rubber past them.

"Get in the truck," Nick yelled, starting the engine.

CHAPTER FIFTY-THREE

Fuck, Nick thought. They had to follow this guy. Had to find out why he was shadowing Houston. The driver knew something, and Nick wanted to know what. But that aside, there were complications—Nick was sure the driver of this muscle car would lead into a pursuit. With no lights or siren on his personal car, it wouldn't be a sanctioned police activity. The liability if anyone got hurt would fall to him. He'd have to be careful, obeying traffic laws. He didn't want to have to report this as an off-duty pursuit to the watch commander—or Meredith's boss, Lieutenant Ferrua.

Why not? He couldn't say, exactly. While they were investigating a crime, they had no authority. He'd long been opposed to cops going rogue. There was a system in place and though it wasn't as efficient as it could be, he respected it. SFPD would re-open the homicide and Sonoma County Sheriff would assist their investigation with the processing of the two bodies and cash found in the storage unit.

By rights, he should've called Lieutenant Ferrua, so he could relay this information to Gareth. At the very least, it wasn't Nick or Meredith's case. And Meredith was past embarrassment about her father's connection to a homicide. Sparing her feelings alone wouldn't be enough to deter him from calling. But he just didn't.

Neither did Meredith.

The gray Charger spun down the narrow lanes, spewing road dust and litter, then out the Evergreen Estates gates, turning north onto Redwood Drive. Nick concentrated on the roadway and traffic while Meredith snapped her seatbelt and called out the Charger's movements.

"Keep straight, now changing lanes to the right, east onto Rohnert Park Expressway—maybe heading to 101. Yep, he's moving to the right lane."

Two car lengths ahead, the Charger's engine was a wall of sound, vibrating back to the truck. Dual exhaust pipes spit a cloud of smoke. Despite the nice body, Nick figured this car hadn't been updated under the hood. Depending on the shape it was in, his truck might be able to keep up. Nick's Chevy had the power to take this vehicle, but not the suspension or maneuverability. A lot depended on the skill of the Charger's driver.

In the right turn lane, the Charger plunged into cross traffic. Screeching brakes, blaring horns, and stunned drivers allowed enough pause for Nick to slip in behind the Charger. Meredith shouted, "Clear. The lane is clear if you go now."

He followed the accelerating Charger onto the southbound highway 101 onramp. The road graduated to a moderately hilly three lane highway bordered by frontage road businesses. In the distance, past tract homes and ranchettes, green slopes were stitched with vineyards.

At least the Charger was off surface streets, where traffic and speed laws would inhibit the chase. Smoke billowed from the Charger as it sped into the fast lane. Meredith kept up a narrative of the Charger's path in relation to other cars on the road. Nick watched the roadway. He hoped they stayed on 101, because it was easier to follow the other car. Still, there was major road construction south of Petaluma. He wondered how this would end. The driver wasn't about to pull over and ask Nick, "Wassup?"

Meredith's voice rose as she asked. "How come you're not calling this into Ferrua?"

"I'm driving." Nick clenched his jaw. "Why aren't you?"

Meredith didn't answer.

Three car lengths ahead the Charger pushed out a lead between the fast and the middle lanes, swerving around slower traffic. With distance growing between them, the Charger decelerated to just above the limit—75 mph—a degree safer. Nick kept the truck running close, staying with the Charger but slow enough to not catch a road cop's notice. CHP's district office was less than a mile from 1807 Arbor; this stretch of 101 between Rohnert Park and Petaluma was always patrolled. It was prudent to keep a close eye on the speedometer.

But the guy driving the Charger wasn't prudent.

"Passing the Highway 116 off-ramp in Cotati." Meredith's voice was strident. "In my side view, there's a CHP unit coming up fast in the slow lane."

"Fuck," Nick whispered. Then, he had a thought.

"The Chippie's spotted the Charger and is changing lanes to catch up." Meredith's voice softened. "You going to back off?"

"Yeah, a bit." The truck's engine slowed as Nick's foot let up on the gas pedal. "I'm going to let the CHP do our work."

They watched the patrol car—now with emergency lights on—slip in behind the Charger. Nick was sure the driver wouldn't pull over. Not for the first time, Nick wondered what the guy had to hide.

Up the Cotati Grade, still southbound 101, bordered by vineyard and cattle pastures, the two cars shot further ahead of Nick's truck. In the fast lane, even keeping a steady speed of 85 miles per hour, 20 mph above the limit, Nick lost sight of the pursuit. He pushed the accelerator as the Chevy crested the hill. He was rewarded with a grand view of the gray Charger, followed by the CHP patrol unit still on the highway. They'd been tailing the car for eight miles.

Meredith pointed, excitement raising her voice. "There, at Petaluma Boulevard North. Passing the exit now." With a corresponding on-ramp on the other side of the exit, there was potential for more cops.

Nick concentrated on catching up. "Keep an eye out for back-up CHP units."

"Yeah," she said. She had been watching. "Got Petaluma PD on the off-ramp."

"They won't join in unless the pursuit goes into town."

Traffic slowed as the three lanes merged into two. Through most of the county, the state had found enough tax dollars to add a third lane, relieving Highway 101 traffic—at least for this generation. But Petaluma south to the Marin County line was being re-built in small chunks. South of town, highway construction was underway. Highway 101 through the Petaluma city limits was only two lanes, resulting in stop-and-go congestion almost all day.

Nick lost sight for a moment, then saw the two cars on the overpass for the railroad tracks in the Denman Flats, north of East Washington exit. The Charger swerved to the left shoulder, passing a slower Camry. The shocked Camry driver slammed on the brakes, throwing the CHP vehicle into a slide on the gravelly shoulder. The Charger was still on 101 and, from the East Washington onramp, had picked up another CHP patrol vehicle. The second patrol car slipped in behind the Charger. The first CHP unit righted itself and followed, now falling second in line.

"The Chippies know something we don't. They couldn't justify continuing this pursuit just for a mere speeding violation because of the traffic. They would've probably shut the pursuit down by now. Maybe stolen? A felony warrant on the registered owner?" Suspect warrants for serious crimes could be noted with a warning notice on vehicle owner registration. "We won't be able to get near the driver if they get the car stopped."

CHP ruled the highways in California. As a state agency, they had roadway authority over county and local jurisdictions. Even if a warrant suspect was detained, most likely he'd be booked into the county jail after all vehicle matters were mitigated. In Sonoma County, highway patrol officers sometimes turned over their criminal arrests to local agencies, so they could stay available for road-related offenses.

From the fast lane, Nick saw the Charger's tail lights with two CHP patrol cars following, still on 101 at the Petaluma River Bridge. They'd followed it nine miles. Pressing on the accelerator, the Chevy engine powered up the quarter-mile incline, the roadway spanning the flats to the cliff two hundred feet above the river.

Nick continued on—he hadn't seen them take any city exits. At Petaluma Boulevard South onramp, Meredith reported, "Two semi-truck-trailer rigs coming on the right.

Real slow. You can pass them easy."

"It's the rest of the traffic that's got me worried." Fast lane traffic had pulled to the shoulder for the lights and sirens. Cars and trucks were now recovering and jockeying to the fast lane. Nick slipped between cars as closely as he could to keep eyes on the last CHP patrol car. Recently laid asphalt kept the ride smooth, but Nick knew highway construction lay ahead.

Bright orange Caltrans warning signs and white concrete barriers appeared on the edge of the road. A pair of dirt lanes now paralleled the highway as bulldozers moved dirt and graded the hillside. At Kastania Road, 101 road surfaces deteriorated to an uneven jumble of old roadbed and new asphalt, especially tricky at high speeds. Nick slowed just enough to keep the patrol cars in view. "Dang," Nick shouted. "This guy knows the area."

"Yeah, but this construction changes daily," Meredith offered. "He could be in over his head."

"Let's hope so."

The Charger veered right, beyond the last concrete barrier, passing several construction pickups using the gravel shoulder. It wobbled back to the asphalt. CHP kept up their tenacious chase. Nick dropped back as traffic thickened with shocked drivers. Disoriented by emergency lights and sirens, most motorists took a few seconds to react, often pulling to the right at the last moment. The errant Charger's reckless speed and changing path set the scene for disaster.

A half mile later, in the incongruous setting of gently rolling pasturelands, the racing vehicles sped over the newly opened San Antonio Creek bridge. They were 12 miles from where they began and 10 minutes into a normal 20-minute drive. More concrete barriers were in place, constricting the Charger's escape. Nick's fingers tightened on the steering wheel as he noted ahead a sedan driving slow enough to cause a bottleneck. A boxy mid-70's Mercedes, it chugged along at 50 mph in the fast lane. This will be trouble.

Nick heard the Charger downshift. It was a shock when metal struck metal, even when he expected the collision. The

Charger clipped the fender of the smoking blue Mercedes, a light tag, more like a PIT maneuver—pursuit intervention technique—than a ram. The Charger backed off, letting the Mercedes steer to the right, out of the way. While the Charger blew past him, the blue car's driver had over-corrected. The Mercedes whirled a 180, then stopped across both lanes facing the oncoming CHP cruisers. The Charger accelerated up the rise and continued through light traffic without a pursuer. The roadway behind him was blocked.

Nick slowed, glancing at the traffic around him. "Hold on," he yelled.

There it was—a small opening to the narrow dirt service road that ran between the old highway and the new.

Nick ground his teeth as the Chevy's frame thumped over the low barricade. He hated damaging his truck but hated letting the Charger get away even more.

CHAPTER FIFTY-FOUR

Meredith yelped, gripping the handhold above the door as the truck rumbled over some construction debris lying between the barricades. Thankful Nick hadn't given up, she righted herself when the truck got to the road. A quick 360-degree survey around the truck revealed no heavy equipment or company pick-ups close by. "The road is clear." Nothing behind, either, except the knot of CHP cars trying to straighten out the mess with the Mercedes.

"This dumps into San Antonio Road, then back onto the highway." He shifted behind the wheel, sitting up a bit taller. "Just keep updating me on that Charger." It wasn't long before the dirt gave way to newly laid asphalt that became the San Antonio Road turn-off. Passing it, Nick kicked the speed up a notch—to 70 mph.

On the highway, the Charger weaved in and out between vehicles. Twice Meredith lost sight when the Charger, still in the fast lane, disappeared behind large trucks.

"Nick, we're running parallel to him." With no traffic on the small feeder road, they'd closed the gap between the Charger and Nick's truck. Nick eased back onto 101, nearly cutting off a plodding Honda Odyssey van. He slipped the truck neatly into the widening space between the Charger and the coupe behind him.

"Get the plate." Nick's fingers were white around the steering wheel. "Damn, wish we had a radio."

"It wouldn't do us any good. This isn't a pursuit." Meredith used her phone to snap a picture of the license number.

Nick snickered, nodding in agreement. "We can't afford to lose him—he's a link we can't explain." The guy couldn't get away. Meredith had seen it before—allied agencies positioned down the 101 corridors made evasion virtually impossible.

"We'll get this guy," Nick said. It was a straight shot

down 101, with no offramps until San Marin Drive in Novato—3 miles max. The car or the registered owner must be wanted.

Up ahead, at a grass covered knoll, a cloud of seagulls announced the county dump. Still speeding through placid dairy pasturelands, Meredith cautioned. "Watch for dump trucks coming from the landfill just ahead."

Concern seeped past the adrenaline rush. There would be consequences for their actions if they were involved in a collision at these speeds. At the very least, reckless driving. Another thought pushed to the forefront. "CHP would radio ahead about the Charger to Marin units." Although a state-wide organization, CHP had clearly defined patrol areas. Fortunately, the Golden Gate Communications Center in Benicia thirty miles away dispatched for the Bay Area. including Marin and Sonoma. Depending how much CHP wanted the driver of the Charger, their Dispatch would've directed units to intercept. The road configuration would allow for an enforcement traffic stop if there was a patrol car close by.

Meredith's scan showed no emergency lights in view. They continued down the highway keeping pace to the northern point of Novato. There, 101 opened from two country lanes to a more freeway-like four lanes. The Charger jerked to the right.

"He's taking San Marin," yelled Meredith. They'd been in it for 20 miles—so far.

CHAPTER FIFTY-FIVE

The San Marin Drive exit was a two-lane roadway in each direction. From east to west, it led through rural hills populated with grazing dairy cattle, small strip malls and suburban homes, cookie-cutter models with three decades of individuality stamped on each.

They followed the Charger, the driver steering lane to lane and veering around slower traffic. Meredith was dismayed at the number of cars ahead of them. At almost a mile in, she noticed pedestrian traffic in front of the tract homes. "This is San Marin High, and it's almost 3 PM. School's out. Kids on the sidewalks and in the street."

Nick slowed to 25 mph, swiveling his glance side to side. "There must be hundreds of kids."

The Charger reduced its speed—just a little. In the school zone, the speed limit had dropped to 25 mph. The Charger was going 45 mph, easy. Meredith saw kids scatter at the ominous rumbling of the vehicle's approach. Girls screamed, dropping books, packs, and purses as the gray car accelerated around a corner.

"We're on Novato Boulevard." Meredith kept Nick updated. "No sign of Novato PD yet. We're headed toward Stafford Lake. We were just here with Gareth."

Nick stared ahead.

The road narrowed to one lane each way, suburban homes giving way to dairy farms. The Charger accelerated even through the turns. The gray car still visible, Nick held back to a speed that kept him on the road and not in a ditch. After two miles and with no warning, the Charger slipped neatly across the yellow line into a Y-shaped lane.

And Nick almost missed it. Meredith saw the flicker of a taillight. "There, to the left. He pulled off."

She looked over and saw a sign. "Indian Valley Golf Club."

Nick decelerated to stay in control on the veiny, patched,

single-lane road, Stafford Lake to the left and oak-covered hills to the right. "No way out of here. We got him." They'd traveled twenty-five miles in twenty minutes on a trip that usually took almost forty-five.

At a turn, they lost sight—for a second. When they rounded the corner, the roadway was empty; smoke hung in the air from skidding tires.

A huge tree limb lay ten feet away, across the asphalt: the driver of the Charger had swerved to dodge it. On the lake side, heavy underbrush lay flattened, mashed by the car that had just barreled through. Swirling dust and indignant insects reeled in the air above. The Charger sank, mired in the lake so that only the top of the roof and taillights were visible.

Nick stopped the truck and flew from the cab before Meredith could stop him.

CHAPTER FIFTY-SIX

Nick ran to the lake's edge, adrenaline streaming through his system. He forced himself to take a moment to consider strategy and the terrain. Only Meredith nearby, but he had to go in.

As he ran into the water, he yanked off his sweatshirt. No one swimming away; nothing floating on the surface. The driver must be behind the wheel. Knee-deep, the mud sucked Nick downward. Glad he was wearing laced shoes, he wrenched his feet free, then got stuck again with the next step. Still, he plodded on, the Charger burping air bubbles.

When he reached the car, the driver's side window was open. It had filled with water up to the last twelve inches from the headliner. The driver, a trim, late-teenaged Hispanic male, lay unmoving, his forehead against the steering wheel and oily water splashing into his mouth. A trace of blood tracked from his cheek.

Nick grabbed a handful of hair, pulling the teen's head well above the waterline. Water sputtered from the kid's mouth as his autonomic response kicked in. His lungs sucked in great mouthfuls of air. Choking and sputtering, his arms flailed out. Nick braced himself on the door panel, getting a better grip on the guy's collar.

Relieved the seatbelt wasn't secured, Nick tugged the semi-conscious kid from the seat. His body floated upward easily. Working with the kid's buoyancy, Nick pulled him through the window. Finally clear of the car, the kid snapped to, his fists flailing against an invisible foe. Kicking and thrashing, a fist soon found Nick's face. A slight glance off his cheekbone, but enough to spike his temper.

Nick looked into the kid's eyes and saw nothing of humanity, only pure animal savagery. Rage rose up. Matching the driver's violence with his own animal fury, Nick pushed the driver's head under water. The kid's hands raked at Nick, then gripped his forearms. He struggled to breathe as air bubbles broke the surface.

Nick's chest heaved, his heart pounding with the wrongness in his hands. Rage and frustration culminated in the moment. He'd never lost it like this. The job held law enforcement to a higher standard, but by his own code, what he had almost done was so wrong. Adrenaline aside, Nick had prided himself on responding to any stimulus with a cool head—and now this.

Nick pulled the kid's head out of the water. The young man gulped a lungful of air. The strength in his grip surprised Nick as the kid latched on to his arms. Nick sensed the electricity between them. He'd almost killed the young man—but hadn't. A specter sinister enough to provoke that response haunted him. But at the moment he couldn't dwell on it. He'd resisted the ugly impulse, thank God. Pushing aside the feeling, Nick concentrated on getting the kid to land. "Calm down, you're safe. Calm down," Nick repeated, quietly. Floating the kid on top of the water, Nick struggled with his footing again as they neared the shore.

Then Meredith was in the water, her hands pulling the kid from Nick. She dragged the exhausted driver, her hands under his arms. Freed from his burden, Nick moved slowly. If he stopped, the mud would suck him under. He stomped on cattails, flattening them to stabilize his balance as he waded to shore. Meredith laid the kid flat on the shore, inspecting his head, looking for injuries as he sputtered and caught his breath. A faint pale scar exposed a repaired cleft palate. His dark hair sported a short, stylish fade and muscular arms told of hours in the gym.

Nick dropped next to them, all three gasping for breath. He'd almost killed the guy. Almost murdered him. He'd have to take him to a hospital. No time for an ambulance all the way out here. A glance to his truck told him he'd have to move the baby's car seat to get the kid in the back.

Nick's breath slowed. "He okay?"

"A concussion maybe." Meredith shrugged. "A small laceration on his cheek; it's already stopped bleeding."

The kid's breathing was evening out, also. He

whispered, "What the fuck—"

Nick sat up. The adrenaline threatened to return. "Why did you run?"

"Because you chased me, fool." The kid brushed a clump of algae from his chest. "Why'd you do that?"

"Chasing you? You tell me: why were you watching us?"

The kid's color deepened to a pale *café au lait*. "Who said I was watching you?" His eyes dodged Nick's scrutiny as he rose to one knee.

Nick grabbed the kid by the soggy plaid shirt, pulling him close. "In the trailer park in Rohnert Park. You were sitting there watching. Why?"

He was even younger than Nick had thought—late teens, at the most. A full face dotted with adolescent pimples, and the faintest hint of a hard-won goatee. Jet black hair— Mexican. Nick's anger surged. He'd run the kid to ground. The kid had wrecked and almost drowned. Nick wasn't sure who he was more disgusted with—the kid or himself. Releasing his grip, he pushed the kid back onto the ground. "I should've let you die."

The kid's eyes focused, trying to understand. "Die?" He finally focused on the Charger's taillights, twenty feet into the lake.

"Fuck me," he sighed as his head dropped into the gravelly shore. "You almost killed me, man."

Nick heard the words over and over in his mind. "You almost killed me."

"But he didn't." Meredith spoke up. "He saved your pimply ass." When the kid swiveled his gaze to her, Meredith yelled, her face a scant foot away from his. "Why were you watching us?"

The kid listened, lifted his head enough to meet Nick's frown. "You saved me?"

Meredith answered. "You're breathing, aren't you?"

"Yeah, yeah. You saved me, 'mano." The kid's face softened with the shortened version of *hermano*, the Mexican word for brother.

"'Mano?" Nick's eyes widened in disbelief. "I'm not your brother." He almost laughed with the irony of it all. But he held his tongue. Nick was reluctant to plant ideas in the kid's head. No telling where this chase was going to wind up—on the Marin or Sonoma County DA's desk? Shit.

The kid sat up, pushing Meredith out of the way. "Yeah, man. Yeah, you are. You saved my life, *hermano*. I woulda died in that water." He looked from Nick to Meredith then back to Nick. "I can't swim."

"You can't swim?" Nick almost choked. He'd chased the kid through two counties. He was the reason the car plunged into the water in the first place.

"Jesus." Meredith shook her head and looked away.

But the boy wasn't having it. "No, man." He sat up. "You saved me. I woulda drowned. I owe you, dude."

What crazy code did this kid live by? Nick made the jump to the kid's history—he talked like he was locked into a life built by gangsters and hoods. Nick had friends from his old neighborhood who'd been sucked into gang life. The gang built a family around an inductee, pledging support unto death for loyalty, replacing absent parents. At ten years old, they started out as sentries; at twelve, if they were conscientious, couriers. This guy couldn't be over seventeen. A juvenile. Another fine mess. "How old are you?"

"I'm sixteen, man." His chin jutted in defiance, prideful. He was a man. "Almost my seventeenth birthday."

"If my partner here hadn't saved you, you wouldn't have a *cumpleaño,* dude." Meredith's sentences were clipped, betraying her irritation. "What's your name?"

"Benny." His hand dripped pond water when he stuck it out to Nick. "Benny Huerta Gaspar."

Nick shook it, deciding to use the kid's compliance. Benny felt indebted because Nick had saved his life—no matter Benny was in the water because Nick had been chasing him. In lessons learned from patrol, Nick got more with cooperation than force—despite his reaction moments ago. "Who told you to follow us?"

"My boss, man—tells me what to do."

Surprised at how forthcoming the kid was, Nick fired more questions at him. "Who's your boss?" He'd take advantage of the help while it lasted.

The brown face sank from indignation to thoughtfulness. "Hector Cruz Granados. He's *mi patron*."

"Granados. I don't know that name."

The kid's chest puffed out. "He's a businessman. He owns a moving company."

"Moving company?"

"Yeah, like, you and the little woman move to Denver for a transfer. We haul your furniture and shit."

Nick digested this as they stood, picking at clumps of algae. Then he searched the kid's face. "Do you move boxes and crates, then?" An easy way to move illegal drugs and any other contraband under the radar.

Benny squirmed under Nick's scrutiny. "Hector wants his money back. A long time ago the guy in the Taurus took it. He lives there in the trailer park. Now he's out of prison. The money's Hector's."

Suddenly this made sense. Granados must be the 2001 robbery victim. He would've gotten word of Jamie Houston's parole. Benny hadn't lied to them—he was watching for Jamie.

"You're from San Francisco?" Nick took a wild stab at finding the origin of his leader. Most of the gangsters in Sonoma were registered with the DA's office—for gang enhancements at chagrin. If you were a cop, you knew most of the important names on the DA's roster. Granados wasn't on it.

"Yeah," For the first time, the kid glanced at Meredith. "And I wasn't following you, 'mano. I was waiting for the white guy in the beat-up brown Taurus. I was watching his house." He looked away, blushing. "But you started chasing me."

CHAPTER FIFTY-SEVEN

With Nick's promise to Benny that his debt was clear, Meredith was happy to see Benny standing next to the lake in her side view mirror. "I hate letting that little dirt bag wannabe free."

"It's better this way." Nick steered the Chevy truck down the country road. Benny had used Nick's phone to call a cousin who lived close by. He'd pick him up and help him figure out what to do about the car. Benny couldn't know about the unforgiving nature of the CHP chase. The Charger was wanted in a burglary out of San Francisco. He swore the car was his cousin's, he didn't have anything to do with the crime.

Except for fulfilling Benny's debt, no promises were made.

Meredith used her phone app to look up the CHP activity. Notes in the incident said a similar model car was wanted in a carjacking in Sacramento. The comments added the Charger was the wrong model. It sounded like there was a mix-up in Sacramento. Until it was straightened out, CHP would be off the pursuit.

Nick and Meredith had to walk away from this. He felt like she wasn't convinced so he asked her, "What do you think we could have done with him, anyway? Nothing to arrest him for: we weren't identifiable as cops, so 2800 VC wouldn't apply—even if we had probable cause to affect a traffic stop." 2800 VC, evading a police officer as defined by the California Vehicle Code was very specific about what constituted evading: willfull attempts to evade a police officer exhibiting a red lights, siren, distinctly marked vehicle or identifiable uniform. No way could Nick's Chevy truck be construed as a police vehicle.

Reckless driving, contributing to an accident. Even as she thought it, the fact registered that this was a misdemeanor unless there was an injury at the scene of the

vital. We'd hit a wall until we talked to him."

After a glance at his watch, Cavanaugh stood. "Time to get up the hill. Wanna get home before dark." With a crooked smile, he swallowed the last of his coffee. "You decide you need to keep the boy out of the line of fire, you call. Jake and I'd love to have him, and Filomena will take good care of him."

Ignoring Cav's discomfort with overt displays of affection, Meredith smiled her thanks and hugged him—she couldn't help herself. This man was a rock in their lives—acting more like a father than Terence ever had. She loved Raymond Cavanaugh.

Cav's voice was gruff as he stepped toward the door. "You guys have a plan?" His brow furrowed at the disruption in their lives. Maybe he disapproved of what they'd done, but, loving them as he did, he still wanted things to go easy for them.

Meredith caressed her son's dark curls. "We'll sit down tonight and put this together. We're working it like it's a case."

"Might this be better handled by the cops? The on-duty ones, I mean."

"They're working the homicides, both Sonoma SO and SFPD. But for now, the rest of this is best done by Mere and me." Nick took Davy and put him in his highchair. "We know more about what happened, and Terence's role makes it a delicate situation. We want the right questions asked—and answered."

Cav nodded. "A little hard to take the emotion out of it?"

Meredith smiled at his insight. "Yes, but I've got help." She nodded at her husband.

Cavanaugh reached out and squeezed her hand. "Those guys don't know who they're up against."

CHAPTER FIFTY-EIGHT

"I'm sorry, Des. I lost them after the storage units. I had to get out of there—the place had cops all over." From Ramona's voice, Desmond got no sense that she was sorry at all.

"They didn't see you, did they? I mean, the two cops who were here." Would they recognize her face from the brief encounter they'd had at the bar?

"No, I don't think so." Now she sounded worried.

"Come on back here." You stupid bumbling twit, he thought. He'd have to come up with a more efficient way of finding the money. He was certain that Meredith would lead him to it, but he needed a way to track her without her knowing, and he must move fast. Granados wouldn't wait any longer. Des was sure Granados would push him. "I'll take care of this."

Ninety minutes later at the bar, Des snapped at Ramona as she grabbed the slip of paper. "Now, don't lose this." He waited for her assent. "You remember where I told you to go?"

"Yeah," Ramona's patience was being tested. "165 Jackson Street, Bay City Moving and Storage, the business office." His stare pushed her to repeat his directions. "Don't hang around. Just give the note to whoever's in the office and leave."

"Make sure the clerk sees this name." Granados was printed on the front. Inside, Des had scratched, "$130,000. Your money. I can get it."

Des wanted to get Granados off his back for a while. He had to concentrate on the money search. Terence had said his daughter was a good detective. The old man didn't pass out compliments often, so Des believed him. He'd watch Meredith, try to guess her next move and get to the cash before her. If she got it first, he'd take it away from her. His advantage was that Granados didn't know about Meredith

Ryan. He didn't know she was a cop or that she was good at what she did. But Desmond knew.

The gangster had been snooping around since Jamie was paroled. Des had to come up with an idea to placate Granados and keep him out of the way. Des had no illusions. Granados would keep a distance for a short time, to see if Desmond could fulfill his promise. Des had a day before Granados lost patience and sent out his own muscle.

This letter would commit him to action, and now the clock was ticking—he had 24 hours, max. He didn't expect Granados to hold to the agreement he planned to propose. But he'd try to find the cash before Granados. Otherwise, he expected to be caught and tortured for the privileged info he kept.

The penalty for dealing with the devil.

CHAPTER FIFTY-NINE

A young Hispanic man pushed the door open. The Mexican was slender, but with noticeable musculature under his cotton shirt. He slipped sideways against the wall, letting his eyes adjust. In the dark, everybody acts the same, Des thought. Two stocky, well-muscled Hispanics followed the young man in.

The sole patron at the far end of the bar never looked up from his draft beer.

Desmond finished drying a highball glass and replaced it on the shelf behind the bar. He was tired of this shit. Tired of all of it. The two-bit toughs coming in for a fight, thinking this was still a cop bar. That was ancient history, dead and buried. No self-respecting cop would be seen going into the Crazy Eights. Along with Terence Ryan, Desmond had pissed off everyone he used to work with. Those guys were retired now, anyway, living in the 'burbs and playing with themselves. The new generation went to nightclubs or live shows. Who the hell knew where the women cops let their hair down? Desmond shook his head. The world had become something he didn't understand. It was better the new generation stayed away.

Even so, he wished for more business. Just for a little while. The bills piled up and he was having trouble convincing himself his plan would succeed. Even if it did, he'd have to make ends meet until he got the money. And if Granados bought into his plan, he'd need some operating cash. For now, he'd use his rent money.

The little Mexican bitch with the cleft palate was the first encouraging sign. Des tossed the towel aside and watched the kid blink.

Des yelled across the room, "What'll it be, Pancho?"

"My name's not Pancho. It's Benny." The kid nodded for the two goons to wait where they were. The kid drew closer to the bar and Des saw that he was young—practically a child. "Desmond Rollins?"

"Yes, I am." Des couldn't help himself. He added, "Pancho."

Des noticed the kid's shoulders broaden. "My boss wants to talk to you."

Fuck, here it comes. "Oh yeah? Who's your boss?" Des knew the kid belonged—locked down to his soul—to Hector Cruz Granados, a low-rent gangster. Des wasn't sure Granados knew of his own association with the 2001 robbery, but his message had obviously caught Granados' interest.

"You should know. You invited him."

Des permitted himself a broad smile. The plan was moving along. Things were looking up. "Then bring him in. I'll buy him a beer."

Benny skittered out. The two guards remained in place, stone sentinels guarding the portal through which their boss would walk.

Des leaned into the storeroom. "Ramona." She appeared, and Des pointed to the drunk at the end of the bar. "Escort this gentleman to the door—the back door."

Three minutes later, Granados entered the bar. He reacted the same way as Benny had but recovered quicker. It still gave Desmond a moment to size him up—a cop strategy learned for survival on the streets.

Granados was a dandy, sporting a flashy street-style that would have daunted a lesser man. Medium height with a tendency to pudginess, the gangster's bleached fade announced his metro-sexuality to the world. The buttons on his charcoal gray suit jacket stretched across his girth. The shoulders must have pinched something terrible. Matching skinny pants accented a large midriff and bird-legs. Varicose veins crisscrossed bare ankles above a pair of plaid loafers.

Des almost laughed out loud.

"Mr. Rollins." Granados tipped his chin, making his jowls shake. A stout index finger flew up, and Benny stepped up to take his boss' jacket. Granados settled his bulk into a barrel chair at a table.

Des sat across from him, thankful that Ramona had found a place behind the bar near the hidden 12-gauge shotgun. He was glad she worked for him; she was better in a bar fight than most men. The muscle named Benny stood behind and to Granados' right, just inside the front door. The two guards were motionless except for their eyes scanning the inside of the bar.

"Can I get you something to drink?" It took an effort to appear civil.

Granados' glance oozed distain. "No, I don't think so." His eyes held Desmond's in a grip to see who'd look away first.

The gangster's scorn of him and his bar spiked Des' temper. But his future was at stake here. He kept his mouth shut.

Granados took the opening. "Let's get to business. Tell me how you can find my money. It's been gone for a long time. I'm interested in seeing how you think you can succeed where others have failed." A small tic quivered in his cheek.

Des smoothed a hand over the walnut-colored Formica, clearing imagined bullshit off the table. "It would be better if you didn't know." Des smiled. "You know, plausible deniability."

Granados' full lips thinned in what could have been taken for a smile, or a snarl.

Des didn't care which. "I have two lines of inquiry going. I expect to find what you want within a day or two. One is a person close to the man who inspired the theft."

The fat man leaned back, taking in the information. "Am I supposed to believe you'll do this because you're a paragon of virtue?"

Des smiled pleasantly while shaking his head. "There isn't much goodness in my heart, sir, no." He straightened. "Here's the part where you offer me a finder's fee."

"A finder's fee?" Granados' face broke into a surprised smile. "Really?" Not expecting an answer, he studied the bar owner.

His cop face on, Desmond showed no emotion. Inside

he seethed, furious at having to bargain with this low-life douche bag. And knowing that if he flinched this guy would have his guts hung up for all to see.

After five seconds, Granados shifted in his seat, plucking at a button on his shirt. "What figure did you have in mind?"

"Half."

"Half?" The fat man leaned into the table, his eyes wide with surprise. "Why am I so generous?"

"Because half of nothing is nothing." Desmond let the words sink in. On Granados' face, Des saw the argument was won. The gangster had nothing in hand. Even half—65 thousand—trumped zero.

"What makes you think I don't have my own lines of inquiry?" Granados finger-quoted 'lines of inquiry.'

"If you're counting on this little dipshit here to find the cash, you'll be looking until the Second Coming."

Granados stared at Des. "Don't underestimate my nephew, Mr. Rollins. He's learning the family business—and he has skills." Granados snapped his fingers and Benny spun out a slim, fixed-blade knife.

With a side glance at Desmond, Benny said, "In front of the lady." He twisted at the waist, flinging the shiv across the room into a wooden corbel at the end of the bar. Staring at the knife so close, Ramona let out a small yelp. But she stayed put, watching the knife wobble from the impact.

Des heard his heartbeat thumping in his ears. Show-off, he thought, forcing his diaphragm to relax. That didn't mean shit. Des jerked his head sideways, dismissing the man's efforts. "If you want it found, you need help."

"Why do I need you?" Granados inspected his cuticles.

"How far have you gotten in your search? It's been what? Sixteen years?"

Granados had no reply. He stared at Desmond.

"You see? You got nothing." Desmond squinted in disgust. Then, like a light switched on, his face relaxed into a benevolent smile. "I have connections you don't. I can have my hands on the money faster than you."

Mercedes accident. She hadn't seen a collision—only a solo spin-out. Still, she couldn't assume there was no injury. "What if—"

"Stop. We have to be practical about this. We leave it here." His voice was flat. He wouldn't give up anything, but she wasn't sure she could let it go. There was no reason she and Nick should abide by whatever code this gangbanger followed.

"But—"

Before she could finish her question, he spat, "Shit." A Novato PD patrol car cruised toward them slowly, the cop's head on a swivel. Nick let out his breath when they passed without stopping.

Meredith was a terrier. "What about the Charger?"

"That car is junk. It would take way more money to restore it than it's worth."

"And the chase?"

"We leave that alone, too." In the absence of injuries or property damage, Nick and Meredith could leave and not tell authorities about the incident. CHP would have to find Benny and the Charger on their own. The car wouldn't be registered to him, but he'd lay low anyway. The car would be abandoned, probably where it lay.

The set of Nick's jaw told Meredith he was losing his patience. "Look, you're way overthinking this. This deal with your father's got you wound up tight." He sighed and reached for her hand. "Just leave that to me. I'll find out and do the right thing." He enunciated every syllable. The right thing, he'd said. Yes, she trusted him.

Back at home a half hour later, Nick had changed into dry clothes. He and Meredith sat at the kitchen table sipping coffee with Raymond Cavanaugh. The older man looked a little tired after watching an almost toddler. "He didn't get an afternoon nap. We were busy."

Meredith recapped their day while Nick got up to warm Davy's dinner. The boy was in his tired mother's lap, happily chattering at a plastic dump truck. "Thanks for Gareth." Meredith smiled at her friend. "Your help has been

"Why do you need me?" Granados squinted in the dim light, glancing around the room.

"I may need some of your muscle."

Granados nodded. "Why should I trust you? What's to stop you from taking the cash when you find it?"

Desmond permitted himself a chuckle. "That money is tainted. It's bad luck. Three people have died over it. Besides, if I took it all, how far would you go looking for me?"

"To the ends of the earth." Granados lips stretched, an unpleasant smile. "To the ends of the earth."

"So, it's a deal?" Des wondered at how easy this was.

The gangster stood. "Unless I find it first," then stuck out his hand.

"Give me twenty-four hours free of interference. If I don't have it by then, we'll re-negotiate our terms."

Would this axe the agreement? No, it just meant they'd both be on the money trail—the gangster's thugs would trail him, trying to get to the cash first. He'd step up his plans. Clearly, if Granados found it first, Des was out plenty. The money would be the least of his worries.

Granados' hand was extended to seal the contract. Des wanted to slap it away and have nothing to do with this slime ball, but he knew there had to be an understanding in place. He'd rely on Ramona for back-up; he could do worse. He'd promised her five Grand from the take. That had been enough to enlist her. Maybe he'd call in Jamie, too. It was for one day. If he got what he wanted, he'd be long gone before this *maricon* figured out what happened. Des touched Granados' fingers in a damp handshake.

Granados' grip tightened, then pulled Des toward him. Des smelled coffee on the other man's breath. "You have a plan?"

Des' nodded and held Granados' handshake.

Granados' squeezed. "Tell me the plan, Rollins." Des groaned inwardly.

Des wondered what the gangster would say if he knew about the plan to kidnap the Ryan kid for ransom. He decided he could tell him this part. There was less chance he'd take over the show if he had a few details, but not the whole picture. "Terence's daughter has access to info that I don't. I have great confidence that she will find the money. When she does, I'm going to take it from her. If she doesn't hand it over, I'll snatch her kid and ransom him for the cash." Des left out, '—and another princely sum.'

Granados' grip eased, freeing Des' hand. "Forcing the daughter to give you the stolen money." The gangster considered the plan, then nodded. "Simple. I like it. Who do you—"

Des put his aching hand up. "Don't you worry your pretty little head about it."

Granados stepped back, taking his measure of Desmond Rollins. The gang boss' tone was nonchalant, but Des heard the menace behind the words. "Don't fuck with me, Mr. Rollins. Two of the three robbers are dead. The third isn't far behind. It would be nothing to make you go away, if you cross me."

Des motioned to Benny for Granados' coat. Still behind Granados, the kid stood wide-eyed, unmoving. Des snapped his fingers and the kid woke up, collected his boss' jacket and escorted the gangster out. The two guards peeled in behind them.

Desmond snorted after them. "Ramona, you want to make some quick money?"

CHAPTER SIXTY

Dinner was over. The dishwasher hummed while Meredith put Davy to bed. The violet sky darkened as Nick collected what he needed. Meredith returned to find Nick at the kitchen table with an oversized drawing tablet someone had gifted Davy. They used white boards at work when he was in VCI, but this would do.

With a felt-tip marker, Nick drew a huge circle. In the center, he wrote, 'robbery/homicide summer 2001.' It became the hub when he drew a line upward connecting to the circle. Like spokes of a wheel, the line said, 'convicted March of 2002-Jamie Houston.' Another spoke to one side said, 'Brenda Houston/involvement?' Opposite, another spoke: 'Terence Ryan/service weapon.' A line dropping from the center to a circle read: 'victim-Mexican gang.'

At the moment, it was a wheel that was going nowhere.

Nick turned at a soft knock on the door to the back porch. He raised his eyebrows to Meredith and reflexively touched his hip where his Glock usually sat. Nothing there. He nodded for her to go to the bedroom. Guns were kept there, in a safe.

He was an easy target in the well-lit kitchen. He flipped off the switch at the door and turned on the outdoor light.

Benny?

The kid's greeting was terse. "*Hermano*." Not waiting to be asked to come in, Benny pushed past Nick. Meredith rounded the corner, her Glock 43 held alongside her thigh. She hesitated, then faded into the darkness of the hall.

Nick grabbed a fistful of Benny's shirt. "What the fuck, *hermano*?"

Benny squirmed away, and his hands flew up in surrender. "Wait. Wait, man." His forehead beaded with sweat. "I gotta tell you something."

Nick released Benny's shirt with a shove. Playing out motives and scenarios, Nick couldn't make sense of Benny's arrival. Nick slammed the tablet closed. Benny was on the other side. No sense in letting him know what they had on this damn case—or what they didn't have. What was this wannabe gangster doing in their home? Knocking on the door?

Meredith's voice was strong but quiet when she turned the corner, standing sideways, gun still at her side. "Benny, what are you doing here? How did you know where we live?"

Benny waved the questions aside. "I had to warn you. You got trouble coming."

"Trouble—how?" Meredith asked. Nick visualized her knuckles whiten gripping her gun. He wondered if Benny knew how close he was to dying.

Benny shook his head, as if he could make the bad images in his brain disappear. He focused on Meredith "They're using you, *chica*. They're going to trail you to find Hector's money. When you get it, they're going to do something bad to trade you for the cash."

Nick's insides turned ice cold. Kidnap?

Meredith slipped her Glock into a back pocket and stood next to Nick.

"Sit down." She pushed him into a chair. "We've got questions."

"Yeah, Benny." Nick leaned over the kid. "First is, why're you here? How come you're telling us this shit?"

Finally, aware of his precarious position, Benny stuttered. "M-m-my patron, Hector. He wants his money back."

"Yeah, we already heard that crap, Benny," Meredith snapped. "You didn't have to tell us about this trade. Why are you here?"

Nick decided he needed to ask the questions. "What's Hector going to do?"

"I could get killed for what I'm telling you." Benny's chin dropping on his chest. "*Mí patrón* sent me to follow you. When you find his money, I'm supposed to take it from you or snatch—something important to you." Benny looked from one to the other, his gaze settling on Nick, his most sympathetic audience. "Something really valuable. Hector said he'd ransom it for the cash."

"Something valuable, or someone?" Nick prodded.

Benny sucked in a breath. "Before, I saw the baby car seat in your truck. I told the boss about it. But I didn't know what he was going to do. Honest."

Shocked by this turn of truthfulness, Nick straightened, fighting disgust with Benny and his boss. If Granados was willing to kidnap a cop's kid, he must believe there was something worth the risk. In a head slap moment, Nick realized Granados didn't know the stolen money had been recovered.

Benny's honesty was worse than unusual—it wasn't to be trusted. Most people, but especially criminals, had an angle. Information was traded for money or a good word at sentencing, but Nick had never seen a gangster volunteer without something to bargain.

Recalling the moment in the pond when Benny's breath evaporated in the bubbles bursting around his panicked face, Nick felt a tug of remorse for almost drowning the kid. It didn't matter that he didn't follow through on his impulse. He'd saved him in the end and Benny felt indebted. In Nick's mind, there was no debt and he wondered how far Benny would go to salve his conscience.

Nick weighed telling Benny the truth about the money. Would it take the pressure off him and Meredith? No way. Granados and his cadre didn't care how, they just wanted the result—the cash. Even without the specific target revealed, he knew they'd hold hostage what—or who—Meredith and he valued above everything—his son. Would Granados go to extreme lengths to get his money back? Nick wasn't prepared to gamble on Davy's safety.

Nick met Meredith's gaze—she got it. He'd take the lead with this guy. She looked away. For now, the gangsters would continue to believe the cash was up for grabs. "Did you hear him planning something, Benny?"

"He was telling some other guy." Benny nodded. "They

were talking about finder's fees and shit."

"What other guy? One of his gang?"

"I didn't know him." Benny's eyes widened. "But he had a plan to get the money, too. Hector stole the other guy's idea. I think Hector's going to punk him."

"So, two guys are looking for the money? No, three with Jamie." Meredith's voice hinted at her skepticism.

"Yeah. Yeah." Benny sounded hopeful. "They're pretending they're partners, but they really aren't. Hector don't trust him. The boss thinks he can get to the cash first, but he gave the guy twenty-four hours."

"Who's the other guy?" Nick had his suspicions.

"Never saw him before. Some gray-haired old fuck." Benny flinched as he looked at Meredith. He'd had a mama who'd slapped him when he cussed. He mouthed, "Sorry."

Nick was sure he knew. "Where did Hector meet this old guy?"

"At a bar on the Avenues, Ninth and Irving. Can't remember the name—something about cards—a real dump."

Meredith's face was stone. "How dare he use his best friend's grandson as a hostage."

Nick cocked his head in a warning. "Why're you telling us this, Benny?"

For the first time, Benny was at a loss for words. "It just ain't right—taking a baby from its mama." Benny cleared his throat. "My little brother died when he was two years old. My mama cried all day for—I don't know how long. She's never been the same. She still doesn't smile." Benny looked at Meredith like he was searching her soul. "I seen your little boy. He looks a lot like Miguelito."

Meredith stared back, her face blank, but Nick saw her mind working.

Breaking the silence, Benny said, "It just ain't right."

"You're right." Nick saw his wife's eyes narrow. "It's just not right."

Meredith spoke up. "Benny, did you ever think you weren't cut out for this line of work?"

CHAPTER SIXTY-ONE

Meredith rubbed her arms as if she was cold. She sank to the living room couch. Rage threatened to boil over. "We're going to need help with this mess."

Nick stared out the front window. Benny left and re-positioned his "new" '70 Camaro across the street and down two doors to observe the Reyes house. As Nick turned to Meredith, the night sky beyond framed his silhouette.

She had a question. "Who's going to brief SFPD?"

"We have to start with Ferrua." Nick winced. "No question it's SFPD's case because the robbery and initial homicide occurred there. But first, Ferrua has to contact them."

Meredith sighed.

Nick reached out, resting a hand lightly on her shoulder. "I know, and I hate to rely on him but he's your chain of command. We need to finish this by the book."

"Yes, we do." Meredith rubbed her hands over her face. Her eyes were burning with fatigue. "We start with the lieutenant. Lay it all out," she paused, and with a half-smile added, "except the chase down 101." Already, not by the book.

"He'll gripe, since this is all happening in our county." Nick knew Ferrua well enough to anticipate his objections.

"Doesn't matter." Meredith stood. "He'll have to defer to SFPD because it was their initial crime. They trump our calls."

Nick sagged into his recliner. "First thing we do is get Davy to safety. I'll call Cav in the morning."

Meredith rose, glancing at the clock—almost eleven. "No, call him now. I'm going to get hold of Christy right this minute and ask her to take Davy up to the ranch tonight, if it's okay with Cav. The car seat is in the Subaru." Before Nick could protest, she said, "I want my son gone while Benny's out there. And I have to be here with you. I don't trust Benny, but I appreciate that he took a big risk telling us." She put a hand on his forearm. "You realize he's burned as soon as they find out we know their plan?"

"Yeah, you're right." Nick stood. Meredith followed as he walked to the refrigerator and pulled out a Pacifico. Then put it back. "We may have to pick up the pieces of that mess, too. Benny's so young. He's going to need help after all this is settled. But right now, we need to figure out how to keep Davy away from Granados and Desmond Rollins."

"Unless they have warrants, there's nothing to hold them on. We can't prove conspiracy. We don't know for sure he intends to kidnap Davy. I'll bet Benny won't testify. And, by the way, you don't owe that kid anything. Just sayin'."

"Yes, we do. We owe him for alerting us to imminent danger to our son." Nick smiled suddenly. "What if we let Granados and Desmond go through with their plan?" Nick's expression hid something cunning.

Her lips pursed in dread as his idea blossomed, growing into a plan. "What?"

"What if we just let their plan unfold and roll with it."

"No, no, no. Too many variables. We don't know what's going to happen."

Nick shrugged. "Not the specifics, but they're coming after you or Davy, right?"

Was he thinking what she was? "You want me to be the bait?"

Nick grimaced. "Not exactly. It won't be a set-up, per se."

"What'll it be—per se?" Really, Nick?

Nick blinked slowly, realizing he wasn't getting his idea across. "Scratch that. Let's just turn this mess over to Ferrua and SFPD and let them figure out what to do."

"Great idea." Meredith looked Nick in the eye, her arms across her chest. "Why do I doubt that's what's going to happen? This is one of those times we should trust our agency."

"Like when Lieutenant Ferrua was supposed to protect you from a stalker?"

Meredith winced, knowing the veracity of his words. Four years ago, a Sonoma County Superior Court judge not only obsessed about her but killed Meredith's husband and brother in a bid to isolate her and drive her to him for consolation. When her administration dismissed her stalking complaint, she realized she was on her own. With Nick's help, she fought him, even as the judge's hit man fired the shot that killed him. Afterward, she'd had such a strong feeling of betrayal that she considered quitting law enforcement. But Nick helped her through the painful months that followed and was able to put Lieutenant Ferrua's negligence in context.

For once, she had nothing smart to say.

"When have we ever gone to Ferrua without a plan?" Nick's brain was engaged, figuring out angles. "You know he won't be able to protect us."

"Yes, but he'll dump this into SFPD's lap. It'll be SFPD's decision how to proceed. And Benny's warning isn't enough to get protection. We have to take care of ourselves."

"We can—should—plan for contingencies. With two loose cannons giving orders to God knows how many gangsters or criminals, we need to think this through. What would we do if we called the shots—hypothetically?" Nick's gaze was fixed on her. When she didn't answer, he ran a hand through his hair. "What if we set it up like Davy was still here. Put a bundle in his bed or something."

"No. I'm not having gang-bangers in my house, even for a set-up." She was surprised he'd come up with something so hare-brained.

Nick thought. "Then we could do it in a car. Put a bundle in his car seat. They won't know until they pick it up. At that point they will have committed a crime."

"I don't like it—playing fast and loose with our child."

"Mere, it's not a child. It's a pillow, tied to resemble a baby." He spoke like he'd known the idea wouldn't fly. "Then we could make that Plan A and do it in your Subaru. Put a bundle in Davy's car seat."

"Okay, smart-boy. When Plan A flops, what's Plan B?"

"Still working on it." He grimaced, looking like a guy getting ready for a beating. "We need to expose them, catch them in the commission of a crime."

"No, we don't. We need to let SFPD do their job. We have to stay safe. I could call Deb and Manolo and maybe Marty Ferguson for manpower." She paused as his eyes widened with interest. "Just not Evelina," she said with a rueful smile.

Nick pulled out the coffee beans and set to making a pot. "No, let's wait to call for help."

Meredith's mind was whirring with a million thoughts and their possibilities. "Or we could find proof from the past that will implicate them—and that's another angle Gareth's working on, right?"

"You mean the muddy fingerprint on your show ribbon?" With a doubtful frown, Nick went on. "It's not enough. Even if the print is determined to be Terence's, it isn't conclusive to prove he was at the horse show during the robbery. Terence's presence there was within hours of the crime. Even accounting for heavy traffic, the travel time between the two locations could make involvement in both incidents feasible. It's not enough to give him a solid alibi, Mere."

"What about the medics who transported Judy to the hospital?"

"Gareth hasn't been able to track either of them down yet. He's got inquiries out but no response so far." He smiled ruefully at Meredith. She was clutching at straws. "There again—even if they're found, nothing says they'll remember a particular call, much less be able to ID someone who was on the outside fringe of the incident. Gareth's not holding out any hope." Nick poured a cup of coffee for Meredith. "Desmond and Granados still think the cash is up for grabs, that you'll lead them to it."

"We could use that, couldn't we?" Meredith sat up, excited.

Nick thought for a moment, then nodded with a grin. "Yep. That just might be the way to bring this to a head. We won't be able to charge them for homicide, but we could arrest them for theft after they take the bait money. It doesn't take much imagination to figure the only way they knew about the money was to be complicit in the robbery and two murders." His face darkened with concern. "But it would put you in the line of fire."

She considered it. "It's worth the risk. We need to put an end to this." She took in a deep breath, pulling her reddish-brown hair into a ponytail. "At this point, I don't even care about exonerating my father. I just want Davy safe and these criminals put away where they belong."

"Then let's map this out so we have a reasonable plan in case this goes sideways."

"Okay but we start with Ferrua. Let him do what he has to. We make our plans contingent on his and SFPD's going south."

"Right."

CHAPTER SIXTY-TWO

"Gareth, good to hear from you. What up?"

The simple fact Gareth sounded like Raymond Cavanaugh soothed Meredith's raw nerves. She'd been waiting for this call, not trusting Ferrua to relay information accurately to SFPD. The priority had been handled: Christy had snatched up her pretend nephew and had dropped him at Cavanaugh's Ranch. She'd texted that she was on her way back to Petaluma. Meredith exhaled in relief. Davy was safe.

She glanced at the wall clock in her kitchen. Eight hours since she and Nick had presented their information to her sergeant and lieutenant—her chain of command. At SFPD's Major Crimes Unit, Gareth was an afternoon detective, but it was just past noon. He was on duty early.

"Jamie Houston's in custody on a parole violation. It seems the Petaluma PD lifted his prints from your windowsill. They picked him up at midnight. I'm up at your jail in Santa Rosa. I tried interviewing him, but he's not talking."

"No surprise there." Parolees considered cops their natural enemies. Jamie had no reason to admit to a hot prowl at a cop's home, much less volunteer information about the Adam Mejia-Isaiah Renton murders.

"He did say something interesting, though," Gareth said. "Seems that his mother, Brenda, has some type of cancer. He tried to claim hardship. Said they can't afford treatment here, but they could in Mexico."

"Well, this opens several new possibilities that speak to motive. Is Jamie looking for the money to get Brenda treatment in Mexico? Is Brenda working him?"

"It's likely. It feels like she's pulling his strings." Meredith imagined Gareth's shrug. "Desmond and Brenda don't seem to have any contact. I don't think they're in this together."

"Des has his own motive. He's got financial trouble with

the bar. Maybe he needs a bail-out."

"I don't buy it. It's too big for bail-out. One hundred and thirty thousand dollars and he spends it on a dive like the Crazy Eights? More likely Des sails off into the sunset." She heard rustling on the phone, Gareth looking through papers. "I'll check on his financials. Might give us a better picture."

"Good idea. But, before you talk to these clowns, you need to know that they all believe the money is still hidden somewhere. They don't know you have it." She had a thought. "You didn't tell Granados that you found his money, did you?"

"No, and we won't." Gareth grunted, moving as he talked. "His holdings were under investigation for fraud and tax evasion—one step away from being frozen. That case never went forward since the money was missing. This must've made him more careful. For now, the money is being held in evidence. Once this case is adjudicated, it'll probably go to the Feds, until they close whatever case they file against him. Wherever it ends up, it won't be to Granados, the supposed victim."

"So, there's your bargaining chip."

"Thanks for the info, Meredith. You've been a real help dealing with these jackasses."

"Doesn't hurt that I have a bit of history with some of them, even if it was kind of distant."

"Which is the reason I called. Will you come with me when I interview Brenda Houston? I want to get more on Terence Ryan's involvement and I'm going to leverage Jamie's arrest to push her. And you know her—"

"She hates my guts, Gareth."

"Still, I'm betting there's a bond between you. She must've loved Terence, and no matter what your history, he was your father."

Meredith thought about it. She didn't know Gareth well enough to dump her family history on him. It had no bearing on the case, anyway.

Smoothing over the silent moment, Gareth asked, "You okay with finding out more about your father's role in the crime?"

Meredith was quiet.

Gareth continued, "Look, I've got no clear picture that he was involved in the robbery. So far, it looks like he knew about the robbery and homicides. That's all."

"But whatever you find out about Terence won't have an impact on the crime."

"It's background, Meredith. I need to know how this all started."

"Yeah, I guess so." She sounded as uncertain as she felt. Why would she want to know more? She'd wanted to exonerate her father, find some reason for his inexcusable behavior. But now, the whole thing was too complicated. She just wanted the case closed, for real and forever, and her son out of danger. She couldn't get excited about Gareth's interest, but he needed to know about Benny's warning. "There's something else, Gareth."

When she finished briefing him, he shouted. "Holy Christ, Meredith—"

She got the chills at the depth of his concern. "I know. We've taken measures—"

"You dig a moat around your house?"

For the first time in recent memory, she laughed. "No. In fact, we're kind of hoping Granados shows up here."

"But Davy—"

"Davy is safe and being spoiled in the hills above Lake Sonoma."

"Ah. Smart move." Gareth sighed in relief. "In light of what you've told me, I'd like to push ahead with Jamie's interview. I need to fill in some of the holes in this case. Meet you at Brenda's about ten o'clock?"

"Okay," Meredith sighed. She wasn't sure why she agreed. She'd planned to stay available for something like this today. She missed her son—no chasing Davy around as he crawled over the hardwood floors of their home. Damn, she hated the sight of Brenda Houston. But if it would help bring an end to this mess, she'd face her.

It was going to be long day. She felt like half of her was

missing without her son. She'd already called the ranch and spoken to Filomena three times this morning. Meredith had tears in her eyes when she disconnected the last call. Davy was safe and happy. Filomena was taking great care of him. He was excited about a swim before lunch.

God, she missed her son.

CHAPTER SIXTY-THREE

The June sun smarted on Meredith's Irish skin, so she moved into the shadows. She'd parked in the four-space guest-parking two doors down from Brenda's trailer. Too warm to wait in the car for Gareth, she leaned against the passenger side of her Subaru, chasing the shade. She checked her phone—9:50 A.M. Gareth should be here any moment.

She was alone today. Nick was off chasing a lead on the paramedic at the horse show—something he said wouldn't be much help but needed to be eliminated. And Meredith hated waiting, hated the idea of facing Brenda again, and hated anything Brenda would say about her father.

Five minutes later, a dark Ford Crown Victoria eased down the narrow lane to Brenda's trailer. Gareth was behind the wheel, but someone else sat in the passenger seat. When the Ford turned into the next parking space, she recognized Jamie. Crap. She felt oddly shocked at the sight of him—were tables turned, she wouldn't want to see him.

She hoped Gareth knew what he was doing.

Meredith heard Brenda's voice yelling at her yapping Chihuahua, then a door slamming, the dog closed up. She answered Gareth's knock, opening the door a scant six inches.

"Brenda Houston? I'm Detective Gareth Cavanaugh from San Francisco Police." He sidestepped on the narrow porch. "You know Meredith Ryan. I'd like to ask you some questions about an incident that occurred—"

Brenda dropped her cane and pushed past Gareth. "Jamie, Jamie my boy." He stood on the sidewalk behind Gareth, in front of Meredith. Brenda wobbled down the stairs to embrace her son. When his cuffed hands blocked her hug, she wailed, "What have they done to you? Oh, my boy."

Meredith observed the tearful mother reuniting with her child. She despised the irony of this. Because of these two—somehow—Meredith had to hide her own son for his safety.

She also had to hide her anger over being here. Damn Terence. Damn him.

Moving Brenda aside, Gareth controlled Jamie. With a hand on her Glock, Meredith brushed past them to the threshold. She scanned inside for other people, obvious weapons, dogs—any threat. The barking dog in the back room added to Meredith's mounting irritation. The home was cluttered with bundles of newspapers and magazines, plastic boxes filled with God-knew-what stacked on top of each other. Meredith wondered if the Brenda was diagnosable as a hoarder.

Finding nothing in the open, she nodded an "all clear" to Gareth.

Three minutes later, the four of them sat at the round particleboard topped with wood grain laminate dining table. Gareth, Brenda, Jamie and her. Meredith had the palest recall of an over-used painting of dogs playing poker around a similar table. Different breeds unintentionally portraying their emotions while cheating each other. She wondered at the metaphor and studied Brenda and Jamie.

The faint rays of sunshine danced through the angular leaves of the Chinese Pistache tree outside, but Brenda's face was dark, unreadable. She was hunched with the burden of age and disabilities as her veined hands picked at a cigarette pack. Jamie sat next to her in a similar posture. His bearing said submission—a felon in the company of two cops. He was at their mercy here, only because he hoped to reduce or eliminate his parole violation and burglary charge. Typical of ex-cons, he was unwilling to meet Meredith's gaze. Heavy-lidded eyes focused on the tabletop as he listened to his mother chatter in his ear. He gave nothing away.

Gareth tapped his phone, spoke into it, then set it in the middle of the table and began the interview. He started by asking Jamie about his relationship with Terence Ryan.

"Terence was my mother's boyfriend," Jamie answered.

"Did you live under the same roof?"

Crap. Another thing Meredith didn't want to know. Why the hell did she agree to this?

With a glance at Meredith, Jamie answered. "No. They lived together for a while but did better living apart."

"Because I wouldn't let the old bastard use me as a punching bag." Brenda's face held a smug grimace as she faced Meredith. "I wouldn't stand for it, and he couldn't live without me. So, we lived apart."

Gareth eyed Jamie. "How did he act toward you, Jamie?" Meredith didn't understand. Why was he asking this? It didn't have a bearing on the case.

"He acted like he was my father." The thirty-five-year-old waved the thought away as if parenting was a fly to smack against a screen door. His words maddened Meredith. It surprised her again that this bothered her—it seemed like a new betrayal, after all this time. She'd constructed a hard shell against her father years ago. Terence Ryan hadn't acted like a parent to David or herself. Except for fostering Meredith's interest in horses, the man had nothing to do with her.

Gareth asked, "How did you know about the courier moving money from the moving company?"

Jamie twisted his mouth in disgust or, perhaps, shame; Meredith couldn't tell. "Terence drove past the business when he was taking me to the dentist. He said they had an illegal card game going on. He mentioned how easy it would be to knock it over. Said they were sitting ducks. I couldn't get it out of my mind."

"Why?" Gareth asked. "You never got into trouble before."

Jamie sighed. "I got to thinking how I could use the money. My mom was always going on about how broke we were. It just seemed like the money was the answer. He made it sound like it would be so easy."

"Did someone coach you on how to take the courier down?"

Jamie was silent for a moment, wrestling with something. "No."

"Did Terence Ryan know you were involved in the robbery on May 11th, 2001, in San Francisco?"

"Yeah, he knew—after." Jamie's head hung in humiliation. "He caught me."

"After? How did he find out?"

"I took his gun. Used it in the job." Jamie wiped his nose with a sleeve.

"Did he say how he knew it was you?"

"I took his gun. Don't you listen?" Jamie slapped a palm on the tabletop. "He knew it was me because I put it back—right after the job. I wanted to get rid of it. He said he figured I'd taken it, because it'd been fired and not cleaned. I didn't know shit about cleaning a gun. He said I was the only one who knew where he kept the fucking thing."

Meredith tried to keep judgment out of her voice. "Tell us what Terence did when he found out."

"He yelled and screamed at me, took the money—the duffel—right outta my hand. The old asshole. That's what he did." Jamie's head snapped up; eyes focused on her. "Maybe he wanted it for himself."

"No." Meredith was confident. "No, I think he wanted to keep you out of trouble. He wouldn't spend the money." She'd found the money he'd said went to savings went to Brenda. Now, every cent was accounted for, even the secret account he'd set up for Brenda. Meredith knew she should've looked at his savings statements. "He cleaned the gun, so your prints weren't on it, but ballistics matched the round that you got off."

The man who'd refused to be her father took very good care of Jamie. She shook her head at the absurdity—Jamie Houston was a felon while Terence's blood daughter had followed in his career.

"You don't know nothing. I never shot no one. You think you're so smart." Jamie's spine straightened. "Oh yeah. You're his cop daughter. You'd know all about him, wouldn't you? Like how he said he'd like to be a father figure to me—bet you didn't know that."

The words stung, but not as much as they could have. There were cracks in the wall she'd built. She shook her head. "No, tell me."

"He showed up after school sometimes, to take me to play soccer at the park. And he liked the Giants." Jamie scrutinized her, assessing how much she knew. It dawned on Meredith that he competed with her. Jamie thought of himself as Terence's son. He knew Meredith was legitimately Terence's daughter, therefore, inheritor of his estate.

Jamie continued a little louder, as if the strength of his voice gave his standing legitimacy. "He tried to teach me right from wrong, like cops always mouth off about, ya know? But then, he'd do something just the opposite—like take my money away." He stiffened with indignation, while a glance to his mother implored her sympathy.

"It wasn't your money, Jamie," Meredith reminded him.

"I worked for it. I helped pull off the whole deal." This was an admission of guilt and Meredith weighed Mirandizing him. Because he'd been convicted and served his time for the robbery didn't mean they couldn't find evidence of any one of the three homicides for which he could be culpable. But an interruption carried the risk of alienating Jamie, shutting down his narrative. A glance at Gareth told her he wasn't going to interrupt, either.

Meredith continued to ask questions while Gareth relaxed in his chair, absorbing the answers. As a detective, Meredith knew what elements the case needed although she wasn't sure what bearing this had on the storage unit homicides. She was pleased that Gareth trusted her to conduct this interview. It could change the direction of the investigation—or not, depending on what info she gathered. And she was in a unique position to make intimate inquiries.

But she wasn't the investigating officer. She was a member of Terence's family in search of answers. Nick might say she used this to get the story while bypassing the suspect's rights. Well, Nick wasn't here, and she wanted to know. "That's when you took Terence's service pistol to use in the hold-up."

"I already told you." His head tipped while he considered what to say. "It was easier than buying one on the street. Isaiah already had a piece. Adam didn't want one."

Meredith wondered why he would admit to this. What was in it for him? The admission could lead to a theft charge. Did the gun belong to SFPD? If so, they would be the victim and undoubtedly charge Jamie, unless the statute of limitations was up. She doubted they'd care. "Where did you take the gun from?"

Jamie found the courage to look her in the eye. "Terence had a locker at the Crazy Eights. I went in the storeroom. The door wasn't latched so it was easy to get in."

Stupid move, Dad. You should've locked up your weapon. But I guess you figured that out. "You said you 'helped' plan the robbery." Meredith's voice was quiet as she leaned toward him, getting ready to coax a name from him.

He shrugged, looking away. "It was mostly my idea. I didn't need any help."

"Okay, how did you come up with the plan?"

"I already told you," Jamie insisted. "Terence was driving me to the dentist. We drove by the moving company. He mentioned how this new gang had started it up as a front for a card room. He said they probably handled a lot of cash and how easy it would be to knock over. He said the pick-up truck out front was probably transferring their take."

Surprised at her father's lack of discretion, Meredith realized Terence had trusted Jamie enough to tell him this. Cops know things—things that society never sees and feels better not knowing about. He'd spilled information to Jamie. That probably made Terence feel complicit in the crime. The robbery wouldn't have happened had he not told Jamie about the card room. Terence would've realized Jamie's role after the police got involved in the investigation.

Again, she wondered: Did Jamie have help planning the hold up? He didn't seem sharp enough to do it on his own. And at the time of the robbery, he was barely eighteen and seemed inexperienced in criminal matters.

She recalled reading in the report that the victims didn't call 911. Bystanders saw the guns and reported the robbery.

Even under the guise of a moving company, the gangster start-up was reluctant to call the police's attention.

Meredith went back to Jamie's version of events. "You told Adam Mejia and Isaiah Renton." Again, it wasn't a question. She made sure her face was expressionless so she didn't appear to make a judgement. Assumptions and judgments for cops were deadly in interviews, unless there was a plan. There wasn't.

Jamie's body slackened, resigned. "I don't know how those fucking gangsters found them two so fast, Adam and Isaiah—they were my friends."

But Meredith felt a charge in the air. He was going to tell her something important. Meredith prayed Brenda wouldn't interrupt them.

Out of the corner of her eye, she saw Brenda straighten with a start. The older woman flung the cigarette pack to the middle of the table with a disgusted snort.

"Jamie! You fuckin' idiot." Brenda pushed herself to standing but leaned her weight on the table. "Get a deal before you tell them anything more."

CHAPTER SIXTY-FOUR

Gareth put a restraining hand on Jamie's arm while Meredith stood, ready for trouble. A little late, Brenda. Even skinny old women could do damage. "Brenda, I'm not here as a—"

"Don't give me that shit." Brenda hollered again. "You can't take the cop out of a person." She squared off with Meredith, her frail body ready to take on an interloper to protect her son.

Jamie yelled over her, emotion shredding his voice. "Shut it, Ma. I know what I'm doing."

"What I know is—you can't trust her." Brenda bowed her scrawny arms, fists on her waist in a warning. "You're spilling to the one person Terence wanted to keep this from. And she's a cop. Just look at her—she ain't gonna give you a break." She spit the words out like she had a mouthful of spoiled food, her face screwed up in a sour scowl.

Meredith realized her expression had telegraphed this to Brenda.

"Mom!" Jamie's voice boomed over his mother's. "Knock it off. It's time she knew. She's Terence's daughter, for Chrissake. And he's dead. He's not going to come after you."

Brenda dropped her arms with a grimace. Meredith felt the other woman's aggression fade. "If you're going to tell her, I better be here to make sure it's the truth."

Jamie squinted at her insinuation that his story wouldn't be accurate.

The old woman realized her mistake and back-pedaled. "I mean, I'll fill in what you don't know." She stuck her nose in the air, avoiding his gaze as she dropped into her chair. "Well, go on."

Jamie blew out a breath of frustration and something else. Bitterness? Meredith couldn't tell, but neither Jamie nor Brenda were eager to tell the story. It was sounding more like a purge. Meredith said, "Start at the beginning—you told Adam Mejia and Isaiah Renton what Terence said. Who helped you plan the robbery?"

With a dare in her eyes, Brenda swept salt off the table with her hand. "This is your story, kid. You tell it."

Ignoring Meredith's question, Jamie murmured. "Des."

"It had to be Desmond." Meredith grasped onto this truth as sacred. "If not Terence, no one else knew, right?"

Jamie nodded. "Des said it would be easy, even handed over Terence's gun. Told me what to do."

"Terence didn't know." Meredith brightened at this one small piece of good news. "Go on," Meredith urged.

"He told me to watch the courier's movements—taking money from one place to another—for a few days until we figured out where to stop the truck. All we had to do then was find Isaiah a gun." He shrugged. "I had Terence's piece. The job started out like we planned except we were all scared shitless. This was a first for all of us. And, we never figured on the driver having a piece." Jamie stopped, his face twisting in an agonized knot as he recalled the moment. "He pulled this fuckin' cannon out. I'd given Adam my gun— Terence's gun—so I could pull out the bag of cash. Adam fired accidently—the gun went off and shot the driver. He didn't mean to do it. Adam was so scared he pissed his pants. I didn't shoot anybody." Another short, silent minute. "Then I grabbed the gun and Isaiah took the money from the truck—it was stuffed in a big duffel bag. We got in my car and boogied. I made Adam clean up his stinking piss from my front seat later. Now I'm sorry I was so rough on him."

"What happened to the money?"

"Yeah, about that." Jamie sniffed. "I hid the duffel in the spare tire well of my car. Adam, Isaiah and me was gonna lay low for a while 'til things cooled off. Isaiah tossed his gun down the drain on the way. I can't remember where. I dropped them off at their cousin's house in the Mission, Folsom Street, I think. Then, I drove back to the Crazy Eights and put Terence's gun back in the locker. Then I drove around, thinking. I had to come up with a safe place to stash the money—it was still in the trunk. Mom was at the doctors' and it would be late when she got home. It was after nine when I got back to her place and she drove in just before me." Jamie focused on his hands, squeezing them into fists in a mesmerizing rhythm. "They—the killers—found my boys so fast. They cut 'em and dumped 'em on our front porch. Isaiah was all sliced up, missing fingers, an ear was ripped off and cigarette burns all over his arm. He'd been shot, too. Adam was bleeding all over the place; his throat was slit. It was," his voice faltered. "It was fucked-up, man."

Brenda picked up the story as if reciting a grocery list. "They were just kids, really. Lying there on the porch, dead. We couldn't believe our eyes. We didn't know what to do. "The killers went through the house, tossed it real good, looking for the money." She shifted in the chair, arms across her chest. "I called Terence. I didn't know what happened before or what to do, and Jamie, here," she flung a hand toward her son. "Jamie was freaking out. There was blood everywhere. They'd peeled—"

Meredith put a hand up. "Wait. I can get those details later." She hated the grisly facts that were bound to come out. Blood and gore always put her off. But she was a professional and knew how to sit on her personal feelings to get the job done. "I want to know what happened next. Did Terence come?" She half hoped he'd told Brenda to get lost, but she knew he wouldn't have. Something else she hated to hear; her father stupid, reckless, leaving the law behind.

"Yeah," Jamie answered. "He came. He always came when mom called."

Meredith clamped down another spike of anger. When he abandoned the family, Terence didn't come back for anything. What hold did Brenda have over her father? What made her so irresistible? Meredith couldn't see anything attractive in the woman. In fact, Brenda Houston was crass, devious, and manipulative. Meredith wanted to scream at these two idiots for being so self-absorbed. Still, she needed to find out what happened.

"He was shitted when he got here. Mom caught him

before he got out of his car." Jamie shook his head at the memory. "He didn't like being interrupted while he was drinking. Anyway, she calmed him down and walked him up to the porch. Once he saw the bodies, he like, sobered up right away. He went to work, checked both for a pulse, said they were dead for sure. Told us Adam was alive when they were dumped—that's why there was so much blood."

Meredith nodded. Mejia would continue to bleed as long as his heart beat.

Jamie continued, "I found a note in Adam's pocket. It said, 'Houston is next.'"

"That's when Terence lost it," Brenda cut in. "He took Jamie by the neck. He knew the boy had the gun, so it wasn't a big leap to figure this mess was related to the Harrison Street robbery. He shook my boy so hard that I was afraid his neck would snap." The woman's gaze turned inward, reliving the moment the man she loved might kill her son.

"But he didn't." Meredith stared. "What happened next?"

Brenda sighed, her face drawn and pale. Meredith wondered what this was costing her, emotionally. Meredith couldn't imagine the burden of having to perform this grisly work to protect her child—living with it and now, the telling of it. "I had to beg him. I couldn't turn to anyone else. Couldn't call the cops—I wasn't sure how, but I knew Jamie had screwed up. There was no one I could trust." Brenda picked up the pack of cigarettes from the table, arthritic fingers tearing at the cardboard. "Terence said it would mean prison for him if anyone found out. Covering up a crime was a felony for a cop. Hell, I didn't know. But I begged him. Jamie and I couldn't do it on our own."

Brenda pulled out a cigarette and leaned over to Gareth. Nodding at the lighter on the table, she held the position until Gareth completed his task. Meredith caught a flirtatious glimmer in her eyes. Twenty or thirty years ago, she might have been attractive. But not anymore. This, combined with what she'd done, put a macabre shadow over Brenda Houston.

The old woman blew a cloud of smoke through her wrinkled lips. "He put the bodies on a tarp in the trunk of Jamie's Taurus—right on top of the money. Then, he made Jamie take his car and go to the corner market and buy a couple of bottles of bleach, dishwashing gloves and all the cling wrap they had. We had two rolls of plastic sheeting we bought for weed block. He found them in the garden shed along with a coil of rope and threw them in the back seat of the Taurus. Terence made me stay here to hose down the porch. Told me to dump the bleach over the blood stains." Brenda frowned. "It took years for plants to grow in front."

Meredith wondered where the woman put a heart. No wonder Jamie turned out the way he had. Any compassion Meredith might have felt evaporated as revulsion took over. She imagined the horror of the scene Brenda described. The disgust bled over to her father. She'd known he was bad, but this was lower than she'd thought anyone could go.

"What did he do with the bodies?" Meredith felt skeptical how much Brenda knew. Terence would've done what he could to keep her out of this.

"I don't know where he took 'em." She shut down; her face devoid of expression. She pointed her chin at her son. Not much loyalty here. "Ask him."

"After we loaded up, we went to dump the bodies." Jamie's voice quavered with the memory of his dead friends. These guys were his buddies, after all. Meredith wondered how she'd feel if her friends were cut up and dead on her doorstep. She mentally shook her head, unable to imagine being in Jamie's shoes. Again, she found no sympathy. And, with Terence and Brenda for guidance, what else could be expected?

"By that time, he was stone sober." Jamie's voice thickened with indignation. "I could see he'd been figuring out what to do." Jamie paused, remembering. "He made me dig out my knit cap, smeared mud on the license plate, got in, and started yelling at me. He made me drive."

CHAPTER SIXTY-FIVE

Jamie's eyes unfocused as he remembered that night.

"You dumb sonofabitch." Terence twisted in the front seat of the Taurus to face Jamie. "What the fuck got into you? Turn left here, then right at the signal. What made you think you could pull a robbery?"

Jamie felt like crying. He'd just lost his two best buddies and now the only man he ever respected was giving him a royal ass chewing. The burden in the trunk weighed as heavily as Terence's barrage. All he saw was blood, tissue and the remains of his friends. The horror pressed on his brain. Who could do this? Isaiah must've been in excruciating pain; Adam, too. The warning resonated—'Houston is next.' They know he was involved. They'll be coming for him—and the cash. How the fuck did they know?

Terence's fury punctuated Jamie's panic. "Not to mention you're a target, you fuckhead." Terence lunged toward Jamie, stopping inches from his ear. "Did you know these guys were working to join the *Brazo Negro* gang?"

"*Brazo Negro*?" Gangsters? If his gut could've tightened any more, it would shatter. "Never heard of them."

Terence sat back, with a smug, self-satisfied grimace. "You couldn't have picked a worse target. From what I hear, these guys are setting up to do the money-laundering for *Brazo Negro*. That means they have security now, thanks to you and your buddies. Their soldiers are likely the ones who took out your friends." He hooked a thumb in the direction of the trunk. "If they dropped the bodies on your doorstep, it's a warning. You're next."

"Well, they scared the shit out of me." Jamie's mind leapt from one scene to another. In each, he was the object of grisly torture schemes. "What do they want—"

"The money, dumbshit." Terence whacked him on the back of the head. "Then they want to kill you."

Jamie looked around, as if the *Brazo Negro* soldiers

were standing outside. "What if I give them the money back?"

Terence looked at him like he was the stupidest person on earth. "Then they'll just fucking kill you."

Two blocks later, Terence told him to turn into the driveway at a storage unit structure—an erector-set building surrounded by a sea of concrete. A motion light flicked on as they pulled up to the gate. "Cover your face." After he pulled his ball cap down, Terence provided the gate code. Jamie had a hell of a time seeing to punch in the code while keeping the cap brim low.

Directed by Terence, Jamie stopped in front of a series of garage doors marching along the entire block. Jamie wondered how Terence knew which one was his target. They all looked the same. Jamie stopped in front of the one Terence pointed out.

The older man had yanked the knit cap down to cover his face, then pulled it off. Using his pocketknife, he sawed eye holes, then put the cap on again. "This thing stinks." His voice muffled from the cap. He got out and stood next to the door. "You're a pig. Now, back the car in."

While Terence opened the padlock, Jamie jockeyed the Taurus around. The storage unit was a 10' X 10' space, plenty of room to get the important part of the car inside. Terence moved off and shoved a stack of three cardboard boxes to a corner, yelling at Jamie. "Get the plastic out and open the rolls."

He did as he was told, dreading the moment he had to touch the bodies of his friends. The sheeting was a thick 6 mil gauge opaque material 4 feet wide by 20 feet long. For packaging, the wide part had been folded into quarters. Jamie rolled the length as far as he could, leaving the remainder in a wad at the far wall. After Terence unfolded the width, he pulled out his pocketknife and cut the plastic in half. Then, he nodded to the trunk. Time to get the bodies.

Shaking, he touched Adam. His skin felt cold even through the latex gloves. Jamie drew back as if he could escape from the gruesome job. "Leave all the shit in their pockets. It won't make a difference when they find the bodies. They'll be easy enough to ID." Terence reached into the trunk, grabbing Adam's ankles. "Besides, I don't want their wallets and personal belongings on me."

Terence nodded to a stretch of plastic. "Get that cling wrap, then put him at this end."

Jamie followed Terence's precise directions. They wrapped both bodies in cling wrap first, then the weed block. It was heavy, cumbersome work and Jamie was covered in sweat when Terence secured rope around the last body. "That should keep them from stinking too much." Terence looked up at Jamie. "Don't want anyone poking around here before we can move them."

They picked up the boxes Terence had shoved into a corner and threw them in the back seat of the Taurus.

"I'll move them—and the money—when I can. As long as the rent's paid, no one'll find them." He said he'd pay up the rent as far in advance as he could afford, then be sure to take care of it when that bill came due. "No bodies, no crime."

Jamie slumped down in the chair, exhausted from reliving the nightmare.

CHAPTER SIXTY-SIX

"You're a lot like him, you know." Brenda Houston thumped the coffee cup down, a smirk spreading across her thin lips. She stole a glance at her weary son, then to Meredith. "Too bad you couldn't forgive him before he passed." Her gaze cut to Meredith.

Ignoring Brenda's disapproval, Meredith forced herself to ask. "What do you want from me?" Hoping for an answer with some weight, Meredith waited for Brenda to speak.

A quiet sigh escaped the old woman's lips, like she was boxed into a corner and fessing up was her only hope for escape. It might be the case. "Help Jamie out. Put in a good word with this guy." She nodded toward Gareth.

Meredith named the crime. "For the parole violation?"

"He's paid his debt," Brenda's lips twisted into a snarl as she finally acknowledged Gareth. "He told you who pulled the trigger. Isn't that worth something?"

Gareth answered. "Jamie offered no proof that Adam pulled the trigger, killing the courier. And Adam can't talk, can he?"

Brenda's tone took on a whiney quality. "Why can't you assholes leave him alone?"

Meredith didn't need to explain the role of law enforcement to her. Petaluma PD had nailed Brenda's son for by his fingerprints. He got caught violating the terms of his parole—breaking into her home—that's a felony. Any felon in California was prohibited from owning or possessing a firearm. Often terms stipulated no alcohol, no association with known criminals. Those clauses were frequently used with gang members. Jamie knew his conditions—they'd been explained prior to his release, and he signed documents attesting to his knowledge. Petaluma PD had identified him by his fingerprints and charged him with criminal trespass. By violating his prison release terms, he will be sent back to prison. He was lucky they'd found him first. She didn't feel sorry for him.

"What the hell were you doing in my house three nights ago?" Meredith was also certain Jamie was the intruder she'd chased out of her home. Finally, justice caught up with him.

"I dunno." Jamie slapped the table, frustration creasing his brow. "I thought you might have hidden the money somewhere. Then when I saw the kid, I kinda couldn't move—until you showed up."

Brenda cut across him. "He didn't harm anything. Nothing was taken."

Meredith shrugged. "He knows how it works." She tried to stay neutral to allow Brenda an easy way to tell her what was on her mind. Meredith had talked to relatives and friends many times throughout her career. Very few admitted their criminal could've "done it." Maybe Brenda had a new take on the theme, maybe she had another reason to go to bat for him.

"I need the boy here." Brenda sat up in her chair, a sulky shadow over her eyes. "I'm disabled. I need his help."

"I'm not the person to talk to about a hardship case. You might speak to his parole officer."

"That no good—"

"Brenda, what do you want?" Meredith leaned into the woman. "Why did you agree to me being here when this is SFPD's case?" Out of the corner of her eye, she saw Gareth sit back, becoming a fly on the wall, taking all this in. Most cops would've jumped in and taken over questioning, but Gareth didn't. So like his Uncle Raymond.

"What if I could trade you something for a get outta jail free card?"

Meredith stared at her. "There's no such thing."

Brenda was silent for a moment. "What if what I tell you is important enough to reduce his jail time?"

"Depends on the value of your info." Meredith wondered what Brenda thought she knew that would change the game. There was no way she could identify who killed Adam and Isaiah. She had no idea the cash from the robbery had been recovered. Any information she held might be valuable to Meredith alone, therefore personal in nature. None of that would sway a prosecutor to lighten Jamie's sentence. "I'll have to hear it first."

"What if—"

"Those are the terms." Meredith cut her off. "What did you know about the robbery?"

A brief glare at the direct question, then the old woman reached for the pack of cigarettes. Meredith didn't stop her, not wanting to interrupt her cooperation. During the familiar cigarette lighting ritual—so like her father's—Meredith made herself sit still. It was the four of them in Brenda's cluttered, stinking trailer. Brenda had no way of knowing what Meredith would say, nor how much weight the DA and State Parole would give her assurance about Jamie.

The woman sat back in the barrel chair and sighed a stream of blue smoke. "The first time I got a clue something was wrong was when Terence came over, spitting mad, looking for Jamie."

Meredith, dying to ask more, kept her silence. Brenda would talk. Meredith would let her tell the story, then she'd ask questions.

Brenda looked away, tapping an ash in the ashtray. "Your father was as mad as I'd ever seen him, and I'd seen him pretty angry before." Another draw on the cigarette, smoke puffing out with her words. "When he divorced your mother, he was pissed all the time." Brenda stole a glance at Meredith. "He loved you, you know. He respected you more than anyone—even me. He knew you'd be okay if he kept being tough on you. Your brother was a supreme disappointment. And he said Nora was a waste of air."

"The robbery, Brenda." Meredith wasn't going to let the other woman sidetrack down that path. Maybe someday they'd have this conversation, but not now.

Brenda sighed at the interruption. "Yeah, yeah. Here's what happened."

CHAPTER SIXTY-SEVEN

"Jamie! Brenda!" The trailer front door bounced open so hard it ricocheted off an end table. "Brenda, where's the boy?"

Brenda marched into the living room, dread and anger at Terence's temper making her voice louder than normal. "What the fuck d'you mean, storming in here like this?"

In his mid-forties, Terence was a tall, trim, handsome man. But he was a black cloud darkening the earth when angry. Now, facing him, he spit when he shouted. "Where's the boy?"

"If I knew, I wouldn't tell you." She knew but she'd be damned if she'd say. Terence needed to cool down before she'd tell him anything. He'd hit her before—once—and she was not about to let it happen again. She took a small step back.

His face twisted with fury as he moved closer. "You know what he did? He fucking took my service weapon. Stole it from my personal locker at the bar."

"Get away from me." Her fear and anger roiled but she resisted pushing him away. If she got physical, he would, too. She backed away, trying to stand tall.

Shouting, he asked, "Where the fuck is he?" Then, Brenda's lack of reaction seemed to crack Terence's hostile approach. He stopped, blowing out a breath of frustration and leaned onto the back of the sofa. "God, I'm sorry for yelling at you." His hand smoothed his short salt and pepper hair. "Look, if I don't get that piece back, I'll get canned." His gray eyes met hers. "You don't want that, do you?"

No, she didn't. Terence had been paying her bills for years. Besides her small social security disability check, she had no income. Des had forgotten she existed after she moved north. Terence had left his wife and kids and Brenda was already deathly afraid her money train would get derailed. Now this. What was that idiot kid thinking?

"Terence," she stretched her hand out to him. "Baby, I

don't know where Jamie is." Her fingers touched his flannel shirt, his muscles taut beneath the fabric. "He hasn't been around for a few days. You can check in his room, if you want."

Terence huffed, his chest deflating as his anger ebbed. "He took it yesterday. I had it for work the day before."

"What makes you think he took it?" She hated to risk firing up his temper again, but she wanted to know if he planned on strangling her kid. "What are you going to do? Can't you borrow someone else's gun?"

Terence crossed his arms, nodding. "I'll have to, for now." She could practically see the gears turning in his head. Suddenly, he stood and reached for the doorknob. "If you see that little prick, call me. If you can't reach me, leave a message with Des."

Des, at the Crazy Eights. Des, who'd introduced them. Des, who'd most likely knocked her up 35 years ago.

But she didn't tell Meredith that. The truth was, she'd slept with Terence the night Des introduced them. She'd dumped Des soon afterward. Maybe Terence had—she stopped the thought. Better to let Des believe Jamie was his. He had more earning potential than Terence. And up until she'd moved, Des had given her cash every now and then and watched the kid to assuage his self-induced culpability.

She never bothered to tell Des that he was probably Jamie's father. She didn't say anything to Terence, either. Poor Terence couldn't squeeze out an extra dime from his shrew of a wife, so Brenda never bothered to guilt him out—it was enough to leave to his imagination. Terence had found the trailer she and the kid lived in. She'd paid for it with the money from Des' Crazy Eights buy out. Terence had even arranged to get her on food stamps. He still paid her every month. Despite the tumor growing inside her, she felt a tingle between her legs. Even after all these years, Terence was a real man. Des was too soft for her taste.

But the truth was, she wasn't sure which man was Jamie's father. Brenda glared at Terence. "Jamie didn't take your damn gun. He's a good son."

CHAPTER SIXTY-EIGHT

Gareth sat up. "So far, you haven't told us anything we don't know." He nodded toward Meredith. "Maybe you gave Meredith something to chew on about her father, but nothing you've told us merits any kind of special consideration for your son's prosecution."

"I haven't gotten to that yet." She straightened in a pitiful posture of indignation. "I know where you can find the money."

Gareth's eyes narrowed. "Okay. Let's hear it."

"Information on that amount of cash has to be important enough to reduce Jamie's time in the can." Brenda toed a gum wrapper on the dingy linoleum. Meredith thought she might pick it up, but it seemed the old woman was just playing coy.

Gareth's arms settled across his chest. "It depends how credible your information is."

Meredith had no trouble imagining Brenda constructing a story to get her way. While she and Gareth knew where the money really was, it might benefit the investigation to hear what she said. She didn't know where the murders took place—time would've degraded the evidence, anyway. But Meredith knew it was unwise to stop witnesses from talking if there was something still to be learned. The detectives waited for the woman to speak.

"Des' place—the Crazy Eights out in the Avenues."

Gareth's neck stiffened as he considered her suggestion. "Where would he put it? Not into the bar. I mean, the place is on its last legs. Why wouldn't he blow town or spend it?"

"Brenda, why would you point us to Des? Did he piss you off?" Tired of Brenda's shoddy manipulations, Meredith wondered how the woman came up with the idea. She leaned toward Brenda. "Detective Cavanaugh is right. Wouldn't he spend any money he had? That old bar of his is a dump; his business is about to go under." Meredith straightened. "No, I can't see it."

Brenda's smirk returned. "I don't think Desmond knows where the money is hidden. Have you searched his back room? That's where Terence lived for the last eight years before he went into the home." She eyed Meredith, a satisfied smirk on her lips. "Your father could be sneaky when he needed to. Bet you didn't know that."

**

Gareth stood to package Jamie up. The felon slumped into the standing position with his hands behind his back. The loud click of the handcuffs overrode Brenda's protest. Meredith rose to keep an eye on Brenda.

"He's going back to jail." Gareth spoke to Brenda over his shoulder. "Your information isn't specific enough to forward the investigation."

From his pocket, Gareth's phone jangled a synthesized tune.

"I'll take over if you have to take that call," Meredith said.

Gareth answered, "Cavanaugh." He listened for a minute, then barked, "I'll be there in an hour. Keep them separated—away from everyone else."

CHAPTER SIXTY-NINE

In her living room, Meredith tossed aside an unread novel and picked up her ringing phone: 9 P.M. The area code was from San Francisco.

"Meredith, it's me, Gareth."

Glancing at Nick, she mouthed Gareth's name, then said, "We've been waiting to hear from you." Nick wasn't much of a reader—he'd been playing solitaire on his laptop.

"I don't have much time, but I knew you'd want an update. Got a minute?"

"I'll put you on speaker for Nick to hear."

"Hey, Gareth."

"First, thanks for transporting Jamie back to jail. You saved me an hour at least."

"No worries. Happy to help."

Gareth continued. "Second, we have good news. We found hair follicle DNA from one of a pair of former Granados thugs on both bodies. Oakland PD picked him up when he was released from jail. He snitched off his buddy right away. OPD found him at a half-way house for ex-felons. We got 'em in a couple of hours ago. Both are one-upping the other to spill on the Mejia-Renton homicides. They've named Granados as the guy giving the orders."

"That's great. You have enough to arrest him?"

"The DA wants evidence to back up these shitbirds' stories, so the forensics people are going over the two bodies. We've got Granados under surveillance for now, pending the results of the tests- more DNA, fingerprints. Given the threat to your family, the crime lab is pushing them through as fast as they reliably can."

"Glad to hear it."

"One more thing: I got zilch when I checked out your father's alibi at either stable. I'm afraid that's a non-starter."

Meredith sighed. "It was a long shot anyway. Thanks for checking."

"I'll let you know if anything else important develops."

"Thanks for the update, Gareth," Nick said. "We appreciate all you've done."

Gareth said, "No worries," and disconnected.

"I'm calling Cav to let them know we'll be picking Davy up tomorrow morning."

"Wait. Des is still out there."

"He's in the wind, don't you think?" Meredith groaned. "He knows he's in crap, so he'll be laying low for sure. He's probably halfway to Mexico by now."

Nick shook his head. "Why am I having trouble seeing that? He doesn't care who he hurts. He wants the money."

"Oh, Jeez. Humor me. Please. I miss our little boy."

"This isn't over yet. Remember, Gareth gave me the address of the medic who might've been on duty at your horse show medical call? I'm going to meet him tomorrow."

"Oh yeah." Meredith groaned. "He's where? Santa Clara? I'm tempted to say forget it. It's such a long shot." She looked into his eyes, searching to see if she could encourage him to stay home.

"Let's get this done. I want it off the table." Nick shook his head. "No, I'm going. I meet him at 11 A.M. I won't be back until late afternoon at the earliest." His face scrunched up in irritation. "It'd cut it too close to go pick up Davy then down to Santa Clara—it would take one accident to foul up my schedule."

"I wish—damn, I'll be glad when this whole mess is over."

"We're close, baby." Nick's arms encircled her. She missed Davy, down to her toes.

She and Nick had begun to settle into as routine a life as their careers would allow. She hadn't realized, until now, how busy and preoccupied they'd been. Savoring his smell, she buried her face in his shoulder, hugging him back. "I know. I'm just impatient."

Nick stroked her hair, calming her. His finger caught her jawline and tipped her mouth to his. She met his kiss and pushed against him, loving the gentleness in this man who would die for her. Pressing into her, his hand caressed her back. Reaching under her shirt, he expertly unsnapped her bra. "Let's make another baby."

He stopped and leaned away from her, turning off the lamp. The room was dark.

Damn. Benny is out there, watching.

The mood was gone.

CHAPTER SEVENTY

Filomena handed over Davy's backpack, laughing as the boy marched around his mother's leg. Davy had fun with Filomena, but he wanted his mommy. That was fine with Meredith. She picked him up, nuzzling his soft neck, inhaling the scent of her son. He'd had a bath last night. Filomena was an awesome babysitter.

The landline rang. Cav answered it and soon said, "She's right here. Nah, no problem. I doubt you could get cell reception up here anyway." He motioned her to the phone. "It's Gareth, for you."

"I knew you'd want to hear this," Gareth began without greeting Meredith. "First, both bodies are ID'ed as Mejia and Renton. The dental records had been entered into the Missing Persons database. But there's more—good news, finally."

"Go on."

"We got Granados dead to rights. Forensics found and matched his DNA from hair found on both homicide corpses to him. He'd been arrested in a sexual assault back in 2010, so his DNA was in CODIS." The Combined DNA Index System blends forensic science and computer technology into a tool for linking violent crimes. Federal, state, and local forensic laboratories can exchange and compare DNA profiles electronically, thus linking serial violent crimes to each other and to known offenders.

"Sexual assault?"

"In Richmond. He raped some poor kid and got caught. He pled to a misdemeanor battery and was fined. But we got his DNA. This means we can prove Granados was at the scene of Renton's murder and was present at the beating that caused Mejia's death."

"Finally, something your DA can sink his teeth into. Has he been arrested?"

"Yes, and he's been cooperative so far, a real surprise.

But we're keeping it out of the press for now."

Relief flooded through her. With Granados off the street, she would bring Davy home. Still, something niggled at her. Some piece of the puzzle hadn't yet fallen into place.

Pushing aside her discomfort, she sighed, anticipating holding her son.

**

The clock was ticking. At the bar, Desmond lifted a glass of Kilbeggan, sorting through the few options to get to the money first. He longed for a cigarette, but he'd quit last year. Nothing like a smoke and shot of fine Irish whiskey to help a man think. A plan took shape in his mind. He couldn't trust a gangster, especially a metro sexual. He glanced at his watch. He needed to keep Granados out of his way for the next sixteen hours. He needed to find someone else do the heavy lifting. Jamie wasn't answering his cell and probably in the wind.

He still had people who owed him at the PD. He'd call Jerry. Yeah, Jerry would listen to him. He'd tell him that Granados ordered the hits on the two flunkies who pulled the hold-up on Harrison Street back in 2001.

Jerry would pass the info on to Homicide Bureau. SFPD would have eyes on Granados until they could find enough evidence to arrest. That left no chance for him to come after the kid. The gangster would be cooling his jets in jail while Des was on his way to finding the cash. Damn him and his truce.

He tipped the last of the whiskey, savoring the burn as it tracked down his throat. He turned and hurled the glass across the room. It shattered against the wall where he'd once had a small dance floor. It seemed so long ago that it had been used.

Now where was Jerry's phone number?

CHAPTER SEVENTY-ONE

After picking Davy up, the drive home from Cav's allowed Meredith an endless dialog with herself. Had she been over-protective? Even in hindsight, it wasn't clear. She felt no shame in hiding her son from Granados. He'd proven he could kill, and she couldn't assume Davy would be exempt. Was she sure he was safe now? As sure as she could be. Des wasn't in custody yet. Although Gareth didn't have enough to hold him, he had a team watching the wannabe gangster.

Besides, it tore her apart not have her son near. It still amazed her how a 21 ½ pound bundle of energy could change her life. The life she'd mapped out before was unimaginable now. Successful career ambition paled next to being a mom. Besides, these days she wondered how much of her "ambition" had been to show her father that she could do his job. She didn't think she was all that different from many kids who were the product of divorce, but Davy's surprise arrival put it in perspective.

His soft sigh from the backseat soothed her built-up anxiety. Her son had been safe at Cav's but having him home with her felt so much better. Now that Granados was in jail and Gareth was putting Desmond under surveillance, she could relax a bit.

Breathing in the scent of home, Meredith walked Davy into the living room. She dropped his overnight bag in the baby's bedroom and hoisted him onto her hip.

"Gotta put Mama's stuff away," she said out loud.

"Mama." Davy jumped from her arms onto the bed with a shriek. Meredith put her Glock away and smiled as she snapped the gun safe door shut. "Yep, and Daddy will be home soon." Actually, he was overdue. She texted Nick, 'Where are you?'

'There's an accident on the bridge, backing up traffic in the City. Might have to go around thru Oakland.' Traffic wasn't unusual this time of day on the Golden Gate Bridge. But a collision on the span was problematic—no shoulder to route traffic around the wreck.

'Granados is in custody and I've got the baby.'

An hour later, Nick texted, 'Going across the bay. Might take longer but at least I'm moving.'

After dinner and a bath, Meredith read her son a story and tucked him into bed. She was so happy to have him back, to savor the smell of his hair, to feel the baby-soft skin and see his tired smile. He lay his head on the pillow and she ran her fingers through his dark locks—so like Nick's. Davy's chest rose and fell in the rhythm of slumber, even before his good night kiss. His chubby little hand clutched Fresno.

It was dusk, with the sun fading beyond the neighboring roof lines. She left the window open for an evening breeze tempered by the newly installed window screen. She remembered the ladder still out next to the house. Darn, she'd have to ask Nick to put it away tomorrow.

At the doorway, she glanced around the room to be sure all was in order. Her eyes settled on Davy's unpacked bag. She sighed, deciding to leave the bag until morning. After toying with turning off the baby monitor, she dismissed the idea. Nick would have a fit if the device was off. Rightly so. Experience made him cautious. They both knew that some bad things were beyond their control. She left it on.

Her phone vibrated in her pocket. A text from Gareth. 'Granados said Des told him about Houston, Mejia and Renton pulling the job. Call me when you can.'

"What the hell, Gareth?"

"Yeah, unbelievable." Gareth snorted in disgust at Des' overt violation of the blue code—the unwritten standard that governed cop behavior; the code that drove decision-making expected loyalty to the law, his community, and his peers. Loyalty to the community in this case meant not revealing confidential information carelessly—you never knew who would take advantage of it. Jamie had told Desmond what Terence said about the Bay City Movers. Terence violated the community's trust with a lack of discretion. If Terence hadn't told Jamie, Desmond wouldn't have snatched up the opportunity with Jamie.

"Granados said Desmond was one of the first patrol units on scene after the shooting. Desmond found Granados—he went looking for him, Meredith. How did Desmond know who the money belonged to? Everything, including the truck, was unmarked."

"Didn't the courier truck's license plate return to the business?"

"No. Registration returned to a shell company with a PO Box address. There was nothing to tie the vehicle or the driver to the business—no paper trail, anyway."

The sheer, glaring evil was astounding. A pig, Desmond violated everyone's trust.

"But why? I can't see why—"

"I'll get Des in here tomorrow and we'll find out."

"Jeez, it's hard to believe even a jerk like Desmond would betray his department, his friends for a woman, particularly Brenda."

"I'll keep you posted. Oh, by the way: It's a dead-end trying to get prints from the horse show ribbon. Too degraded."

"Crap. But thanks for trying." She disconnected.

Meredith wrestled with calling Nick to update him but decided to wait until he got home. She was pleased that Gareth was going to follow up with Desmond. Telling a victim who committed the crime was always a mistake, but this was the exception to the rule; Des betrayed everyone and facilitated the entire caper. Not to mention, the victim was a gangster with something to prove.

A minute later Meredith sat at the kitchen table, a steaming cup of coffee beside her laptop. Her fingers flew over the keyboard as she created a synopsis of what had happened, from the robbery/homicide in 2001 until today.

Jamie steals Terence's duty weapon early May 2001

Robbery/homicide May 2001 of gang courier in SF

Missing persons reports Renton and Mejia May 2001

Jamie arrested June 2001

Terence relieved of Mounted Patrol, put on a desk June 2001

Terence's sidearm confiscated and logged into evidence July 2001

Terence's official retirement date August 1, 2001

Jamie convicted for 211PC, sentenced to prison March 2002 served 16 of a 20-year sentence.

Terence hospitalized December 2002.

Jamie paroled April 14, 2018.

Terence Ryan died May 30, 2018. Natural causes.

Focusing on the details of Jamie's parole, it took her a second to register sounds coming from the back of the house. The window? But it wasn't the back porch window.

The baby monitor. Davy!

Meredith reached to her hip for the Glock. Locked in the gun safe. Damn, right where she had put it. The reedy sound of rustling came from his room, maybe bed clothes moving around. It echoed oddly from the kitchen speaker.

She listened to the sounds in her house as she crept down the hall, willing her eyes to adjust to the darkness faster.

Davy groaned.

Holding her breath and wishing she had her Glock, Meredith rounded the doorway.

Screen gone, a solidly built woman stood inside the room at the wide-open window. With Meredith's sleepy son slung over a shoulder, the woman dropped the baby's bag to someone below. That damn ladder was still up.

The woman cocked her ear—she'd heard Meredith. In a fluid motion, the woman swung the sleepy toddler toward the window. Ramona—from Desmond's bar.

With a split second to decide, Meredith chose the lesser of evils. She launched herself across the room and into the woman, reaching for her son. He slipped from her grasp and fell. Davy landed on the floor with a grunt, then erupted into a wail as he tumbled in a heap beneath the window. Meredith pushed him away from the window—out of the woman's reach—then grabbed Ramona's arm. Davy screamed. Meredith didn't have time to react.

Ramona rose and grabbed Meredith's neck with both hands. Meredith swung both arms in a windmill rotation from below that knocked the woman's hands away. This old-school move had served her well on the street more than a few times. Physical fighting wasn't new to Meredith after seven years in patrol. But this was different—her child was at stake.

Ramona leaned back toward the window, but Meredith grabbed both arms. At the sill, Ramona braced herself, then using her feet, shoved Meredith through the window.

Meredith felt weightless as she plunged into the dark. A frightening disorientation threatened until she heard her son screaming for her. Snapping to, she twisted to lean into the fall as she'd learned to fall from a horse. But there wasn't enough time. Pain shot through her as one hip banged into the aluminum ladder still propped against the house.

Meredith landed on her back with a thud, the hard patio concrete knocking the breath out of her. Davy's wailing cut through her shock. Davy. She must catch her breath, to save Davy. Where did the cop-thinking end and the mom-thinking begin?

Nearby, a man's voice, familiar but sharper. She'd heard that tone once before. Desmond. "Get back in there and get that kid."

From the window, Ramona cursed at him and ducked into the bedroom.

Meredith twisted, trying to get up, intending to stand and face Desmond. But a heavy boot slammed across her neck, pinning her to the concrete. The weight cut off her breathing—already uneven. Damn, she'd been complacent in underestimating Desmond's threat.

"Hurry up," he shouted to Ramona. Then to Meredith, "Tell me where the money is and I call this whole thing off."

Damn the money. He mashed her cheek into the patio. She struggled to reply. "Money's gone." She heard the front screen door slam shut. Ramona had gotten Davy out of the house.

NO.

"You fuckin' liar. You want it for yourself." Desmond had to be off-balance, with some of his weight resting on her neck. Not knowing where the strength came from, she found enough to swing a fist at the back of Desmond's knee. Buckling, he stumbled away, but just three steps.

Meredith gulped air, swallowing in great, huge mouthfuls. Then, she heard the woman's shout. "C'mon on!"

Desmond recovered and kicked at Meredith, the strike glancing off her shoulder.

Shards of pain flashed through her even as Desmond scrambled off. It was as if her life was showing on two screens, one with stars above in a peaceful night; the other with Davy's distant screams while some low-life scum kidnapped him.

The thought brought her to her knees. Dizzy, she grabbed a trellis to steady her.

"Mere, what the hell's going—"

Nick. Above, Nick shouted at her from Davy's open window.

Meredith pulled together all her energy and rasped, "They've got Davy."

CHAPTER SEVENTY-TWO

Nick jumped from the window, the six-foot drop giving him time to anticipate his landing. Keeping his knees flexed, he landed hard on his left hip, but rolled upright beside Meredith. He gripped her arm as she struggled to her feet—coughing, rubbing her throat.

He put a hand on her shoulder, then in the dim light saw the scuffs and scratches that tracked across her neck. She'd been fighting. "You okay?"

She gulped in a breath, nodding. Her arm flung out toward the street, where Desmond and the woman were running toward a parked car across the street. "Go. Desmond has Davy," she croaked.

But Nick was already in motion. He put his hand on his right hip, feeling for his Glock. Satisfied, he kept it holstered. He wouldn't endanger his son. He couldn't lose another child.

Nick ran as if his life depended on it. He sprinted over the grass, took the hedge in a leap, skipped over the walkway to the fence and through the small gate. His legs pumped over the neighbor's front lawn toward Melvin Street. Thank God he had the advantage of knowing the neighborhood terrain.

Mere yelled behind him. He hoped she'd called for help—this was going south quick. Springing over a short hedge, Nick caught sight of Desmond. Across the street, Des stood by the open. driver's side door of an old Corolla, pointing a handgun at him. Nick saw the flash as he ducked and felt a red-hot jab of pain above his elbow. The impact felt like a knife slice as he dropped to his knee.

Righting himself and ignoring the pain he re-oriented to the target. He got up and ran on. "Oh no you don't," Nick shouted. No way this scumbag takes our son. No way.

Behind him he heard Meredith calling for Davy. She was following. Relief washed over him. She had his back.

Together they'd get their baby back. Together—like they did everything.

CHAPTER SEVENTY-THREE

Meredith knew Desmond wouldn't hesitate to kill Nick. There was no need to keep her husband alive; Des only needed her and Davy. Her heart froze when she saw the man raise a small revolver. The blast sent shockwaves through her. Nick jerked sideways and went down to a knee as the round struck him. By the way his arm dropped, he'd been hit, maybe in the arm. Only when he got to his feet and took up the pursuit again was she able to take a breath.

Nick kept moving toward Desmond, trying to run but not having the energy. The older man fired again, missing. Meredith heard a plunk when the round hit a parked car to her right. With his off hand, Nick pulled his Glock. "Put the gun down, Desmond." To Meredith's relief, Nick side-stepped to take Davy out of his sights. Damn, she wished she'd had time to get her Glock.

Des waved him off, a farmer swatting a pesky fly. "I want the money. I get that, and you get the kid back."

Nick yelled across the road, "The money is in police evidence. We've had it since yesterday."

Desmond's furious scream shattered the night, "Liar."

Then, she heard distant sirens. Meredith turned, scanning the area for the blonde woman carrying Davy. She heard the baby's cries coming from the Corolla. Ramona was holding him in the front seat. No, wrestling with him. Her boy was putting up a good fight.

Sirens grew louder. Help was on the way.

But Desmond heard it, too. "Get the woman," Des shouted to Ramona, rushing Nick.

No need. Meredith, the woman was sprinting toward the Corolla. Meredith saw the two men rolling around on the asphalt. She heard her husband grunt, then a thump.

The blonde tossed Davy into the back seat. She opened the console in the front, then met Meredith on the sidewalk, a small .22 revolver in hand. "Get in the car."

Davy tried crawling between the seats to get up front. She had to get him to safety.

At Meredith's hesitation, the blonde grabbed her arm, twisting around. The gun moved away from her field of vision. Then the barrel tip jabbed the skin under her jawbone.

Damn, that hurt.

"Get in the fuckin' car."

**

Meredith crawled in behind the driver's seat, pulling Davy towards her. Her arms encircled him as she watched Ramona stow the handgun in the console. Having seen the weapon, Meredith knew an equal threat would come from Ramona. She glanced out the window looking for Nick.

On the asphalt behind Des, Nick rolled onto his side with a fist clamped across his chest holding his bloody forearm. He'd been hit.

"Nick!"

Des stood and broke into a run to the Corolla, shoving his gun into his front pants pocket. At the passenger door, he slid inside and yelled, "Move!"

Ramona slammed the idling car into gear, and they lurched forward. The woman's knuckles whitened as she gripped the wheel. Her foot jammed the accelerator, sending Meredith sprawling across the back seat as they sped off, turning left toward town. Davy whimpered in his mother's arms. His big brown eyes, so like his father's, caught movement and his head swiveled toward it. Confused by the car's sudden lurching, he broke into a sob.

Des hollered, "Slow down before you wreck the fuckin' car, stupid."

Ramona braked. A Petaluma PD marked unit approaching from Dana Street, the opposite direction, shut down the siren and slowed to the curb three houses away from the Reyes home. Looking out the back window as the Corolla drove off, Meredith prayed PPD would find Nick in the street and get him help.

"Turn right," Des yelled at Ramona, then softer, in that

fake Irish brogue. "Stop with lights out. Everybody get down." The front head rests had been removed. They had to hunker down to hide. Meredith ignored his orders and held her son close.

Davy changed everything. She'd wrestled drunks by herself before and wasn't afraid to fight. But her son's proximity made her consider every possible action. What could happen? She had to be careful.

"Now drive up the hill," Des ordered. The road was an old narrow street leading to La Cresta Ridge. Little illumination fell from the retrofitted streetlights.

Three police units, darkened and silent, turned right to the opposite side of Melvin Street—100 feet away from where the Corolla had pulled over. From the sirens in the distance, more were coming.

With an exasperated sigh, Des whispered to Ramona. "Go on up the hill a bit more." He pulled out his phone and studied the map on the screen. "We won't be able to get down this way—too damn many streets that wind around." He decided. "Back down the hill and turn right at Webster."

"You'll have to tell me when to turn. I'm too busy driving," Ramona groused. She turned right on Webster when told to. They passed Bassett Street, ramped up to 50 mph on the long block of Webster. A right turn that led to the dogleg around Petaluma High School and up to Pearce Street. Slowing to 20 mph to negotiate a narrow one-way street then careening around the corners, they turned onto B Street, then to El Rose Drive. Ramona was getting frazzled, her driving skills deteriorating, not trusting Des' directions. Reaching D Street, she stopped, in a panic. "Where the hell are we? Where's the fucking highway?"

"Trust me."

"Are you kidding?" Ramona choked out an ugly laugh. "You don't even know where we are. A measly five grand ain't worth it, old boy. I should kick your wrinkled old ass outta this car."

"Big talk, girlie," Desmond sneered. "You're in this up to your neck. Now drive."

In the back seat, Meredith tested the door handle, thinking she and Davy could make a run for it. No luck, the child safety lock prevented the door from opening. Pushing away all the horrible situations that came to mind, she redirected her focus to her son's safety. She must keep him safe until she could do something to get help. And she'd figure something out. No way was she going to wait for Desmond. Who knew what he had in mind?

Davy whimpered at the harsh voices from the front seat. Meredith belted him in. It would have to do. Even though Davy was small, there was little space for her to maneuver.

She had an idea and would have to make it happen soon.

Des pointed suddenly. "This should be D Street. Turn left." He turned his phone upside down and shouted, "Fuck. You turned the wrong way."

"Asshole, you told me to go down here." Ramona swerved to the curb, setting up to pull a U-turn.

"Headlights. Stay where you are. Lights out!"

A sheriff's marked SUV barreled down D Street past them, silent but with the light bar flashing its urgency. As it passed, Meredith peered out the side window, catching a glimpse of the driver. A grim-faced Evelina.

Damn.

"Now move out," Des snapped. "Turn around and go up the hill."

Tires screeched behind them. Meredith's breath caught as Ramona jammed on the accelerator and flipped a U-turn.

Evelina had seen them. The Sheriff's SUV was turning around.

CHAPTER SEVENTY-FOUR

Nick's head bounced off the asphalt when he fell. Road rash grated on his forehead and the warm trickle of blood tracked down his face. Fighting to clear his mind, he winced as he rolled over onto his back. He did a quick wound inventory. He felt like someone had sliced his forearm. Ah, it hurt like a sonofabitch. The bullet had cut through, but he still had one good arm.

"Nick, are you hit?" Someone asked.

When he could answer, he said, "Right arm."

"Jesus," Patricia Doran whispered. "Take it easy, Nick."

"They've got my wife and baby." Nick rolled over, getting to a knee. Someone said an ambulance was on the way. "No ambulance. Help me up."

Strong hands pulled him to his feet. His skull hurt, but his arm throbbed. He looked at the Petaluma officer who'd helped him. Officer Doran and another PPD cop stood by, patrol cars parked a half block away. Kyle Lockford, one of the two sheriff's deputies assigned to the south county, skidded to a stop ten feet away, slamming the transmission into park. He ran to Nick and inspected him, focusing on the small trail of blood from Nick's head. Nick gasped as the deputy touched his blood-soaked sweatshirt sleeve. It didn't matter. He had to move fast.

"Wait," Doran flicked on a flashlight. "You're hit. Let me see your arm."

Nick pushed the officer's hands away. "They've got Meredith and my boy." Nick pulled his shirt back in place. Ignoring the stabbing pain, he turned to Lockford. "They're in an older model gold Toyota Corolla sedan; three aboard and a baby. Driver's a white female, blonde, 40's maybe; passenger's white male, 60's with white hair." Nick shouted at Doran, "Get that on the air. They just left on Melvin to English Street, less than two ago and my wife and son are hostages."

Lockford leaned into his car and grabbed the mic. Following instructions, the deputy updated dispatch. Nick heard Lockford's suspect broadcast coming from the Petaluma units a split second after he put it out—all the PPD cars had the SO channel selected.

On the radio, a female deputy's voice spoke up. "Sheriff's one, George 20," Evelina. "I just saw that vehicle, blacked out, turning onto D Street from El Rose. I'm trying to catch up to it now."

Nick closed the ten feet to Lockford's unit in less time than it took to tell. Grabbing the steering wheel, he threw the gearshift into Reverse, flipped a U-turn and jammed on the accelerator. Lockford barely made it into the passenger seat.

Patricia Doran yelled as they passed her patrol car. "Nick, wait a minute." She sprinted the five feet to her car and popped the trunk as Nick slowed. She threw Nick a tactical vest through his open window. "Take this. It's made for a woman, but it'll do the job."

Nick caught it and wrestled the vest's Velcro straps around his upper body while Lockford grappled the wheel from the passenger seat. Nick was on the gas pedal before Doran's smile reached her eyes. He sped down the street.

CHAPTER SEVENTY-FIVE

Desmond's aggravation was growing. "Get moving." He stared at his phone.

"I thought the highway was the other direction." Ramona swore as she flipped on the headlights. "Put that thing away. You're hopeless. You can't read a map, much less work your phone."

"Just go straight here. It'll get us to onto back roads that'll go to the highway."

Ramona jammed the accelerator, jerking Meredith in the back seat. Her moment had passed. She couldn't do what she'd planned, because now they were moving, building up speed.

Maybe he'd listen to reason. "Uncle Desmond?"

"Shut-the-fuck-up." Not a trace of the brogue.

"You know how this will end—with you in the hospital, prison, or dead." She grabbed the small door-mounted armrest, trying to stabilize herself. "You can't win."

Davy's face scrunched, frightened by the yelling and the motion of the car. He was scared, and tears threatened. She was surprised he didn't cry. He certainly had a double dose of cop genes. Meredith wanted to hold him, soothe him, but he was safer belted in. Besides, she had to be ready.

"Desmond, it's the money you want—" Meredith's voice faded. Des was focused on the road. They were just outside the Petaluma City Limits, going into the country. Meredith knew D Street—bucolic in the daytime with lush green dairy pastures on both sides. Deceptively twisted roads made driving a challenge during the day. The rural road had no streetlights, making travel even riskier after dark.

Des was giving orders. "Watch out for the ditch on the side, there's no curb." Then, "Put on your high beams."

"Desmond." Ramona yelled. "I'll drive. You talk to the bitch in the back seat. She knows where the money is."

Desmond raised his eyes from the road, glancing to the

side-view mirror. "Fuck me, a cop's following us. Step on it."

CHAPTER SEVENTY-SIX

Nick had Lockford call dispatch to inform them they were on their way to back up the primary pursuit unit—Deputy Evelina Marquez. Lockford handled the radio while Nick drove one-handed. They listened to Evelina broadcast her pursuit of the kidnapping vehicle, their location and speed. Nick's indignation spiked when she used the term, "victims" for Meredith and Davy, instead of using their identities. Sensible, but he didn't want to think of Meredith as a victim. And he sure as hell didn't want to picture his son as such. Anger would do him no good. He shut the feeling down and went into work mode.

Within minutes, Nick had spotted Evelina's patrol unit. A half mile in front of her, taillights were visible. Even at that distance he was sure they were from the Corolla. There hadn't been any other traffic on the road.

They followed. Nick steered the Ford with a passion, knowing that failure wasn't allowed. The Ford Police Interceptor 3.5-liter engine roared all 280 horsepower into the straightaways, screeching to slow around corners, as he followed Evelina as close as he dared.

Evelina's SUV slowed. Lockford updated dispatch. "They're westbound D Street, just passing city limits. Notify Marin County SO and CHP. Speed up to about 60 now."

The calm voice of the dispatcher, replied, "already done. We're updating them with locations. They're trying to get into position for a spike strip."

Nick's heart froze. A car could still roll after tearing through spike strips. The possibility of a wreck increased. He grabbed the mic. "Tell them to hold off on that. The two victims are a Sonoma deputy and her son." He almost choked on the words.

A pause. "1David Six?" Meredith's call sign.

Nick sighed. "Affirm."

"Copy, we'll update allied agencies with this info."

Using the right-hand spotlight, Lockford got a bearing from an address marker. "Passing 4421 D Street now, speeds up to 65, no traffic." In the darkness, Nick saw the taillights ahead. Between the Corolla and Evelina's unit was another country block and a road leading up the hill to a housing tract. They entered the county jurisdiction now, an area filled with winding narrow roads bordered by cattle pastures. Not that it made any difference. He'd keep after the Corolla until he had Meredith and Davy safe. "See if you can get CHP to set up a roadblock before San Antonio Road." Nick wasn't sure of the road configuration because of the construction, but he'd seen the San Antonio Road exit off 101. It was a safer stretch for a spike strip, although he doubted anyone could get into position in time.

"Fuck," Nick whispered as they rounded a curve, losing the taillights. He caught them, then lost them again below a hill. He leaned forward, as if his anxiety could push him in front of the Corolla.

CHAPTER SEVENTY-SEVEN

"Desmond—" Meredith pleaded.

He turned toward her. Desmond's twisted face was illuminated by the blue and red light from the Sheriff's unit behind. "Where's the fuckin' money?"

"It was with the bodies of the guys who pulled the robbery. We found it all in a storage unit in Santa Rosa." She felt more than a little satisfaction in telling him. "Terence lied to Jamie—told him that he'd move it. Not that Jamie knew where the storage unit was."

Des stared at her, not moving. Silent.

"You've got nothing to gain here, Desmond." She tried another tactic—flattery. "C'mon. You're smarter than this. You know how this plays out. It won't be good for you—or Ramona."

Meredith saw a crack in his arrogance—was it desperation? "Just pull over. It'll go easier for you if you let us out."

He half-turned and hit the console with his fist, his fury palpable. Then, he kicked at the dashboard, snapping the brittle plastic.

"What do we do now?" Ramona screamed. She took her eyes off the road, her foot off the accelerator, her voice rising. "You told me this was going to be easy money. You're a fucking idiot."

"Shut up, Ramona." Des shouted.

"You better come up with some way to get us out of this mess, Des." With a quick glance at the road ahead, she slapped Desmond's chest. "You're nothing but a bullshitter, Des Rollins. Look what you've gotten me into. My probation officer hears about this and I'm back in jail. Des? Are you listening? How the fuck're you going to get us out of this?"

Meredith knew what she was going to do. The road ahead was dark, but she'd been watching and was familiar with the twists and turns of this road. They'd been rising to a knoll. Meredith could just make out the shadows of a eucalyptus grove on the downhill side. There'd be a fenced slope on the other side.

The car slowed against the inertia of climbing a hill with weak acceleration.

She might not get another chance.

The Corolla was small enough that Meredith could reach as far she needed. She braced herself against the back seat. Lifting her legs, she kicked a heel against Ramona's head. The other foot jammed against Des'.

The car slowed as the Ramona's head slammed against the steering wheel. Ramona sighed—out cold and laying limp against the driver door.

Now, for Des. Shaking his head, he'd reached one hand for the steering wheel, trying to control the driverless vehicle. The other hand grabbed at Meredith.

Wedging her body weight against the back seat, she kicked at Desmond's head with all her strength. Her foot met Des' jaw, snapping his head back.

Recovering—not showing pain—he grabbed at Meredith's foot, latching on with a firm grip. She wriggled loose, pushing on his shoulder with her other foot. Then, she leaned over Ramona, stretching for the wheel to steer the decelerating car into the ditch.

Desmond reached for Meredith again as the car slammed to stop against a wooden fence post. She fell against him. He gripped her—one shoulder and a handful of hair. As his fingers dug in, Meredith shouted in frustration and pain at being pinned. Writhing loose, she found Desmond too close for her to get another kick in.

CHAPTER SEVENTY-EIGHT

Meredith launched herself between the front seats. Her sore hip banged the console—Ramona's gun was still inside—as her hands found Desmond's head. Ignoring the pain, she slammed him against the side window. This was an all-or-nothing fight. As far as she knew, Des still had his handgun in his pocket. Davy screamed, calling for his mother, adding to the chaos. The car interior was lit up like daylight, with wailing sirens approaching.

Help was near.

Desmond shook his head, stunned, and leaned his shoulder against the door window. He threw clumsy slaps at Meredith as she tried to restrain him. Suddenly, the door behind him fell open. Desmond spilled out to the road, twisting face down, hands beneath him.

Meredith struggled to right herself halfway into the front seat. She heard someone yelling warnings—Evelina had opened the door, her weapon drawn. "Let me see your hands—empty hands! Show me your hands!"

"Gun in front right pocket," Meredith shouted. She kept her eyes on Desmond. He raised his head; his mouth was a grim line of anger. But his sharp gray eyes had already made an assessment—he was cornered. Still, Meredith didn't trust that he knew he was defeated. She eased out of the car to stand beside him. "Put out your hands and you won't get shot, Desmond."

Des lifted a shoulder and pulled out one hand, laying it flat on the asphalt. Then the other. No gun. Meredith stepped aside while Evelina holstered her weapon. The deputy bent to roll him over and reached out to snap on the handcuffs with a satisfying click.

Meredith glanced back at Davy, who had quieted but was still calling for his mommy.

From the Corolla, a moan. Crap, Ramona.

Meredith whirled and faced the woman in the car. The

console snapped open. Ramona pulled the small revolver from inside. The 2" barrel wavered as she focused on a target.

Meredith.

"Gun," Meredith shouted.

Somewhere in the background, tires scrabbled against the road's small shoulder. Foot falls, people running. Meredith didn't dare look away. "Evelina," she warned the deputy.

Then Nick was there, diving in front of her.

A shot rang out, a blast that filled the small space of the car and overflowed outside. The bullet knocked Nick backward into Meredith, who fell on top of Desmond.

Stunned, Meredith scrambled to her feet. She grabbed at Nick and, grasping the vest's shoulder straps, pulled him to the side of the road and out of range. She went to her knees and tugged him to her lap. Outside her mind, she heard Davy screaming again. Another round, then two, three.

Evelina had fired at Ramona. Voices shouting. "Shit, shit," from Ramona. Then someone telling Ramona to drop on the ground, another shout, "Gun!" The sound of a fist on flesh, and yet more approaching sirens.

"Nick."

CHAPTER SEVENTY-NINE

Nick was dizzy with pain. He remembered the shot, the woman in the car. He didn't feel blood. The vest! His wife's face loomed over his own. He squinted to focus. Had he lost consciousness? No, just disoriented, he thought. Damn, he must be down. He inhaled. A sharp pain sliced through his sternum.

"Fuck," he hissed, rolling over into a ball. "Uh, God. That hurts." Was that Davy fussing? He couldn't see his son.

Meredith stroked his forehead, whispering, "The ambulance is on the way."

"Davy." Nick struggled to his elbow. "Where's Davy?"

"He's right here, Nick." From behind, Patricia Doran leaned into Meredith, then passed Davy to her waiting arms. Doran had kept the boy turned away while his father lay on the ground. Now, Meredith swiveled so Nick could view his son. Davy's eyes were red and puffy, but when he saw his daddy, his face split open with a smile.

"You're going to be fine, Sarge," Lockwood said. "The vest saved you."

"Christ. It doesn't feel like it. I got shot twice tonight."

The Petaluma Fire Department ambulance pulled up, guided in by a deputy. Meredith and Davy moved aside so the paramedics could treat Nick. He answered the questions he'd heard asked of others so many times, then watched his family standing by quietly as he was loaded into the ambulance. Meredith shouted over the engine, "I'll see you at the hospital. I'm getting a ride from Lieutenant Lyons from Petaluma PD."

Davy snuffled into her T-shirt as she turned away.

CHAPTER EIGHTY

Lockford had Ramona handcuffed and laying on a gurney in the second ambulance. Desmond was cuffed and locked up in Evelina's vehicle. Meredith took a moment to get Lockford's attention. "Thanks for securing her."

"Lucky for her Marquez' a crummy shot. She's got nothing but flying glass wounds. The tall deputy smiled. "Besides, you did all the hard work."

Meredith shrugged. Credit didn't matter. What mattered was her son, safe in her arms. And Nick, too, safe in the back of the ambulance.

The dark-haired Petaluma PD Lieutenant, tall and sharp-looking in his neatly pressed uniform, walked toward her. "Ready to go to PVH? I've got a car seat for the little guy all hooked up." Petaluma Valley Hospital had the closest emergency room.

She had something else to do. She held up two fingers. She needed two minutes. Stiffening, bracing herself, she turned. "Evelina?" For an odd moment, while Meredith's brain tried to put off what she needed to say, she noticed how pretty the woman was. Evelina's eyes widened—just a little, in expectation of what?

"I want to thank you for this." Meredith nodded to Desmond, sulking in the back seat of the SUV.

"Just doing my job." Evelina's smile was tight. She flipped her notebook closed and stuffed it in a breast pocket. Meredith's own tension made it easy to see the deputy was still pumping adrenaline.

Meredith weighed getting personal; trying to express her gratitude or complimenting the deputy on a well-done job, but finally turned away. Her emotions were a jumble. She was furious at Evelina's past behavior, but she'd saved their lives. Meredith figured she'd said enough.

"Wait." Evelina's hand landed on Meredith's forearm. They both looked down at the hand. Evelina jerked it away.

"Wait a minute."

As Meredith turned to listen, Davy's head wobbled in sleep. Meredith pulled her arm away and braced it on Davy's back to keep him stable.

"Meredith, I need to say this to you." Evelina met Meredith's gaze. "I made a big mistake—before." She seemed to search for the right words but failed.

Meredith resisted the impulse to sock her in the jaw. She took a moment before replying. Was she really sorry? Or just sorry she got caught? In the end, nothing would absolve Evelina, but the damage was done to all women in the profession. Meredith couldn't say she'd suffered from Evelina's actions. But chasing a married man around was bad enough. Chasing a man married to a co-worker was heinous. She finally said, "Look, what you did cheapened the profession, but especially for women in law enforcement. We fight and hold on by our fingernails to do a dirty job that is also a noble profession. We get enough flak from the public, not to mention the dinosaurs in the department who doubt our ability. To have one of our own devalue my position reflects badly on all women law officers. I'm embarrassed for you."

Evelina's jaw jutted out. "I was wrong, I know."

Meredith couldn't find anything to excuse the deputy's actions. In the end, she said. "Yes, you were. You made a big mistake." A glimmer of compassion waggled through her brain. Should she let Evelina see it?

"I never knew anyone who'd take a bullet for the woman he loved." Evelina's face broke open in soul-wrenching candor. "I can't compete with that."

Davy's head rested on her shoulder. "No, you can't." Would Evelina ever get it? Maybe someday she'd see the honor in her profession—not just a place to rock and roll, then find a husband. Maybe she'd see that she was held to a higher standard by the public, her administration and profession and herself. Maybe not, but Meredith had done what she could. She extended her hand. "Peace?"

The deputy smiled tenuously, taking Meredith's.

"Peace."

Meredith tightened her grip, yanking Evelina close. Their noses almost touched. "We won't ever speak of this again. It's history from this moment on." Meredith's eyes narrowed. "But you will never get close to my husband again. Understand?"

Evelina's eyes widened. She tried to pull away, but Meredith doubled down on her grip. "Do you understand?"

The deputy nodded, struggling to keep the shock out of her face. Meredith released her grip, turned and walked away.

CHAPTER EIGHTY-ONE

"I'm so very sorry for your loss." Donna Moran slipped an arm around Meredith's shoulder, cutting off her own expression of sympathy. "I understand you just lost your father." The widow's smile was sincere, her eyes filled with understanding. She hadn't known Terence. She hadn't known about Terence. But she'd heard her friend had lost her father within days of her own.

How like Donna to put others before her own grief.

"Thank you, Donna." Meredith looked into Donna's reddened eyes. "I wish there was something I could say or do to ease your pain. Please know that Nick and I are here for you."

The funeral was not a line of duty service but was executed with the same reverence. Eddie Moran had been a respected member of the Sonoma County Law Enforcement community and his department and colleagues honored him as such. Almost a thousand emergency workers attended, standing at attention for the hearse bearing the casket.

Inside St. Eugene's Catholic Church on a dais to one side of the altar, Nick stood beside the sheriff, undersheriff, and three captains. As the priests said Mass, each man carried the weight of guilt and grief over the loss of their brother. All were proud to honor their friend, unabashed at the pain on their faces as Nick got ready to deliver the eulogy.

He rose to the podium. He'd been up most of the night preparing for it. Strain lined his face, and his eyes were still red. He began, "Monsignor Nelson. Father Chavez. Sheriff Flannery. To Eddie's wife, Donna and children, Amber and Jason. And to all the members of Eddie's family. On behalf of the Sonoma County Sheriff's Office I extend our deepest condolences to you.

"Today, as we honor the memory of Edward Moran, we recall the words engraved on the national law enforcement memorial in Washington D.C.: "it is not how these officers died that made them heroes; it is how they lived."

Sadness shook Nick's body. He took a second, then resumed. "Eddie lived a life full of passion for his family, for his friends, and for his fellow officers. He could be counted to defend the weak against the strong and to fight for what was right. He believed good should prevail over evil, and he worked to make it so. Other deputies felt safer knowing Eddie had their back. He was the guy you wanted to show up if one of your family members ever needed help. He loved this life, his career, his people.

"I'd like to illustrate something about Eddie's life, if you'll bear with me a few seconds. Would everyone here who serve public safety please raise your hands." The room blossomed with hands.

"Eddie shared some of the same characteristics of those of you with raised hands. He was unique because of his dedication and self-imposed standards. It's hard, demanding work.

"So, what makes a person do this for a living? If you know this is how it ends, why bother to show up? Police officers, sheriff's deputies, firefighters, highway patrol, dispatchers, and medics will say this is why people like Eddie come to work every day: because they know there are people who depend on them. You know you make a difference in lives that would otherwise be filled with chaos. You honestly care about the welfare of others." Nick's voice quivered. "Don't forget for a moment why you signed on."

"Donna, Amber, and Jason, please stand and look around the room at these men and women with their hands up. Don't just look at the number of people. Look into their eyes. They signed on because they care, about the public and about their own family. Know that they will always be there for you. It is who we are. It is what we do, and Eddie will always be a part of this family.

"Please remember that Eddie Moran sits in Heaven to watch over us and guide us for all of our days. In closing, I'd like to quote from Jesus Christ's Sermon on the Mount, one of the Beatitudes, from Matthew 5:9: 'Blessed are the peacemakers, for they shall be called the children of God.' May God bless his family and bless and protect his fellow officers."

CHAPTER EIGHTY-TWO

A light breeze riffled through the oak leaves sheltering the food-laden table in the yard of the Cavanaugh Ranch. It was dinner time, four days after the arrests. The family, including Christy and Gareth and his wife, Jenna, gathered in a sort of celebration. Although not decorated with balloons and party-favors, it was manifestly a feast. Everyone wore smiles—even crusty old Raymond Cavanaugh.

Cavanaugh took off his Stetson, laying it carefully on a clean area of the brick barbeque behind him. He sat down at the head of the redwood picnic table with family and friends surrounding him. Filomena bustled from the kitchen to the patio, bringing out the last of the condiments. Nick's bandaged forearm barely slowed him from pulling the steaks off the Traeger, then divvying them up according to preferences. When done, he slid beside Jake to face Meredith. Filomena took a seat and said, "Can I say grace?"

At Cavanaugh's nod, Filomena and Nick crossed themselves. "Dear Lord, thank you for the blessings you have given this family—all of us." She sneaked a smile and a glance at everyone around this table, with three families represented. "Thank you for our *patrón*, Mr. Raymond and his grandson, Jake, nephew Gareth and wife Jenna Cavanaugh. Thank you for the Reyes family—for their safety during the past dark days, good friend Christy Ryan, and thank you for my boys, who are all healthy and happy. Bless us, O Lord, and these thy gifts which we are about to receive from thy bounty through Christ, Our Lord. Amen."

The table erupted in a cheery "Amen," and "Pass the potato salad."

Thirty minutes later, Jake tipped his chair back and burped. "I'm done."

With a growl, Cav threw a soiled bar towel at him. "There are ladies present."

Davy wriggled off Meredith's lap and, hanging on to

those seated between, waddled to Cav. The baby put his arms up in childish supplication for a lap to loll around on. Cav smiled and picked him up.

Jake sat up, a grin across his freckled face. He tossed the towel back at his Grandpa. "Mere, okay if I take Davy for a ride on Rocket? I'll stay in the pen, I promise."

"I need to clean him up first." Meredith looked at the mustard on her child's face, thought about what she said, then laughed. "Forget that. A little horse dirt might do him good." Davy had been clingy since his abduction, uncertain about new people and situations. But this was Jake, and they were at the Cavanaugh Ranch—their second home. Davy loved horses, too. Jake scooped up the boy and headed for the barn. He'd be fine.

"I can give the little man a bath after his horsey ride." Filomena jumped up from the table, gathering empty plates.

"I'll help you in the kitchen, Filomena." Jenna waved to Meredith and the men. "That'll give you guys time to fill Cav in." Christy stood. "I'll help, too." Filomena nodded her thanks and loaded dishes into Jenna's and Christy's arms. The three walked off to the house.

Cav rose, stretching his back. He reached in a cooler and pulled out three Pacificos, handing one to Nick, another to Gareth and keeping one for himself.

Meredith tipped her iced tea toward them in a mock toast. "Let's go sit in the shade by the pool."

Cav leaned into a green metal patio chair, old enough to be an antique. "So, how'd they figure out which car you were kidnapped in?" Meredith smiled as she saw Cavanaugh settling in for the long haul. He had questions, Nick, Meredith and Gareth had answers.

"Evelina—the deputy with a crush on Nick—she saw me in Ramona's car. I looked out the window to see where we were when she drove by."

He nodded, his lips thinning with understanding. "I'm glad Gareth could help out."

Gareth tipped his beer at his uncle. "Me, too. I cleared a cold case and two more homicides."

Nick chuckled at Gareth. "Good for stats, no?"

Gareth had an answer for that. "You two did most of the hard work."

Meredith said, "Still, you made things happen that we couldn't have. Can you answer this: Did Desmond say why he gave up Jamie to Granados?"

"He's lawyered up. I can only speculate—with Jamie out of the way, he'd have a chance to win Brenda's attention again." He shrugged. "The crew was just collateral damage."

"Damn." Nick grimaced.

Gareth continued, "Desmond knew who the robbery victim was, because he'd set up the whole thing. Terence's indiscretion by mentioning it in passing to Jamie instigated the whole mess. Terence figured it was his mistake out and had to do something, so he helped conceal the homicides. But Des orchestrated the robbery. Then Jamie got the rap, Terence got forced out and Des let them take the fall."

"Some friend," Cav said.

They were silent as they listened to Davy's baby belly-laughs in the distance. Jake was taking good care of him. Meredith sighed, as content as she'd ever been, even after the drama of the past several days—the threat to their son, the discovery of two bodies in a storage unit rented to her father, the exposure of Terence's involvement in the homicides, and just this morning, the funeral of their good friend, Eddie Moran.

Meredith saw Cavanaugh eyeing her. She knew a provocative question was coming. He squinted like that if he had something important to say.

"Tell me, then, Meredith. Did you get the answers you wanted about your father?"

She'd been thinking about little else in the time since their abduction. Her face scrunched up. "There's no clear answer," she said, more to herself than anyone. She took a second, then looked at them. "I suspect I know why he left our family. Mom was very strict, with little tolerance for mistakes. She wouldn't have forgiven him his indiscretion with Brenda. I have this ugly thought that Jamie and I might be related. But Brenda's not talking." She considered it all for a moment. "I'll never know what he saw in that woman."

"She must've had something on them both. Why Terence stuck with her is a real puzzle. Then, he was no prize himself," Nick said. It was as close as Nick had ever come to admitting he disliked her father.

"Jamie admitted he broke into our house," Meredith smiled at Cav's disgusted huff. "His mother hinted to him that he and I might be related. He said he was curious, and because I'm a cop, he didn't just ring the doorbell. I think he believed we had the money hidden in our house." Meredith leaned forward, her irritation building. "Brenda's a scheming, self-serving bitch. I can't believe Terence didn't see that. I'm sure she manipulated—no, used emotional blackmail—to force him to give her money. She would've hinted that Jamie was his kid. Jamie was in prison because of Terence's indiscretion. He must've felt guilty enough to pay her."

Cav asked, "What happened to Benny?"

Nick snorted. "He wasn't charged. He didn't do anything except to ally himself with his shithead cousin." Nick nodded with approval. "He's on his way to San Diego, where my sister and her husband have a small plumbing business. They've offered him an apprenticeship. Benny says he's going to try making an honest living. He wasn't much of a criminal."

Cav took a drink of his beer. "Did you ever find out who provoked your father into having a heart attack at the con home?"

"Jamie admitted to it. He tried to pressure Terence into telling him where the money was stored—he hadn't found it at our house. He couldn't remember where he'd taken the bodies of his friends that night, and Terence wouldn't tell the truth. He said the money was safe but wouldn't tell where. Terence must've thought he could change Jamie—even in the last seconds of the game. Who knows? Maybe he thought he was protecting Jamie." She sighed, realizing the improbability of that idea. Her father didn't have it in him to properly protect anyone. "If Terence had been honest, this could've been avoided. Jamie would've told Brenda or Desmond where the money was. Who knows if they'd been smart enough to get the key from him? No doubt the cash would be gone by now." Meredith swirled her tea glass. "Messing with people was like a second calling for Terence."

Cav's eyes were soft yet probing. "Was your mother like that? I mean—conniving?"

Meredith was quiet, looking inward at the wisps of ugly realization, completing the fragmented memories of her mother. She'd known Nora Ryan as a loving woman who never argued with her. As Nora's daughter, Meredith had always looked the other way at her mother's flaws, particularly around her father. She'd even thought of Nora as weak for refusing to admit the level of his abuse. How could anyone let her husband walk all over her? Meredith knew all the clinical reasons for domestic abuse, but this was personal. This was her mother—the woman who'd literally been slapped out of the way so Terence could be with another woman. Nora had died pining for a man who didn't love her.

Brenda despised Nora Ryan, so her observations were skewed—but maybe not totally inaccurate. Des? Well, Des may have paid to give her mother a good old Irish wake, but he showed Nora no respect while she was alive.

"I always thought of Mom as an emotional doormat. Brenda told me Terence couldn't see David and me after they split up because my mom refused to let him. I guess Mom figured if she had something Dad wanted, she could trade us for something." Meredith shrugged. "I don't know. You think you know someone, but you don't really. I had no idea she used us kids as bargaining chips, but I guess I shouldn't be surprised. Lots of divorcing parents do."

Nick asked, "Why do you think Terence hid the bodies in the storage unit? They were sure to be found at some point."

"You mean, why not dump them in the Pacific or

something?" Cav nodded. "I wondered that, too. Bodies always get found, except in the ocean, right?"

Meredith shook her head. "Jamie told me Terence wanted to get rid of them fast. A stopgap turned into a long-term plan. He intended to move them, dump them somewhere they'd never be found. Then he got sick and couldn't do it. Jamie didn't know where to look, and then he wound up in prison."

Gareth leaned forward, swirling the dregs of his beer. "How come *Brazo Negro* didn't reach out to Jamie while he was inside?" A wry smile said he had the answer.

"Haven't heard anything about them, right? There aren't any registered *Brazo Negro* members in Sonoma County. Probably the same in San Francisco." Meredith looked at the younger Cavanaugh as he nodded. "Maybe the robbery knocked the wind out of them. Didn't you say they were a start-up?"

"Yeah, but it didn't seem probable a gang would let the theft go unpunished. So, I checked on them. Turns out they're unorganized and unaffiliated with any another gang. Pretty much defunct now." Nick squinted. "Granados and his guys weren't worth the attention of a larger gang. While he intended to launder gang money, the stolen cash was from the card game he had going in the back room. Besides," Gareth's mouth twisted in a wry smile, "Granados didn't inspire loyalty like gangsters try for. He must not have had the resources to get to Jamie in prison. But back to the story: Once Jamie got paroled, he asked Terence to tell him where the money was. For some reason, your father refused to. Jamie got him so agitated it pushed him into a heart attack. Jamie had nowhere to turn but you, Meredith. By then, we were all over him, so he couldn't."

"That we were." Nick grinned with the satisfaction of a job well done.

"What happens next? Will Jamie go back to jail?" Cav observed the last of his beer, then swallowed it.

Nick handed Cav another Pacifico. "Yes, probably prison, thanks to you and your nephew."

At Cav's quizzical look, Nick explained. "You put Gareth on the trail. It seems my wife has met her crime-fighting match. Gareth took the challenge and found the answers to the many questions in this case. Granados and two of his goons are in jail for the two murders—due to Gareth's thorough follow-up with the existing evidence. And Jamie has admitted to concealing a crime—the two homicides and breaking into our house. He's back in the can as we speak."

Meredith didn't get all the answers she hoped for about her father, but it turned out he wasn't as bad as she'd imagined. It made no difference in his interment—he wouldn't get a flag from the department, nor would there be any effect on his pension benefits—Brenda would get those. For her part, Meredith got as many explanations as possible.

Some little peace of mind, such as it was. She didn't believe Brenda's assertion that Terence was hard on her because he loved her and wanted to keep her tough, to stand on her own two feet. Not for a moment. "So, yes. I think I have solved part of the secret that was Terence Ryan."

She still had to live with the memory of her father. He'd been a challenge while alive, and Terence, as the specter of an abusive and ultimately absent father, would continue to cast a shadow over her life. She vowed to keep her son from turning out like Terence. Would a fraction of her father's or her mother's parenting ways seep into her own? She glanced at her husband and felt reassured. With Nick in the mix, Davy's odds were much better than hers had been.

She recalled vestiges of her mother's personality appearing in her own relationship with Richard, her first husband. After their third year of marriage he'd grown domineering and demanding, becoming less than supportive of the late nights at work and missed family events—they inconvenienced him. In retrospect, she realized she never stood up to him. She remembered picking shifts based on the least impact to her home life. She'd thought everyone did that.

Until Nick.

He'd been listening to her, rolling the cool beer bottle against his forehead in the afternoon heat. Cav slumped in a poolside chair at his sanctuary of a home, an ear cocked toward the barn. Meredith's attention wavered between these two men she loved so much. She smiled at the burgeoning respect she felt for Gareth. It dawned on her that she was in a completely safe place. No one had a hidden agenda or was out to get her. In fact, these men had put their lives on the line to keep her safe.

And she'd responded in kind—with complete trust. With Davy and Jake laughing in the distance, she felt happy.

Acknowledgements:

With my grateful appreciation for time and expertise in your specific area are Michael A. Black (Matteson Illinois PD retired) , Jim Guigli, Reegan (San Francisco PD retired) and Rhonda Fitzgerald who wrangled his cooperation, Mike (SFPD patrol), Jerry and "Fred" (SFPD Mounted Unit), Karen Lynch (SFPD retired), Mike McBride (Marin County DA, San Rafael California PD retired), Mike Brown (Sonoma County Ca. SO retired), Will Wallman (Sonoma County Ca. SO retired), Terri Mazzanti (Rohnert Park Department of Public Safety, retired) and Judy Melinek (Forensic Pathologist San Francisco Ca.). A special thank you to Chief Dana Wingert, Des Moines Police Department for "loaning" his elegant words to form a eulogy.

My patiently enduring critique group have made this a better book: Andy Gloege, Billie Settles, Fred Jonas Weisel, my thanks. To my family, especially Pat and Nancy, Sandie, Wallace and Chere, many thanks for the words of encouragement through the years.

To my readers who have reached out and given me the reason to sit at the keyboard, my humble gratitude.

CPSIA information can be obtained
at www.ICGtesting.com
Printed in the USA
LVHW010702180121
676771LV00001B/64